MW00529746

PEACE

By Gene Wolfe from Tom Doherty Associates

Novels
The Fifth Head of Cerberus
The Devil in a Forest (forthcoming)
Peace
Free Live Free
The Urth of the New Sun
Soldier of the Mist
Soldier of Arete
There Are Doors
Castleview
Pandora by Holly Hollander

Novellas
The Death of Doctor Island
Seven American Nights

Collections
Endangered Species
Storeys from the Old Hotel
Castle of Days

The Book of the New Sun
Shadow and Claw
(comprising *The Shadow of the Torturer* and
The Claw of the Conciliator)
Sword and Citadel
(comprising *The Sword of the Lictor* and
The Citadel of the Autarch)

The Book of the Long Sun
Nightside the Long Sun
Lake of the Long Sun
Caldé of the Long Sun
Exodus from the Long Sun (forthcoming)

PEACE

GENE WOLFE

A TOM DOHERTY ASSOCIATES BOOK
NEW YORK

This is a work of fiction. All the characters and events portrayed in this novel are either fictitious or are used fictitiously.

PEACE

Copyright © 1975 by Gene Wolfe

All rights reserved, including the right to reproduce this book, or portions thereof, in any form.

This book was originally published in 1975 by Harper & Row, Publishers.

This book is printed on acid-free paper.

Cover art by Tony Roberts

An Orb Edition
Published by Tom Doherty Associates, Inc.
175 Fifth Avenue
New York, N.Y. 10010

Library of Congress Cataloging-in-Publication Data

Wolfe, Gene.
        Peace / Gene Wolfe.
            p.   cm.
        "A Tom Doherty Associates book."
        ISBN 0-312-89033-8
        I. Title.
    PS3573.O52P43   1995
    813'.54—dc20   95-15464
                                                                  CIP

First Orb edition: July 1995

Printed in the United States of America

0   9   8   7   6   5   4   3   2   1

To Rosemary

1

ALDEN DENNIS WEER

THE ELM TREE planted by Eleanor Bold, the judge's daughter, fell last night. I was asleep and heard nothing, but from the number of shattered limbs and the size of the trunk there must have been a terrible crashing. I woke—I was sitting up in my bed before the fire—but by the time I was awake there was nothing to hear but the dripping of the melting snow running from the eaves. I remember that my heart pounded and I was afraid I was going to have an attack, and then, fuzzily, thought that perhaps the heart attack had wakened me, and then that I might be dead. I try to use the candle as little as I can, but I lit it then and sat up with the blankets around me, enjoying the candle-light and listening to the sound of the dripping snow and to the icicles melting, and it seemed to me that the whole house was melting like the candle, going soft and running down into the lawn.

This morning, when I looked out through the windows, I saw the tree. I took the cruiser ax and went out to it and chopped a few broken limbs finer still and put them on the fire, although it was no longer cold. Since my stroke I have been unable to use the big double-bitted Canadian ax, but at least twice a day I read it; "Buntings Best, 4 lb. 6 oz., Hickory Handle" has been burned into the wood. It was, in other words, branded, as though it were a steer; the three- or four- or five-hundredth time I read it, it finally came to me that this must be the origin of the phrase "brand new"—tools like my ax (and no doubt other things as well, more when more things were made of wood) were branded with the manufacturer's trademark after passing inspection, or by the inspector as a sign of approval. This would be the last manufacturing operation—they were then ready for sale and were "brand new." It seems a pity that I have only thought of all that now, when there is no one to tell it to, but that may be for the best; there are many questions of that kind, as I have observed, to which people would sooner not know the answers.

While I was still living with my aunt Olivia, her husband bought her a Dresden figure of Napoleon for her mantel. (I suppose it is there yet—it may well be; I should find her room and see.) Visitors often wondered aloud why he kept one hand thrust into his waistcoat. As it happened, I knew the cause, having read it a year or so before—I believe in Ludwig's biography of him. At first I used to tell it in the hope of satisfying curiosity (and so obtaining those real though impalpable satisfactions, sweet at any time, but sweetest at thirteen, which accrue when we appear knowledgeable and thus, at least by implication, effective). Later I continued it as a psychological experiment, having observed that the innocent remark invariably offended.

My little fire is only smoldering now; but, dressed warmly as I am, this room is not uncomfortable. Outside the sky is leaden, and there is a breeze blowing. I have just taken a walk, and the weather feels ready for rain, though the ground is already so sodden by the melting snow. The half-warm wind is fit for spring, but I saw no other sign of it; the roses and all the trees still have hard, tight winter leaf buds; and, indeed, some of the roses still show (like mothers holding up their dead infants) the softly rotten shoots they put forth in the last warm weather of fall.

Sometimes I walk as much as possible, and sometimes as little as I can, but the difference is not great. I do it to comfort myself.

If I have decided that walking will bring death closer yet to my left side, I plan each errand with care; first to the woodpile (next to the china elephant whose howdah is a cushion for my feet), *then* to the fireplace, then to my chair again, before the fire. But if it seems to me that exercise is required, I deliberately include small side trips: first to the fire to warm my hands, then to the woodpile, then back to the fire, and sit down glowing with hygienic virtue. Neither of these regimes seems to improve my condition, and I change physicians regularly. There is this to be said for doctors: they may be consulted though dead, and I consult Doctors Black and Van Ness.

I consult Dr. Black as a boy (though with a stroke), but Dr. Van Ness as a man.

I stand straight and six feet tall, a fine figure of a man, though twenty (Dr. Van Ness will say thirty) pounds underweight. It is important, going to the doctor. Even in some mad way more important than a board meeting. As I dress in the morning, I remind myself that I will be undressing not, as usual, for bed, but in the doctor's office. It is a little like knowing I am going to be with a strange woman, and I shower after shaving and choose new shorts and undershirt and socks. At one-thirty I enter the Cassionsville and Kanakessee Valley Bank Building through bronze doors, more bronze doors to the elevator, and a glass door for the waiting room where five people sit listening to Glinka's *A Life for the Czar.* They are Margaret Lorn, Ted Singer, Abel Green, and Sherry Gold. And me. We are reading magazines, and the magazines are *Life, Look, Today's Health,* and *Water World.* Two of us are reading *Life.* Different issues, of course, and I am one of these readers, the other being Margaret Lorn. There is (as a matter of fact) a whole pile of *Life*s before me, and I play the old game of trying to arrange them chronologically without looking at the dates, and lose. Margaret tosses down her copy and goes in to see the doctor, and I know, somehow, that this is a mark of contempt. I pick it up and find an area of the cover that is still warm (and slightly damp) from her hands. A nurse comes to the window and asks for Mrs. Price, and Sherry, who is sixteen now, tells her that she has already gone in, and the nurse looks aggrieved.

Sherry turns to Ted Singer: "I have . . ." Her voice sinks to a whisper. Ted says, "We've all got problems."

I go to the nurse, a woman I do not know, a blond woman who might be Swedish. I say, "Please, I've got to see the doctor. I'm dying."

The nurse: "All these people are ahead of you."

Ted Singer and Sherry Gold are both obviously much younger than I, but there is no use arguing with that kind of thing. I sit down again, and the nurse calls my name—into a cubicle to undress.

Dr. Van Ness is slightly younger than I, very competent-looking in that false way of medical men on television dramas. He asks what seems to be the matter, and I explain that I am living at a time when he and all the rest are dead, and that I have had a stroke and need his help.

"How old are you, Mr. Weer?"

I tell him. (My best guess.)

His mouth makes a tiny noise, and he opens the file folder he carries and tells me my birthday. It is in May, and there is a party, ostensibly for me, in the garden. I am five. The garden is the side yard, behind the big hedge. It is a large yard, I suppose, even for adults, big enough for badminton or croquet, though not for both at once; for five it is enormous. Children come in boxy, tottering cars, as though they were toys being delivered in little trucks, the girls in pink lace dresses, the boys in white shirts and navy shorts. One boy has a cap, which we throw into the blackberries.

Today it is spring, a season that in the Midwest may last less than a week, leaving the jonquils to droop in the heat before they are well opened—but this is spring, true spring, the wind whipping the first dandelions for their birthday, once for this year, once for last, ten to grow on, and a pinch for an inch.

Mothers' dresses are a hand's-breadth above their ankles, often of sensible colors; they like wide-brimmed, low-crowned hats, and jet beads. Their skirts flutter and they laugh, bending to gather them, holding the hats with one hand when the brims flap, the wind rattling their beads like the curtains in a Tunisian brothel.

In the wind-shadow of the garage, on the smoothly mown lawn, there is lemonade for them and a pink-frosted pink cake whose five candles blown at a breath grant every wish. Violet-eyed and black-haired, my aunt Olivia takes ice water in a large goblet instead, swirling it in her hand as though she were warming brandy; Cassionsville water from the Kanakessee River, around and down, lonely for its catfish. There is a white Pekinese as big as a spaniel at her feet, and it snarls when anyone comes too near. (Laugh, ladies, but Ming-Sno will bite.)

Mrs. Black and Miss Bold, sisters, sit side by side. They have —together, as though they were the goddesses of nations joined to blast the fields of that foreign power, myself—brought Bobby Black. Barbara Black has chestnut hair, regular features, and long soft lashes; since bearing her child she has—so my grand-mother, whose ghost vaguely, pinkly, haunts my party, says— "put on twenty pounds of healthy flesh"; but it has not height-ened her color, which remains that soft and only delicately pink-tinted hue which is the heritage of all the Bolds. Her sister is radiantly blond, slender and flexible as a willow—too much so for the other women, for to them a physical pliancy implies moral accommodation, and they suspect Eleanor Bold (assigning her, in their own minds and in sewing-circle, sugar-lending, Methodist-social conversations, the most improbable of lovers: farmhands and railroad firemen, the rumored sons of departed ministers, the sheriff's silent deputy).

This high, white house was my grandmother's and since our mothers on the lawn can see what we do there, we are—largely— in it, clattering up and down the steep and narrow and carpetless stair leading from the second floor to the third that we may stare in giggling silence there at the huge picture of my father's dead brother, which leans, unhung, against the wall of the farthest, coolest room.

It was, as I know from some occult source that, beneath the sleepless and probing lenses of the Cassionsville Spiritualist Society now so recently organized by my aunt Arabella, might be found to be Hannah (once my grandmother's cook and now my mother's)—it was, I say, painted almost precisely a year before his death. He appears to be about four, a sad-eyed, dark-haired child standing willingly but without joy to have his portrait done. He wears loose red trousers like a zouave, a white silk shirt, and a black velvet vest, and he smells of apples, from having been stored so long with them, and of quilts (hand-stitched with incredible fineness so that each in its own fabric of being stood a soft, warm monument to the endless labor of Tuesday and Thursday afternoons—just as so many did, in their designs, to the genius of William Morris); and afterward, when I had not seen my father's dead brother—whom he himself had never seen—for years, I came to imagine that he stood wrapped in a quilt (just as I, as a child, had been made to wrap myself in a large towel after a bath) with apples rolling at his feet. I went, I think at about the age of twenty, up into that house again and disabused myself of the notion, and at the same time recognized—with a start of surprise that might almost have been shame—that the dreaming landscape before which he stood as though upon a windowsill, a region I had always associated with the fairy tales of Andrew Lang (particularly those of the *Green Fairy Book*) and George MacDonald, was in fact a Tuscan garden.

That garden, with its marble faun and fountain, its Lombardy poplars and its beeches, has impressed my mind always far more strongly than poor dead Joe, whom none of us except my grandmother and Hannah had ever seen, and whose little grave in the cemetery on the hill was tended mostly by the ants that had built a city upon his chest. Now, when I sit alone before my fire and look out at the wreck of the elm revealed by the lightning flashes, confused and ruinous as a ship gone aground, it seems to me that the garden—I mean little Joe's garden, basking forever in the sunshine of its Tyrrhenian afternoon—is the core and root of the real world, to which all this America is only a miniature in a locket in a forgotten drawer; and this thought reminds me (and is reinforced by the memory) of Dante's *Paradiso*, in which (because the wisdom of this world was the folly of the next) the earth stood physically central, surrounded by the limbus of the moon and all the other spheres, greater and greater, and at last by God, but in which this physical reality was, in the end, delusive, God standing central in spiritual truth, and our poor earth cast out—peripheral to the concerns of Heaven save when the memory of it waked, with something not unlike an impure nostalgia, the great saints and the Christ from the contemplation of triune God.

True; all true. Why do we love this forlorn land at the edge of everywhere?

Sitting before my little fire, I know, when the wind blows outside, moaning in the fieldstone chimney I caused to be built for ornament, shrieking in the gutters and the ironwork and the eaves and trim and trellises of the house, that this planet of America, turning round upon itself, stands only at the outside, only at the periphery, only at the edges, of an infinite galaxy, dizzily circling. And that the stars that seem to ride our winds cause them. Sometimes I think to see huge faces bending between those stars to look through my two windows, faces golden and tenuous, touched with pity and wonder; and then I rise from my chair and limp to the flimsy door, and there is nothing; and then I take up the cruiser ax (Buntings Best, 2 lb. head, Hickory Handle) that stands beside the door and go out, and the wind sings and the trees lash themselves like flagellants and the stars show themselves between bars of racing cloud, but the sky between them is empty and blank.

Not so the Tuscan sky: it is of an untroubled blue, once or

twice touched with thin white clouds that cast no shadows on the ground below. The fountain is sparkling in the sun, but Joe does not hear it, nor will it ever damp his clothes or even the flagstones about its own basin. Joe holds a tiny gun with a tin barrel, and a stiff-legged wooden dog, but Bobby Black is coming and will, if he gains this room, throw apples that, striking the walls, will break, spattering picture and floor with crisp, fragrant, tart fragments; and these in turn, eventually, become brown, dirty, and sour, and will be discovered (most probably by Hannah) and I blamed, for it is impossible, unthinkable, that I should clean the floor, like asking a pig to fly or a mouse to play on the mouth-organ—we pigs, we mice, we children do not do such things, our limbs would not obey us. I stand at the top of the stair, inferior in strength and size but superior in position, silent, my eyes nearly closed, my face contorted, ready to cry, and I defy him; he jeers at me, knowing that if he can make me speak his battle is won; the others look over my shoulders and between my legs—my audience, not my allies.

At last we close, grunting, each grasping the other's pudgy body like wrestlers, red-faced and weeping. For a moment we sway.

Outside my aunt Olivia has lit a cigarette in a mammoth-ivory holder (tooth-of-the-devil) as long as her forearm. Mrs. Singer says, looking not at her but at my mother, "Have you the skin?" and my mother: "Yes, it's in on the piano; I'll have Hannah bring it when she comes out again," and Mrs. Green, who is somehow—I am too young to know—something of a slavey to my mother because we own her husband's farm: "I'll get it, Princess White Fawn," and my mother: "Fly swiftly, Princess Little Bird," and everyone laughs, for they are all *Indians*, and Mrs. Green, who is not little at all but short and big-boned and heavy, has chosen to be Princess Little Bird (when she might have been something suitable like Princess Corngrower, which was what Princess Star-Behind-Sun—my aunt Olivia—suggested for her) and has an expression of foolish joy when referring to herself by that name, as she must on ceremonial occasions (standing with her hand over her left breast while my mother places a feather in her hair for baking brownies for the Pow Wow).

"It's a shame, I think," my mother says. "They ought to have taken care of the old one."

Princess Singing Bird, whose husband is a building contractor, says, "They should have put it in a cornerstone," and Princess Happy Medicine, sister to Eleanor Bold, "They wanted the schoolchildren to see it."

Mrs. Green comes back, reverently carrying a soft roll of deer-hide; it is pale brown and almost as soft as chamois. My aunt Olivia, olive-skinned, oval of face, the most attractive woman there if we call Eleanor Bold a girl (which she was: the railroad firemen and traveling salesmen, hardware drummers and hired men are mythical as centaurs), takes it from her and unrolls it, her cigarette holder clenched between her teeth to the dazzlement and scandalization of the others. "There's nothing on it, Della."

My mother says, "I know. That's up to us, isn't it?" And Mrs. Singer asks, "Where did you get the skin?"

"John shot it," says Aunt Olivia. She smiles. "I mean, Chief White Fawn."

"Oh, Vi!"

"Just having fawn with you," Princess Star-Behind-Sun says, scratching Ming-Sno's ears.

"Oh, Vi!"

Hannah comes, clearing cake plates, bringing coffee. "Where are the children, Hannah?" "Inside. I don't know. Behind the vegetable garden, I think, some of 'em." Her arms are red, her hair white, her face large and square. She remembers covered wagons, but she will not say so. My mother talks to her husband, Aunt Olivia to her dogs, the Methodist minister's wife to God, and Grandmother talks to Hannah, but Hannah talks to no one but me, and because of this I, in front of my fire in bed, can hear her still when so many others are silent. I go to the old house, to my grandmother's house, to the kitchen where the old blue linoleum is worn to the boards in the center of the floor, and Hannah is washing dishes there, Princess Foaming Water. I sit on the little stool close to the iron stove. . . .

"It isn't the same. It's not the same place. I used to be there and now I'm here, and everyone says—would say if I asked 'em —that it's days and nights going, turning around like that electrical clock with the little hole in the face that goes black and then white every second so you get dizzy to watch it, but it's not that. How can everything change just because the sun goes down? That's what I want to know. Everybody knows it doesn't. I remember when I was just a little girl, just a little bit of a thing, and Maud—that he married after my own ma died, and made me to wear a dish-clout around my head so my ears would be flat—got the hired girl, that Irish girl, to telling her stories, and I was afraid, so afraid I wouldn't go out in the night, in the night after dark, and wasn't it dark there on Sugar Creek with nothing but the coal-oil lights and no other house that you could see, and the stars! The stars so bright it was just like they were hanging right over our house, only when I did go out, out on the back stoop, I could feel the corn under my feet that had dropped out of my apron when I'd fed those chickens, so I knew then it was the same place, and I went clear out to the pump and there wasn't anything—it was brighter, even, when I got off the stoop—and I walked back with long steps, holding up my skirt so I could.

"Now it's all gone, and when I went back there with Mary, Sugar Creek itself was gone, just dry rocks where it had been. It was May—no, it wasn't; it was June—the last part of May or the first part of June, it doesn't matter. . . . And that house; so small. We never all lived there, we never could have. Falling down, falling to nothing, little narrow doors you couldn't hardly get through. I never in my life been a hundred miles off from that little house, but it's gone now, and I never saw it go."

And I feel just as she does, yet differently. This house has grown larger, not smaller. (Nor is it falling down—not yet.) I wonder now why I asked for all these rooms—and there seem to be more and more each time I go exploring—and why they are so large. This room is wide, and yet much longer than it is wide, with two big windows along the west side looking into the garden, and along the east side a wall that shuts out the dining room, and the kitchen, and my den, where now I never go. At the south end is the fieldstone fireplace (which is why I live here; it is the only fireplace in the house, unless I have forgotten one somewhere). The floor is flagstone, the walls are brick, and there are pictures between the windows. My bed (not a real bed) is before the fireplace where I can keep warm. When summer comes—it is an odd thought—perhaps I will go up and sleep again in my own room.

And then, perhaps, the old days will really come back. I wonder what would have happened if Hannah had slept at Sugar Creek Farm (I will call it that; no doubt the neighbors called it simply "the Mill place")? Would Sugar Creek have flowed again, babbling in the night, wetting all those dry stones?

"Hannah?"

"Well, what's the matter, what do you want? That little boy, sitting there with his big eyes, what does he know? Work? Why, you never worked a day in your life. Look at that plate. Working for other people. Well, it's not your fault. I ain't got much longer to go, Denny. What does it matter? Want to wash these, and I'll run out and play tag with the others. Wouldn't your ma be surprised—she'd say, 'Who's the new girl?' I was just about to say I remembered her when she was just a little bit of a girl herself, only I don't, she's not from around here; it was another girl, that your dad used to play with when he was small. When it was warm summer sometimes, there was more children around the gaslights out on the street than there was millers around the mantles. It will be warm summer again pretty soon and I guess you'll be out there yourself, and I'll bake gingerbread to

go with the root beer; I've lived through another winter, and I've never figured to die in summer."

I don't think I have ever seen anyone wash dishes in our kitchen. There is a dishwasher there—they always used that, scraping the plates first into the sink, to go down the disposer, making the sink a kind of garbage can. I cook my food in the fireplace now, and eat it there, too, and I eat so little anyway.

"You are thin, Mr. Weer. Underweight."

"Yes, you always check me for diabetes."

"Strip to your shorts, please. I'm going to have the nurse come in and weigh you."

I undress, conscious that Sherry Gold is in the next cubicle, probably stripped to her bra and panties. She is a small girl, a little plump ("You seem to be putting on weight, Miss Gold. Strip to your bra and panties, please, and I'll come in and weigh you") pretty, a Jewish face—Jewish faces are not supposed to be pretty, but pretty anyway. If I were to make a hole through the partition with my jackknife, I could see her, and if I were lucky she would not see the bright blade of the leather punch coming through the wall, or the dark hole afterward, with my bright blue middle-aged eye behind it. Knowing that I will not, in fact, do any such thing, I begin to go through my pants pockets looking for the knife; it is not there, and I remember that I have stopped carrying it months ago because I went to the office every day and, because I no longer worked in the lab, never used it; and that it wore the fabric of my trousers where its hard bolsters pressed at the corners of my right hip pocket, so that they wore out first there.

I stand, holding on to the mantel with one hand, and look again: it is not there. The rain patters down outside. It might be good to have it again. "If I *did* have a stroke, Dr. Van Ness, what should I do?"

"It is quite impossible for me to prescribe treatment for a non-existent ailment, Mr. Weer."

"Sit down, for God's sake. Why the hell can't you talk to a doctor as if he were a man?"

"Mr. Weer—"

"There's not a man in my plant I'd talk to the way you talk to every patient you've got."

"But I can't fire my patients, Mr. Weer."

I dress again and seat myself in the chair. The nurse comes in, tells me I ought to be undressed, and leaves; after a few moments, Dr. Van Ness again: "What's the matter, Mr. Weer?"

"I want to talk to you; sit down."

He seats himself on the edge of the examination table, and I wish Dr. Black were alive again, that formidable, heavy man of my childhood, with his dark clothes and gold watch chain. Barbara Bold must have gotten fat just cooking for him; after seeing him eat, she would lose all sense of proportion, since her own meals, however large, would be so much smaller; how could she have realized that a second baked potato, or a bowl of rice pudding with cream, was too much when her husband ate as much as three such women? My mother gives her another slice of pink cake, technically my birthday cake.

"Thank you, Della."

Barbara's sister Eleanor says, "All right, we can write on that, but what do we write, and what *with*?"

"Oils, I suppose," says my aunt Olivia. "You can use mine."

Someone objects that the Indians had no oil paints, and Mrs. Singer points out that the children won't know.

"But *we* will know," Mother says. "Won't we."

"Listen," says Mrs. Singer, "I have a fine idea. You know when they met? The settlers and the Indians? Well, they had the *Indians* do the writing, but what if *they* had done it? Then it would be *ordinary* writing and we could do it."

One moment, please. Let me stand and walk to the window; let me put this broken elm branch—shaped as though it were meant to be the antler of a wooden deer, such a deer as might be found, possibly, under one of the largest outdoor Christmas trees—upon the fire. Ladies, this was not what I wanted. Ladies, I wish to know only if in my condition I should exercise or remain still; because if the answer is that I must exercise I will go looking for my scout knife.

"Mr. Weer! Mr. *Weer!*"

"Yes?" I poke my head around the edge of the door.

"Oh, you're dressed; I can see by your sleeve."

"What is it, Sherry?"

"Don't come in, I'm not dressed. Oh!" (Dr. Van Ness is coming back, and Sherry withdraws, slamming the door of her cubicle.)

"Doctor, for a stroke—"

"Mr. Weer, if I answer your questions will you cooperate with me in a little test? A game with mirrors. Then will you look at some pictures for me?"

"If you answer my questions, yes."

"All right, you have had a stroke. I must say you don't look it, but I'm willing to accept it. What are your symptoms?"

"Not now. I haven't had a stroke now; please try to understand."

"You will have a stroke?"

"I have had it in the future, Doctor. And there is no one left to help me, no one at all. I don't know what I should do—I'm reaching back to you."

"How old are you? I mean, when you've had this stroke."

"I'm not sure."

"Ninety?"

"No, not ninety, not that old."

"Do you still have your own teeth?"

I reach into my mouth, feeling. "Most of them."

"What color is your hair?" Dr. Van Ness leans forward, unconsciously assuming the position of prosecuting attorney.

"I don't know. It's gone, almost all gone."

"Do you have pain in your fingers? Are they knobbed, swollen, stiff, inflamed?"

"No."

"And do you still, from time to time, feel sexual desire?"

"Oh, yes."

"Then I think you're about sixty, Mr. Weer. That is to say, that your stroke is only fifteen or twenty years off—does that bother you?"

"No." I have been standing in the door of my cubicle. I withdraw and sit down on the chair; Dr. Van Ness follows me in. "Doctor, the side of my face, the left side, is all drawn over—I have an expression I have never seen, and I have it all the time. My left leg seems always crooked—as though it had been broken and misset—and my left arm is not strong."

"Are you dizzy? Do you frequently feel the urge to vomit?"

"No."

"Is your appetite good?"

"No."

"Do you find it painful to move about? Very painful?"

"Only emotionally—you know, because of the things I see."

"But not physically."

"No."

"Has there been only one stroke?"

"I think so. I woke up like this. It was the morning after Sherry Gold died."

"Miss Gold?" The doctor's head makes an unintentional and almost imperceptible movement toward the partition that separates us. I wonder if the girl is listening; I hope not.

"Yes."

"But it hasn't gotten any worse."

"No."

"You need exercise, Mr. Weer. You need to get out of the house, as well as walking around inside the house, and you need to talk to people. Take a good walk—several blocks—each day, when the weather permits. I believe you have a large garden?"

"Yes."

"Well, work in it. Pull weeds or something."

And that is what I so often do, pull weeds or something. And the something is usually flowers when it is not vegetables; or often I discover later that the weed I pulled was nicer than the blossoms I cultivated. There is one in particular that I have not seen in years, which used to grow just between the fence and the alley at my grandmother's house, a very tall weed with a tender, straight column of green stem and horizontal branches at the most regular intervals, airy and slender, each perfect and each carrying its tiny group of minute leaves to stare happily at the sun. I have sometimes thought that the reason the trees are so quiet in summer is that they are in a sort of ecstasy; it is in winter, when the biologists tell us they sleep, that they are most awake, because the sun is gone and they are addicts without their drug, sleeping restlessly and often waking, walking the dark corridors of forests searching for the sun.

And so will I search now for my knife, thus getting the exercise Dr. Van Ness prescribes. It was large, and stamped with the words "Boy Scout." The scales were of simulated black staghorn, bringing to mind (at least to mine) the image of a simulated stag, his horns held proudly as those of any elm-deer, ranging the forest among the now-waking trees, trees whose leaves are dying with the summer in every color, like bruises, but bruises beautiful as the skins of races unborn, withheld from us because God, or destiny, or the bland chance of the scientists (whose blind, piping ape-god, idiot-god, we have met before; we know you, troubler of Babylon) has denied us the sight of all these scarlet and yellow—truly red, orange, russet-brown—races on our sidewalks, and all the wonderful richness of stereotypes we might have entertained ourselves with if only they had been permitted us: the scarlet people with tight fists and loose women, gobbling dialects, a talent for paintings done with chalk upon the sides of newspaper kiosks, and high abilities in the retail merchandising of hobby supplies such as tiny-toy jet engines, and model garbage trucks whose hungry rumps, trundled about the wooden tops of retired dining-room tables in basements, will devour the dross of train-station quick-eat restaurants; the orange people with their weird religion demanding the worship of sundials (as our own seems to others that of telephone poles), so that in friendly locker-room conversations, when we have at last and at the threat of certain legal pressures admitted them to Pinelawn and are discussing the round now past, they out with strange oaths. What is a wabe?

And all of them, since all the lands of this earth are occupied, must be from strange and farther countries, from Hi Brasil and the Islands of the Sun, from the Continental Islands and the Isles of the Tethys Sea. Only the rarest, the russet browns, belong here, native to St. Brendan's land, and they are dying; the things they are famous for are not strange oaths, or ability at any art, or cunning in a trade, but alcoholism and gonorrhea and dwindling. They make good soldiers and that is fatal, just as is the bravery of the simulated stag, which will bring him to death, answering the call of the simulated war cry to meet bullets in the dry autumn woods and fall, his lungs hemorrhaging substitute blood at the edge of the potato fields. The imitation huntsman shouts and dances for joy, and then, having learned very well to shoot, but never to butcher, and being, in his own opinion, no longer of an age to carry heavy burdens, leaves him to rot and stink, the bait of plastic flies with fishhooks in their bellies. In time his flesh, torn by such fur-like foxes as remain, and by the teeth of curs, falls away, and only his horns and his celluloid bones remain, the prey of the boys'-knife maker.

The bolsters—those hard bolsters which, when my life was over and I had come to my desk, wore out so many gabardines and serges—were of German silver, of *Funfcentstucksilber*, like the buttons of the SS. It is a metal soft yet tough, and incorruptibly dully shining. Do not confuse us with pewter, which is a thing of plates and platters and drinking vessels.

But these things, the scales and bolsters, were on the exterior; they were the trim, as it were, of the knife. The truth within was prefigured by the plate in its side, which was of steel.

I remember very well the Christmas my knife was given to me; it was the one—the only one—I spent at my grandfather's, my mother's father's. That house stood high on a bluff overlooking the Mississippi and had many wide windows, though like my grandmother's narrow-windowed house it, too, was of white-painted wood. The Christmas tree stood against certain of these windows, so that, through its branches, among the trumpery dolls and tinsel and brilliant mock-fruit balls of painfully thin glass, one could watch the steamboats. It snowed that Christmas, I am sure, though it was rare to have any snow that far south, and when it came, if it came at all, it was usually later in the year. My mother had brought me; my father had remained behind at home, no doubt to hunt. There were, then, four of us in the house: myself, my mother, my grandfather (a tall old—as I thought then—man who dyed his beard and mustache black), and his housekeeper, a plump blond woman of (I now suppose) about forty. My mother would have been twenty-five, I six. It was the year after Bobby Black was hurt.

We came by train, arriving at a station already lightly powdered with snow, my mother's coat with fox fur around the neck, a black man—who grinned whenever my mother looked at him—to help us with our bags, help us into the wooden-bodied car that would take us, so my mother told me, to Granpa's. "You're cold, aren't you, Den?"

I said that I was not.

"Cold and hungry. We'll get you warmed up there, and into bed, and then it will be Christmas and you'll get your toys."

The driver said, "I guess you're Vant'y's daughter." He had long cheeks like a face seen in the back of a spoon, and blackheads at the corners of his eyes.

Mother said, "Yes, I'm Adelina."

"Well, you'll find he's fine; he's stronger right now than most men ever get to be. Guess you heard he's got Mab Crawford keeping house for him now."

"She wrote me."

"She did? Well, I guess." The man turned away from us, leaning forward, and the wooden-bodied car, which had been shaking and chattering to itself, lunged ahead, stopped almost as abruptly, exploded under the place where Mother and I had our feet, then began to move in a more or less normal manner. "Earl run off from her—you heard?"

Mother said nothing, drawing her coat more tightly about her. The tall windows beside us rattled and let in cold air.

"I guess he's gone to Memphis; but your pa is fine—he's fit as fit, good as any younger man." We were passing among stores with dark windows, down a street that, perhaps only because it was empty, seemed very wide. "That's what he says, and what I believe; that's the way it is. She went to Memphis, too—you heard? Leastwise, that's where *she* went, and that's what made everybody to think that's where he did. 'Bout three months after he was gone. She stayed till pretty near the Fourth of July; then she come back—well, she has to do something, is what I say, I guess a woman that has had her own house like that isn't ever going to want to be a hired girl to no other woman, not that it was much of a place with Earl."

No doubt the house—my grandfather's house—had exterior architecture, but I do not remember it. It was a wooden house, as I have said, and I believe white, though that may have been the snow. I had been afraid, just before we arrived (or, actually, for some minutes before we arrived, since I thought, as children I suppose usually do, that we were at our destination almost as soon as we had begun the trip), that it would not be a real house—that is, a house of wood—but one of those somehow unnatural brick or stone houses that (like stage sets, but more unreal to me, because I was unfamiliar with the term and even with the concept at the time) served, as I felt, only to wall off the margins of streets from something else; inhabited by people, so far as I could see, but fit homes for trolls (of whose existence I remained convinced for years after this visit, as I remained, for that matter, convinced of the reality of Santa Claus).

But the house was of safe wood, which being nailed together would not tumble down, and would not be heavy if it did. My grandfather and his housekeeper met us on the porch; I am certain of that. Everyone's breath steamed, and while my mother fumbled in her purse my grandfather paid the man who had brought us. Mrs. Crawford, who had not worn a coat outside but only her long dress, hugged me and told me to call her Mab; she smelled of scented powder and sweat, and the laundry-day smell of that time: dirty water reheated on a coal stove. All this sounds unpleasant, but actually was not. These—except for the scented powder, since my mother and my aunt Olivia and the other women I knew used different brands—were familiar smells, much less foreign than the odors of the railway coach in which we had come.

I remember a great deal of moving about, of circling each other on the creaking porch boards, while all this hugging and paying, baggage unloading and greeting took place, the white plumes of breath, the blown snow clinging to the dirty screen door still in place in front of the real door, which stood a quarter open. There was a potbellied stove inside, and when we got to it the blond woman, Mab, tried to help me off with my galoshes, but could not get them over the heel, so that my mother had to come in the end, leaving my grandfather, for the moment, to take them off. The ceilings in all the rooms were very high, and there was a big Christmas tree, with toys and balls and candles that had never been lit to decorate it, and cookies painted with egg white colored with beet juice and dotted with small candies.

At dinner I noticed (that is to say, in all of this, I think, I believe in some sense much akin to the belief of faith, that I noticed, felt, or underwent what I describe—but it may be that the only reason childhood memories act on us so strongly is

that, being the most remote we possess, they are the worst remembered and so offer the least resistance to that process by
which we mold them nearer and nearer to an ideal which is
fundamentally artistic, or at least nonfactual; so it may be that
some of these events I describe never occurred at all, but only
should have, and that others had not the shades and flavors—for
example, of jealousy or antiquity or shame—that I have later
unconsciously chosen to give them) that though my grandfather called Mrs. Crawford Mab, which I felt sure was what
he always called her, she called him Mr. Elliot; and that this
was new between them, that she valued herself on using it and
felt herself to be humbling herself in a noble cause—an emotion
that in those days, when it was discussed among adults, always
evoked the phrase "Bible Christian." My grandfather, I think,
was embarrassed by this new deference; knowing it to be false,
he felt my mother knew it to be false as well (as she surely
must before the meal was over) and was shamed and angered
by it. He insulted Mrs. Crawford in the rough country style
both of them understood, telling my mother (as he wolfed down
dumplings) that he had not had a tolerable meal since her
mother "passed over," that some people had little enough to do,
with only one other to take care of, unlike herself "with that little scamp to keep you on your feet all day and all night, Della,
and a church husband to look out for, too." This of course
ignored the existence of Hannah, about whom he must have
known, who did all the cooking and heavy housework at home.
The walls of the dining room were hung with sepia photographs
of trotting horses, the only exception being that part of the wall
which was directly behind my grandfather's head, and thus completely out of his view when he sat at the table: this held a large
picture of a woman in the majestic and complex costume of the
eighteen-eighties—my other grandmother, Evadne.

When the meal was over, I was undressed and put into bed
by the combined efforts of my mother and Mab, who had come
with us carrying a lamp—not, as she said, to show the way,

which she avowed my mother would know far better than herself, but because "it isn't right you should go up without no one to take you when you've just come, it wouldn't *seem* right, and I couldn't sleep if I did that; I couldn't sleep a wink, Mrs. Weer." My mother said, "Call me Della," and this so flustered Mrs. Crawford that she nearly dropped the lamp.

When she had gone, my mother began an inspection of the room, which she told me she had occupied as a child. "That was my bed," she said, indicating the one she had been sitting on a moment before, "and that other was your aunt Arabella's." I asked if I had to sleep in it, and she said I could sleep with her if I preferred. I trotted over, across a cold floor not much mitigated by a rag rug, and sat in the middle of the bed watching her. "We had a dollhouse here," she said, "between the dormers."

"Will I get a dollhouse for Christmas, Mama?"

"No, silly, dollhouses are for girls. You'll get toys for boys."

I regretted this; a playmate (a girl, though I had never before realized that this was other than incidental to her possession of it) owned a large and beautifully painted dollhouse with removable walls. I had assisted her several times with it, and because I had seen it so often I could visualize it quite well—now never to be found at the base of any Christmas tree of mine, floating away, just when I had thought it so near, into the misted realm of the impossible. I had planned to put my toy soldiers in it, firing from the windows.

"A book," my mother said after a long silence, during which she had been examining the interiors of cabinets. "Santa might bring you a book, Den."

I liked books, but I was far from sure that Santa Claus visited any house but ours—or at least any house outside Cassionsville. Surely not this strange, silent house, with its smells of old clothing hanging in closets year upon year. I asked my mother, and she said she had told Santa we were coming.

"Will Santa bring stuff for Granpa?"

"If he's been a good boy. Turn around, Den. Look at the wall. Mama wants to undress."

When the lamp went out, the whole house was plunged in quiet. Even with my eyes closed in the dark, I was aware of the snow sifting down outside; aware, too, that we were the only people on this floor, until at last, very late as it seemed to me, I heard Mab come wearily up the stairs to sleep in the room that —so my mother told me much later—had been Grandmother Vant'y's mother's when she was a girl. I was warm where my back pressed against my mother's, dreadfully cold everywhere else despite the crushing weight of quilts and feather beds; this partly, no doubt, because I was so tired, partly because the Southern house was unaccustomed to the cold that fell on it now, an airy, drafty house that even in the depth of winter dreamed of still, hot evenings, of rocking on the porch and the hum of mosquitoes. My mother slept, but I did not. There was a chamber pot beneath the bed; I used it and returned to the warmth of the covers again, unrelieved.

At last, quite certain in my own mind that I had lain awake almost all the night and that the dawn must even now be graying the windows (though my "dawn" was nothing more than the moon on the new-fallen snow outside), I crept down to warm myself at the parlor stove and to look at the Christmas tree, though I think I still expected my gifts—if I received any at all that year—to be at home, in the place where our tree would have been had we had one, or piled beneath our stockingless mantel. I had only a vague idea, I suppose, of the plan of the house; I know I blundered several times into the wrong rooms—the big kitchen, the dining room with horses trotting all around its walls, the museum-like front parlor with some large bird beneath a glass bell jar on the center table, as though the company (if company ever came again, if there could be company grand enough to merit that parlor, with its cut-glass bowls and wax fruit, its horsehair furniture and morning-glory trompe-l'oeil phonograph horn) would be expected to sit studying its dust-free molt, as though this were the simurg, the last bird of its kind in all the world, as though my grandfather were expecting a company of naturalists, and perhaps it was, and perhaps, indeed, he did.

The door to the correct room, the "everyday parlor," was shut; but even before I opened it I saw, yellow as butter, the line of light at the base of the door. Whether I thought it was light from the isinglass window of the stove, or that someone had left a lamp burning, or that it was the sun in an east window—for I was firmly convinced, remember, that it was morning—I am no longer sure; probably I did not stop to speculate. I opened the door (not with a knob that turned, as we had at home—as we had also gaslights and only used kerosene when a light had to be carried about, so that I thought, when I first came, that my grandfather's house was in a constant state of emergency—but with a strange latch that lifted to the downward pressure of my thumb) and as I did so the soft yellow light, as soft as a two-day-old chick, as soft as the blossom of a dandelion and more radiant, came pouring out, and I saw to my astonishment that the Christmas-tree candles were all lit, each standing erect as its own flame near the tip of a limb, a white specter crowned with fire. I walked toward the tree—halfway, I believe, from the door—and stood rooted. It shone against the dark glass of the window; behind it, far away, shone the stars, and the river below with the stars reflected in its water; a steamboat, blazing with lights, but now, at this remove, tinier and brighter than a toy, passed among the branches. There were presents under the tree, and more thrust into the lower boughs, but I hardly saw them.

"Well, I guess you're late," my grandfather said. "Old Nick, he's already been here." His "well" was *wa-ul*.

I said nothing, unable at first to see him in the corner in which he sat in a huge old oak rocker with a mask carved in the towering headrest.

"Come, left his stuff, lit all these here candles, and gone on out the chimney. Look at that clock yonder—past twelve. He 'most always comes here at twelve, and goes then, too. I just come down myself to have a look at these here candles before I puts them out and goes up to bed. I used to do that, years ago, after he was gone. Can you tell time, young Weer?"

My name was not Young, but I knew he meant me and shook my head.

"I guess it won't hurt you to look, too. Then you can go back up to your bed. Got your eyes full yet?"

I said, "We don't have candles on our tree at home."

"Your pa, I guess, is afeared it will burn his house. Well, that might be. I come pretty quick after Nick and blow 'em out, and I cut that tree myself not two days gone. When your ma was little, her 'n' her sister would come down to see it. I guess she's forgot now—or maybe she sent you."

"She's asleep."

"You want to see what Nick brought?"

I nodded.

"Well, I can't show you your own, but I guess you could see what other folks is getting. Now look here." He got up from his chair, a tall figure in dark clothing, his chin whiskers as stiff and black as the end of a fence post dipped in creosote. Assisted by his cane, he knelt with me at the foot of the tree. "This here," he said, "is yours." He showed me a heavy, square package with its ribbons and trimmings somewhat crushed and flattened. "And so is this'n here." A small box that rattled. "You'll like that'n. I fancy."

"Can I open it now?"

My grandfather shook his head. "Not till breakfast. Now you look here." He held up a large and heavy box, which gurgled when he tilted it. "That's toilet water for Mab. And look here" —a smaller box, held shut with a single loop of red ribbon. "You look here a minute." Painstakingly he removed the ribbon, slipping it down until the box could be opened like a blue leather

clamshell. "These are for your ma. Know what they are? Pearls."
He held up the string for me to admire by candlelight.
"Matched, every one. And a little silver catch with diamonds in
it at the back." I nodded, impressed, having already been made
aware by my mother of the importance of her jewelry box and
the wisdom of leaving this sacred treasury strictly alone.

"You think these here are bright?" my grandfather said. "You
wait till she sees them and look at her eyes. When Vant'y passed
on, I took everything we didn't send down with her and shared
it out between Bella and Della. So I saw it all, but there wasn't
anything half so fine as this, not anything I got her or anything
she brought from her ma. Now you go up to bed."

And as if by magic—and it may have been magic, for I believe America is the land of magic, and that we, we now past
Americans, were once the magical people of it, waiting now to
stand to some unguessable generation of the future as the name-
less pre-Mycenaean tribes did to the Greeks, ready, at a word,
each of us now, to flit piping through groves ungrown, our
women ready to haunt as lamioe the rose-red ruins of Chicago
and Indianapolis when they are little more than earthen
mounds, when the heads of the trees are higher than the hun-
dred-and-twenty-fifth floor—it seemed to me that I found myself in bed again, the old house swaying in silence as though it
were moored to the universe by only the thread of smoke from
the stove.

The next morning I woke with my mother's arm about me, my
face cold but the rest of me warm. We carried our clothes to the
kitchen and dressed there, finding Mab already up and cooking,
and heating the water my grandfather would use when he
trimmed the stubble around his beard with his big razor, for
today was Christmas, a great day, and though he seldom shaved
thus once a week he would do it today. She gave me a sugar
cookie with an enormous raisin in the middle to stay my appetite
before the grits and ham and eggs, the icy milk from the "larder"

abutting the back porch, the coffee—for me, too, for by custom I got coffee here, I discovered, though never at home—and the biscuits and the homemade doughnuts were ready. I wanted, indeed, not breakfast, but to see what was under the tree; but this—by the rule of the house, as my mother explained—was out of the question. Breakfast first. This her own mother, the dead and by me unremembered Vant'y, had imposed upon her and her sister throughout their childhood; and this she and her father were determined to impose upon me, though I strongly suspected there would be oranges (which I have always loved) and nuts in my stocking that would make a more satisfactory collation than any sugar cookie. Even my mother, who made several journeys of inspection to the parlor between her brief bouts of assisting Mab (in the same vague way she assisted Hannah at home) with the preparation of the meal, swore that she went no farther than the parlor door, and I was not even permitted to leave the kitchen. My grandfather came down and shaved around his beard in a corner where a mirror hung—for the first time I noticed that he was smaller than my father. He ignored the women until he had finished, then seated himself at the head of the table, where my mother at once poured him coffee.

"Coldest Christmas I can remember," Mab said. "Snow out on the stoop's that deep." She made an exaggerated gesture, her hands three or four feet apart. "I suppose we're going to be snowed in."

"You're a fool, Mab," my grandfather said. This made her smile, her plump face dimpling, made her push her fingers, slightly damp from the eggs she had broken, into her butter-colored hair. "Why, Mr. Elliot!"

"This will be gone by noon," my mother said. "I think it's a shame. It's so pretty."

My grandfather said, "You wouldn't talk like that if you had to go out tramping through it to fork down hay for them horses."

Mab jostled my mother with her elbow. "I bet you wish that Miss Bella was here! Wouldn't you and her throw snowballs at him!"

"I might anyway," my mother said. "I'll get Den to help me if you won't."

"Oh, I couldn't do that," Mab said, and giggled.

My grandfather snorted and said to me obscurely, "Runnin' around without any stays on."

We breakfasted, the adults with a deadly slowness, then trooped into the parlor. There were oranges and nuts, as I had envisioned. Candy. A pair of suspenders for my grandfather, and a box of (three) bandannas. For me a weighty book, bound in green buckram with a highly colored picture—an art-nouveau mermaid, more graceful and more sea-born than any wet girl I have seen since, signaling with languid gesture to a ship of the late Middle Ages manned by Vikings—sunk in the front board, and a multitude of other, similar pictures, the equal—and in some cases the superior—of the first, scattered throughout a text black-printed and often confusing, but to me utterly fascinating; and a knife. Just such a knife, I feel sure, as my grandfather would have selected for himself, a man's knife, though it bore the words "Boy Scout" on that plate let into its side. Closed, it was longer then than my hand, and in addition to a huge spear blade that, once opened (I could not open it without his assistance), was held so by a leaf spring of brass, it had a corkscrew and a screwdriver, a bottle opener, a smaller blade which my grandfather warned me was very sharp, a leather punch, and an instrument for removing pebbles from the hooves of horses—this last, I think, is called a stonehook. Unlike the blades of boys' knives to come, all these were of high-carbon steel and rusted if they were not kept oiled; but they would take and hold a good edge, as the bright and showy blades will not.

For my mother a large bottle of toilet water, and for Mab a small string of pearls, which made her first dance with joy, then weep, then kiss my grandfather several times, and at last rush from the room, upstairs to her own room (we could hear her feet pounding on the steps, so rapid and unsteady that she might have been a drunken roisterer fleeing the police), where she stayed for nearly half the day.

As a child I believed that my mother, from that unquestioned generosity children so readily assume in a good parent, had exchanged gifts with Mab. At some time before I entered college, I realized (as I thought) that my grandfather himself must have made the exchange—not when I had spoken to him the night before, but later in payment for some sexual favor, or in the hope of securing one imagined as late that night he lay alone in the big first-floor bedroom.

And now that I am older—myself as old now, I suppose, as he was then—I have returned to the opinion of my childhood. Old men, I think, do not make such gifts; and I wonder what the town thought, and if he allowed her to keep them; if she was buried in them.

"They ought to have put it in a cornerstone."

And Barbara Black, mother of Bobby: *"They wanted the children to see it."*

But they cannot see them now at least, not on her; she is dead now, that florid Rubens woman. When my mother died, I found a picture of Mab, standing beside my seated grandfather, among her things. She had something then of the appearance of a nurse, very much a nurse chosen to please an old man, a nurse who could giggle and pout until he had taken his medicine, a sort of walking regret. I cannot imagine her last illness, or someone taking care of her.

I remember that when my mother died she seemed to me to be still rather young for death. Now, in retrospect, I feel that she lived on and on through whole ages of the world, as though she might have lived on forever. (As perhaps elsewhere she has.) It is too late for it now, but it sometimes seems to me that we ought to have kept records, by the new generations, of our remoteness from events of high significance. When the last man to have seen some occurrence or personality of importance died; and then when the last person who knew *him* died; and so on. But first we would have the first man describe this event, this thing that he had seen, and when each of them was gone we would read the description publicly to see if it still meant anything to us—and if it did not, the series, the chain of linked lives, would be at an end. Tell us about going to see the Indians, Princess Foaming Water.

"Oh, you don't want that old story. You've had that old story a hundred times."

Please, Hannah, tell me about the time your poppa took you to see the Indians.

"Lord, you make it sound like it was a show. It wasn't no show. He just had to go there to trade, and he was afraid somebody'd come; I was too small to leave alone, anyway. It was just after Ma passed away, before Mary was born. Before the hired girl, that Irish girl, come; before he even married that other one at all.

"I suppose it's a terrible thing to say, Denny, but looking back on it now I would have to say I think I like that time the best of all—I don't mean I didn't pine for my mother. But it was terrible toward the end, with her so sick and all and me so worried about her and what could I do, just a little bit of a child. Then she was gone. He slept alongside of her so he could help her if she needed anything, and she must have gone in the night, and he didn't wake me up. He'd pegged up a box for her—we didn't use nails much, they were made by the blacksmith then and cost a lot. But he had his drill and he bored the holes in the wood and whittled pegs for them and drove them in with a big hammer that he had made for himself. The head of it was wood, too. He told her he was building a house for chickens, and she said that was good, she'd be glad to see eggs. He said he'd get some chickens when the house was finished.

"By the time I woke that morning, he had the lid down—

that's what woke me, his pounding in of the lid pegs. You know, Denny, all the times I told you this before I never remembered it, but that's right, that's what woke me, his pounding in those pegs. I guess I never thought of it, not even then, because by the time I got woke up and I set up to look at him, he was finished and was just standing there with that wooden hammer in his hand. He told me later that he used cherry pegs for it everywhere, but the boards were pine. We had a cherry tree in back of the house—not the kind you could make pies out of, but a wild tree: what they called a bird cherry or bear cherry. My ma wouldn't never let him chop it down because it looked so pretty when it bloomed, and he never did, not even after she died. But he'd cut pegs off it because the little branches grew round and straight and the wood was hard. He made pipes out of them, too; he made all his own pipes, and he grew his own tobacco. Made the bowls out of corncob and left them soft on the outside."

Hannah, I can make you say a Indian word.

"How? Oh, I see. Aren't you the scamp. I know a story like that—I bet you'd like to hear it. This is the story that that Irish hired girl we got when they was married used to tell. It was better, though, when she told it; we didn't have any neighbors, you know, or any telephone—none of what they have now. There was a road past our farm, down at the bottom of the hill, but sometimes it would be a week before anybody'd come. . . ."

"Well, once upon a time there was a poor boy named Jack, and he loved a girl named Molly; but Molly's father didn't want the two to marry, because Jack had nothing to bring to the wedding but his own two hands and a smile; but he was a fine, strong boy, not afraid of anything, and everyone in the neighborhood liked him. Well, Molly's father he plotted and schemed how he could get rid of him, but he was afeared to throw him down the well, for he was too strong, and besides he thought they might hang him. Now, this farm he had was so big it had every sort of land on it."

Katie, is this a really true story?

"As I breathe, darlin'. And—"

Was this in Ireland, Kate?

"Oh, not a bit of it, Miz Mill. It was in Massy-chusetts, where me father worked makin' shoes.

"There was medders and woods, fields for plowin' and fields for hay—much of everythin' and the richest you ever saw, but rocky bits, too, and dells among the woods where never a bit of sun shone from one year to another. So big it took a man all day to walk across it, and ten would be hired at wages to plant, and forty to harvest.

"Now, away back in the wood where nobody saw, there was a stone barn; and you'd think they'd be using it for this or for that, wouldn't you? But they did not, and it stood empty as a churn on Sunday from one year to another. And the reason of it was that it was haunted, and the haunt was a banshee, and that's as bad a ghost as there is of any sort, and I've often heard it said, when they talked of driving out ghosts, that you could away with most any sort but that. And them you burn the house—or whatever it might be—down around their ears and they'd haunt the ashes; and you could bring the holiest man that ever lived, or even the bishop, but they'd be back; and you'd quicker get rid of the landlord than a banshee. Ugly old women they are, with long fingers to scratch you and teeth like thorns on a bush, and they're the spirits of midwives that have killed the baby because someone gave gold to them to do it that it might not inherit, and never a day can they rest until whatever land it was is under the sea.

"Now, every night as soon as the moon shined in at the window, the banshee would come. And if there were cows in the barn she'd milk them and pour out the milk on the ground; and if there were horses she'd gallop them all night, or drink their blood so they'd be too weak even to stand in the morning. And if a man tried to stay in that barn all night she'd grab him and choke him until he named somebody, and then that person that he named—whoever it was—they'd die that same night, and him she'd tear the clothes off of, and beat him with a wagon tongue till he was black all over so everybody'd know who done it."

Anybody he said would die, Katie?

Why didn't the bad man just go to the barn, and when she
"That was just the way of it. Well—"
came he could say the boy's name?

"He feared her too much. No, but he plotted and planned and cast his mind forward and back until at last he thought of a way to get free of Jack, that was always botherin' him about his daughter Molly, while he sat safe as could be beside his own fire. You've guessed it yourselves, sure as I stand here. Even little Mary in the cradle knows. He told Jack he'd have to spend the whole night in the barn and never be throwed out, and if he did he could have Molly and half the farm.

"So the first time Jack went and he sat with his back to the wall where he could watch for the moon in at the window, and never a wink did he sleep. Betimes the moonlight came—just a little spot, it was, movin' across the floor—and no sooner was it there than somebody knocked at the door. Knock . . . knock . . . knock."

I don't think you have to hit the table like that, Kate; you'll wake the baby.

"Well, Jack he was never afeared and he called out bold as you please, 'Come in with you, but shut the door after, for there's draft enough now.' And that door, it opened ever so slow, and the banshee come in. Her gown was all windin' sheets from graves, and she walked like this. She said, 'I'll be leavin' it open if it's all the same with you, Jack, for you'll be needing it shortly.' Then it was on Jack's tongue to say something about Molly and how he'd stay there no matter what until the sun shone for he loved her so, but devil a word of it could he get out before the banshee had him by the neck, yellin', 'A name! A name!' For they're hungry all the time for the souls of the livin' but they can't get them till they know their true names, and they

forgets everyone they know when they die. Jack wasn't going to
name anybody, not if she choked him to death, but she kept hitting him against the wall, and the way she had his neck his
tongue was slappin' at his belt buckle, and he thinks what if he
was to say Molly, all dizzy as he was with the chokin' and the
bangin'; and then he thinks to say Molly's father, but that was
to be his own father-in-law if they were ever wed, and he
couldn't turn on his relations like that, so to be rid of her he
says the name of the meanest man he can think of, a man that
robbed everybody and never gave poor folk a penny, and then
she let him go; but she tore a board out of a stall that was there
and gave him such a beating with it he couldn't walk, and then
she threw him out the door, and there they found him in the
morning, and Molly's father he brought him a bottle of witch
hazel, but he told him he didn't ever want to see him again.

"Well, you think that's the end, but it isn't. By and by, Jack
got better and he still loved Molly and he said could he do it
again; well, her father didn't want to, but she cried and everything and finally he said all right, and then she cried some more
because she thought Jack would be killed for certain this time.
Well, he waited like before, and she came, and this time he said
the name of a real old lady that was goin' to die anyway and she
beat him so bad he like to died.

"Well, you think that's the end, but it isn't. The next time, he
promised Molly's father that if he didn't stay in that barn till
sunup, banshee or none, he'd go to Texas; so her father said yes.
Well, she come in just like before, but uglier and bigger. Her
fingernails was as long as knittin' needles and he thought she
was going to scratch out his eyes with them, so he raised up his
arm like this so she couldn't scratch him blind, and when he
did she got him by the neck. Well, he struggled and fought ever
so—just like Kilkenny cats, I was about to say, but it was really
more like St. Brandon and the Devil. Well, finally he knew he
was going to have to say somebody, so he said Molly's father,
and you'd think that would be the end of the mean old man, but

Jack had noticed before that after he said somebody there was always just a little bit of a holdup while she looked about for something to beat him with. So this time when she let him go he grabbed *her* by the neck straight off. 'Now,' says Jack, 'I've got you good. Spit up that name I give you or I'll mash that ugly gizzard till 'tis no bigger through than a broom straw.' And she did. She coughed a couple of times and out came Molly's father's name, and lay there on the floor of the barn, but mighty sick and dirty it looked for having been in her. 'Let me go now,' says she to Jack, 'for I've given back what I got from you tonight, and the dead, they never rise.' 'No,' says Jack, 'but there's others to come, and a babe in the cradle and a old man in the chimney corner forever. I've heard it said banshees have the second sight.' 'Well, that's so,' says the banshee, 'an' if you'll be lettin' up on me poor neck a trifle I'll be tellin' you about it.' 'Never mind that,' says Jack, and he beat the wall with her like a man beatin' a carpet, 'I've a question for you. Thrice you've asked me who's to die—once I'll ask you, who's to be born.' ''Tis the Antichrist,' says the banshee, quick as a snake, 'an' you to be the father of it.' "

Don't be blasphemous, Kate.

"And the last word hadn't left her lips but what she exploded like a barrel of gunpowder and threw poor Jack head after heels. When he picked himself up, she was gone, and never a man saw her after, and when they came in the morning they found Jack sittin' on a grindstone and pickin' at his teeth with a splinter. Only it wasn't Molly's father that come, because after the banshee swallowed his name he never raised from his bed again, and he died the next year. Well, Jack took Molly for his bride in church, but he had himself a little house built beside her big one, and there he lives, and now they're both old, and no children."

Did the banshee ever come back, Katie?

"Never to show her face, but the cattle do poorly in that barn, and Jack just stores a bit of hay in it mostly, and most years

that's sour. Molly's a old woman now, and they say she resem-
bles the banshee more than is common."

*That's enough, Kate. In fact, it's too much. Get Hannah ready
for bed now. I'll see to Mary myself.*

"Here, darlin', and off with your gown, an' come out back
where there's a clout for your darlin' face, for there's half your
supper on it."

Not so hard, Katie.

"I've been wantin' a word with you, darlin'. Who's that I see
behind you?"

It's just little Den, Katie. He's been there before.

"Yes, but there's another, dimmer yet, behind him."

I can only see the one behind me, Katie. "And that's the story
the Irish girl used to tell, Denny. Or one of 'em. You see, it's not
always well to make someone say what they don't want to."

*I know another one, Hannah. See, I say: I one dirt, and you
say: I two dirt—like that.*

"You ate dirt yourself, you dirty child."

You never finished telling me about the Indians.

"Well, it isn't as if I was Buffalo Bill, Denny. Those were the
only Indians I ever saw in my life, except when I was a grownup woman and the circus come. They were the last Indians
around here."

Tell me.

"They had a little house. It wasn't one of them pointed tents
like you see in books, but a little house made all of sticks, with
bark on the outside. It was so small a grown person would have
to get down on hands and knees to get in, and my father never
went inside it at all, but I did while he was bargaining with the
Indian man, and the Indian woman was inside there, with a tiny
little bit of a fire that went up through the roof where a piece
of the bark had been taken down, and she had a little Indian
baby on her lap—it was laid on a piece of real soft leather, and
it didn't have nothing on. There was a Bible pushed over against
the wall that I guess some missionary gave them, and a little

bundle of feathers, and some wood for the fire, and that was everything that was in the whole house. The man had a gun and a knife, but he was outside talking to Pa. The Indian woman wouldn't even look at me, just kept rocking back and forth, with the baby on her lap there; that baby never moved and I think maybe it was dead—just a little baby. I told Pa about the woman afterward and he said probably she was drunk."

Doubtless she was, but meantime the Indian has his knife, but I do not have mine—and Dr. Van Ness says I could use more exercise. There was never a time when I could feel sure of drawing the floor plans of this house correctly; that is the fault of building late, of moving into a new home at a time when the various old ones have settled into the brain and become a part of its landscape, their walls like those old romantic walls in nineteenth-century paintings, with bushes and even cedar trees sprouting from the crumbling stone. I remember Eleanor Bold once told me that the rose called Belle Amour was found growing from a wall in a ruined convent in Switzerland; the walls of those old houses in my mind are like that, rotting and falling, yet at the same time armed with thorns and gay with strange flowers, and bound tighter with the roots of all the living things that have grown there than they ever were with mortar and plaster.

Furthermore I made the mistake, when the company at last came into my hands and I had funds enough to build, of duplicating, or nearly duplicating, certain well-remembered rooms whose furnishings had fallen to me by inheritance. It would have been better—and I could well have afforded to do so—to have restored the houses themselves, buying up the lots on which they had stood (in those cases, too frequent, in which they had been demolished to provide space for third-rate apartments and parking lots) and building them anew. Old photographs by the thousands might have been found to guide the builders, and surely I might have discovered many tenants, childless couples of orderly habits, who would have been happy to maintain and cherish these possessions in return for a reduced rent.

Instead I made the error of interspersing among the functional rooms of my home certain "museum rooms"; but when I try to recall where they lie—or, for that matter, where the stairs are—or the closet in which I once kept an umbrella, I find myself lost in a maze of pictures without names and doors that open to nowhere. "The nine men's morris is fill'd up with mud, and the quaint mazes of the wanton green for lack of tread are undistinguishable." (I remember the architect unrolling his blue plans on the table in the dining nook of my little apartment, and indeed he unrolled them many times there, for there were changes and consultations—as it seemed then—without end. I remember the squares and rectangles that were to be rooms, and his telling me over and over that those that were to be windowless would be dark, despite the windows we had arranged for them in appropriate places, windows that would be curtained always, with diffused light behind the shades; or blocked—for my aunt Olivia had arranged some of hers so, in imitation, I think, of Elizabeth Barrett—with painted screens; or which would open on illusions like those of a puppet theater. But I do not remember their positions with reference to this long, walled porch in which I live, or even upon what floor they were. I should, I suppose, begin by going out, and walking all around the house, if I can, peering in through windows like a burglar while I note the damage winter has done. But it seems too much, too elaborate, for a man who only wishes to walk about in his own home, behaving as though it were the fun house at a carnival, a place in which all the walls not glass are mirrors.)

"You promised me, Mr. Weer, that if I would prescribe for your stroke you would cooperate with me—take certain tests."

"I had forgotten all about you. I thought you were gone."

"Wait a moment, I have to move this aside. There. It's a mirror, see? With little wheels on the side."

"Like a fun-house mirror."

"Exactly. Stand in front, please. See, as I move the wheel, the area of the mirror adjacent to it becomes more or less distorting; do you understand what I mean?"

"It's metal, isn't it? It couldn't be glass."

"I believe it is actually plastic, with a flash coating of silver. You understand how it works?"

"Of course."

"Very good. Now I want you to stand right there and adjust the wheels until your reflection appears just as it should."

I spin the magic wheels, giving myself first a suggestive immensity in the region of my sex organs, then the corporate gut expected of a major industrialist, then the narrow waist and exaggerated shoulders of a working cowboy, and at last setting everything to rights. Lips pursed, Dr. Van Ness notes the numbers on each dial (there are five) and compares them with numbers on a slip of paper he takes from his desk.

"How did I do?"

"Very well, Mr. Weer. Perhaps too well. Your image of each of the psychosomic body areas is perfect; in other words your I.D.R. is zero. I would say this indicates a very high level of self-concern."

"You mean that's how I look?"

"Yes, that's exactly how you look. Frightening, isn't it?"

"No, I don't find it so. I hadn't thought I was quite that tall —I mean, on reflection; when I adjusted the thing, of course I did the best I could."

"You aren't a particularly tall man, Mr. Weer."

"No, but I'm taller than I thought. I find that comforting."

"You used the word 'reflection,' a moment ago, in a rather ambiguous sense. Were you aware of it?"

"I meant to make a joke. For myself. I'm afraid I do that often—I don't expect the people I'm talking to to understand them, and they seldom do."

"I see." Dr. Van Ness writes something on his pad.

"You know, all I really wanted from you was advice about the effect of exercise on my stroke. I've got that, and now I really should wipe you out."

"Do you really think that you could do that, Mr. Weer?"

"Of course. All I have to do is turn my mind toward something else—naturally I can't prove that to you, because you wouldn't be there to see the proof."

"Do you feel you can control the whole world—just with your mind?"

"Not the real world—but this world, yes. In the real world I am an elderly man, sick and alone, and I can't do anything about that. But this world—your only world now, Van Ness—I have conjured from my imagination and my memories. This interview between us never took place, but I wanted advice about my stroke."

"Could you make me stand on my head? Or turn blue?"

"I prefer to have you remain yourself."

"So do I. You may recall, Mr. Weer, that when I advised you —about this future stroke—you promised to look at some cards for me. Here they are."

"What am I supposed to do?"

"Turn over the first card. Tell me who the people are and what they are doing."

2

OLIVIA

BOBBY BLACK DIED, in time, from the spinal injury he suffered on my grandmother's stairs. Shortly after his funeral, I went to live with my aunt Olivia. I was then (I think) eight or nine years old. The Blacks were—understandably, no doubt—bitter and troubled, and the social situation must have been quite tense. My parents decided to spend half a year or more touring Europe, but I was judged too young to go. Whether my aunt volunteered to care for me or was in some way dragooned into doing so (she was, I think, at that time dependent on my father for at least a part of her income), I do not know. Certainly I felt unwelcome initially, and though that in time changed I do not believe my aunt ever accepted me as a more or less permanent resident in her home—to all intents and purposes, at least as far as she was concerned, I was an overnight guest who would, or should, leave the next day; a day that was long coming, so that, for me now, my whole stay has become one enormous morning, interminable afternoon, and unending evening, all these spent at a house across the alley and five lots down from my mother's (grandmother's) old one, to which I must have tramped a dozen times, in the first weeks after my parents' departure, to peer beneath the shades of its curtained windows. I was mocked mercilessly for this by my aunt whenever she discovered me, and I have seldom felt more abandoned and alone than I did then.

Aunt Olivia's house was quite different from my grandmother's, horizontal and sprawling (though there were two stories, a cellar, and an attic) rather than high, vertical, and secretive. In my grandmother's house I had always felt that the house knew but would not tell; in my aunt Olivia's that the house itself had forgotten.

The windows were wide. There was a bay window facing the street, and another, on a side wall, overlooking the rock garden; there were window seats before these, and at several other windows as well—window seats that, so it now seems to me, were mostly filled with sheet music, though it may be that I am confusing them with the piano bench, which, opening in the same way and possessing the same sort of padded top, must have seemed to me then to be akin to them, a receptacle equally alien and magical —my grandmother's house had had no window seats, and pianists sat at a stool whose particular virtue it was to go up or down when spun.

The walls, rambling walls that never ran straight for more than one room at a stretch, were undecided in other ways as well: sometimes of wood painted white, sometimes of brick—and the bricks not always of a family but various, some soft old crumbling building bricks—in other walls the hard, glassy, vitreous paving bricks for which the local kilns were (locally) famous. The shutters were green. The roof green, too, the cedar shingles welcoming, in spots, bright mosses, and the dome over the Doric-columned cupola above the parlor green as well—*vert de Grice.*

The house extended nearly to the sidewalk, so that there was, properly speaking, no front lawn, only two flower beds given over to ferns, since nothing else would grow in the shade of the elm trees that stood between the sidewalk and the street. One side yard held the rock garden with its tiny toppled elves and gnomes, and the birdbath pool from which the neighborhood cats, climbing the fence and equally contemptuous of the ceramic guardians and the penned dogs, regularly abstracted the goldfish from Woolworth's my aunt as regularly replaced.

The other side yard, which received more sun, boasted green grass and a blaze of zinnias and marigolds and similar flowers. The back yard held kennels for such of the dogs as were not currently permitted the house, and wire runs.

For my aunt raised Pekinese.

And, indeed, she raised them in the most literal sense, and while every other breeder sought diminution, my aunt's dogs, though they retained the pugged faces, bulging eyes, and bowed legs characteristic of the breed, were selected and bred for size, for she was intent upon restoring the "Lion Dogs"—those ancient, ferocious T'ang dogs and Foo dogs which were to medieval China what the mastiff was to Europe; and of which the present Pekinese are only toys, miniature copies, lifetime puppies, intended to amuse and flatter the children and the sheltered, silly women of the Forbidden City.

As such, my aunt felt that they were not for her. She was not sheltered—she had lived alone and more or less independently since the death of her father, treating my grandmother, her mother, a good deal more distantly than my own mother did. Nor was she silly. Indeed she might be said to have been one of those people who are driven to a sort of absurdity for want of silliness, for she made herself ridiculous by caring nothing for so many of the things valued by us—the people about her, her relatives and friends, and the very now-grown girls with whom she had shared a desk in that pleasant brick school at the upper end of what was then a village, a school at which she had somehow learned (or at least taught herself) such a different curriculum than the one her teachers held important. She was a feminist of the sort who despises women, and a bluestocking of a blue that was nearly black, an amateur of every art, of music (she played the piano, as I have indicated, and the harp, too), of painting, of poetry and literature of every kind; she sculptured clay, arranged flowers—begging sweetly from neighbors and friends those materials (and they were many) her own garden did not provide, and using, as well, wild flowers, and branches broken from wild flowering trees in their seasons, and cattails—and furniture and pictures, and this last not only in her own house, but in the home—when the mood struck her—of anyone who would allow her past the door. She subscribed to intellectual and scientific periodicals that would never otherwise have been seen in Cassionsville, and when she had read them gave them to the library, so that a stranger to the town—a drummer, say, just disembarking from a train and seeking an hour's innocent reading before a night spent at Abbott's hotel—would have thought the town to be a very hotbed of intellectuality when the fact was that you might have killed it all, if you were so fortunate as to possess a motorcar, on any spring day when it proceeded, with pansies and lily of the valley on its small hat, from Macafee's Department Store diagonally across Main Street to Dubarry's Bakery.

She had never married. She lived alone with her dogs in her big house, had her laundry done by a washerwoman, and twice or three times a month had another woman—seldom the same one twice running, as there were five or seven of them she, as she said herself, "spread her trade over to make it interesting for them"—in to clean, a slavey with whom she would gossip for two hours at lunch, overpay, and accuse, as soon as she had left, of theft.

In bad weather particularly she might never venture out of doors for days, and I remember, in the year before I went to live with her, hearing—on frosty mornings when I was on my way to school—her harp across the snow. When the mood was on her, and especially on Sundays, she might pay calls on everyone; but other women seldom called on her. She frightened them a little, I suspect, and made them envious with her freedom even while they feared her detachment from all those things that gave meaning to their own lives, from husband and children and cooking and sewing, from the farmwife mentality without the farm, from vegetable gardens (which nearly everyone had except my aunt Olivia, because if you had no vegetable garden, what would you have to can?) and chickens (which many vegetable gardeners had as well) and relatives who came to dinner and brought the children.

We were my aunt Olivia's only relatives, and no one ever came to dinner at Olivia's, because she did not cook, and often had for her supper (I recall how shocked I was when I was first there) only a pickle (from the gift jar of some pickling neighbor) and a cup of tea. Her suitors—she had three when I was staying with her—came in the evening, having, like everyone else, eaten dinner in the early afternoon. She would give them tea and cake, or tea and cookies, cake and cookies from Dubarry's, telling them, laughing, that as she would not cook for herself she would not cook for any man, that they would have to starve if they took her, and they, one and all, swearing that she should have a cook, and a maid, too, if she were to marry them. Professor Peacock—that lean, good-natured man—offered, too, if she preferred, to starve with her, and even proposed that they should set up housekeeping in the boarding house (an entire two towns off!) in which he lived, declaring that they would chop a hole in the wall between their rooms so that they might say they lived, "like the troglodytes known to classical writers" and "to Montesquieu," in a hole, eating dumplings on Sunday and creamed chicken on Monday, and hash and tongue on other days save when some new arrival, some promising new member of the faculty, was at table and the future of the whole establishment turned, as upon less than a hair, on his judgment— when they would have roast pork and dressing, particularly if it was July. This professor, whom I had seen on the street once or twice without identifying before I came to my aunt Olivia's (for he arrived by train, sometimes as often as twice a week, to call on her, staying the night at the hotel and returning to his classroom in the morning by an early train), was the only evidence we had that there was—as there was—a university only thirty-five miles off, a green and living branch borne by the winds and currents of love far out into a sea of ignorance, a sea of chickens and pigs and beef cattle, of corn and tomatoes, where it could be lifted dripping from the water by the weary mariner who, pressing his face to its foliage, might still smell the chalk, without ever knowing to what point of the compass (if indeed it were to any point of a merely human compass) the fabled land of learning lay.

(I have just been describing, without knowing it when I began —or I should say burlesquing—an engraving that hung in my grandmother's front parlor. Its place, I believe, was next to a girl who gripped 'mid perilous seas the Rock of Ages; and it depicted Columbus plucking from the wave, to the amazed delight of his onlooking men, a sprig of dogwood, with the setting sun sinking in a most promising welter of light in the background. When I was a boy, this picture always gave me the impression, as I believe it was intended to, that the New World was uncreated prior to its discovery.)

Just what it was Professor Peacock taught I never learned, but from what I recall of his conversation I should say it was anthropology, or American history, though it might as well have been half a dozen other things, and those subjects only his avocations, the things he did best rather than the thing he was paid to do. For after all, if the lives of most men are examined in detail, it will be found that they have been experts of immense stature in some unremunerated field, the strategy and theory of some sport or the practice of some craft, have had an exhaustive knowledge of old circus posters or eighteenth-century inn signs or the mathematics of comets; and nothing so distinguished Professor Peacock from the ruck of men as his air of amateurishness. He was a man who seemed to love everything he did too much to do it well. His shoes, as an example (and the most typical—the point at which he was clearly most like himself), were always either too loosely tied or not tied at all, the laces dragging the ground like the laces of a very small boy's. But, unlike that small boy, Professor Peacock never tripped over his.

He took long strides, and he was, in any event, agile of body without being graceful, a flurry of elbows and knees as he nearly, but not actually, dropped his umbrella or his spade, or went, with a startling quickness that frightened my aunt Olivia as much as myself, over the edge of a cliff (we called them "bluffs") on a rope, a leggy brown spider that never fell.

And at this point I had better describe Cassionsville and its surroundings more fully than I have yet done. I have just been outside refreshing my memory, though there is not a great deal to be seen from the garden behind my room, and I have not— not yet—walked around the whole house as I proposed. Only to the far side of the fallen elm, where I thought for a time, as I leaned on the handle of my ax, that I would climb into the branches; but in the end I did not. This damp early spring hurts my bones. The weather? Oh, yes, the weather. The south wind doth blow/so we shan't have snow/but I think rain is quite likely.

Cassionsville is situated on the Kanakessee River. The valley is open to the west, typical Midwestern bottomland of which a hundred acres will support a family very comfortably. To the east, where the river is narrower and swifter, the land grows progressively stonier, and the farms (surprisingly) smaller as well as poorer, with more cattle and more woodlots, and less plowing. The graveyards, as I have often noticed, are older in the east, for the first settlers came from that direction and the poorest farms are often owned by the oldest families—the farmhouses often with walls of logs, covered now by clapboards or horsefeathers. The Weers—our family is supposed to have originated in Holland, the "Black Dutch" descendants of Philip II's Spanish soldiery—at one time operated a water mill on the upper river.

Cassionsville was built at the first ford. This no longer exists; the river has been bridged, and the wide, low banks (still visible in old photographs of Water Street) narrowed and filled in to make more space for buildings. The longer, more important thoroughfares run east and west, following the river. They are River, Water, Main, Morgan, Church, Browning, and so on. The north-south streets are all named for trees: Oak, Chestnut, Willow, Elder, Apple, Plum, and Sumac. And others. The town is hilly, and the streets—the north-south streets particularly—are steep. Several creeks once ran through the town on their turbulent way to the Kanakessee, but they were long ago confined to conduits, and paved over, and now are merely storm sewers, their very names forgotten, though they still empty, through wide, round mouths, their floods into the river. West of the town, in broader, quieter water, there is a long, stony island which used, at about the time I imagined myself visiting Dr. Van Ness, to harbor a hermit called Crazy Pete.

To the north and south, above the valley, are rugged and even picturesque hills, too rough for farming. Much of the timber there was cut fifty years before my boyhood and, by the time I first saw these hills, had been replaced by a second growth which was then approaching maturity; but lost among the small, dark valleys there were still (then, and I suppose some remain even now) untouched pieces of the original climax forest of America. Small streams ran through these valleys, chuckling over rocks; and there were deer and rabbits and foxes and even, I think, some wildcats; but the bears and wolves and mountain lions were all gone, gone so long ago that I believe Hannah was the only person I have ever heard speak of them, and even to her they were only a childhood memory.

Like some of the trees, the rocks remain; they are the soldiers, the Knights Templar, of the country, who if they were unable to save all the forest at least saved some of it, and the land itself, from the plow: three-foot rocks like humble infantrymen buried and half buried in the poor soil, tall columns of stone like generals and heroes visible for miles, crowned with hawks. I have seen a lovely pine tree there embracing a stone with her roots as though she were kissing the gallant who was going to war for her, and on her own time scale she was. But among these stones (as Professor Peacock would remind me, were I still a boy and he—whom I never remember as other than a young man—still alive) "there are others, Alden. Projectile points and hand axes, and even others—like this."

His long-fingered, knobby hand pushed to one side the coil of of rope slung across his shoulder and rummaged in a trouser pocket, jingled coins, and at last produced a long, narrow, and very thin flake of hard brownish gray. "Do you know what this is?"

I took it and held it between my fingers, feeling suddenly and foolishly that it was a feather from a bird petrified. I shook my head.

"Have you ever seen a man plane a board? Do you remember the long curly wood shavings, Alden, that come out of the plane? Once someone was shaping a stone, to make a flint knife or an arrowhead. To do that, he had to—"

My aunt Olivia called from upstairs, "I'll be down in just a moment now, Robert. Is Den entertaining you?"

"Oh, yes, we're having a fine time."

I said, "There's a picnic lunch. Aunt Olivia made us a picnic lunch."

"That's quite an honor. She never cooks, does she?"

"Sometimes, just for me and her. There's turkey. She made the lady that comes in to clean pluck it. But she cooked it herself. Sandwiches."

"Are you hungry? Shall we raid the basket before she comes down?"

"You'd better not." Aunt Olivia was on the stairs, wearing the old pink dress that, as she had explained to me the night before over a supper of tea and cheese, she always wore on these expeditions "because it isn't good enough for anything else but it still looks nice," and on her small feet a pair of very fashionable, high-laced lady's hunting boots. The dress was not, as I saw now, nearly as worn-looking as those she put on to dust in—or wore when she was expecting no company—when there was and would be no one in her house but myself. "Ready to go, Robert? Den's been ready for hours, I know." Suddenly (it was something I was still unused to) she whistled piercingly, and Ming-Sno and Sun-sun came bounding, panting with pleasure, their deformed heads seeming almost split by their wide "kylin" mouths.

"Are you going to take both of them?"

"Why not? I'll hold Ming-Sno, and Den can hold Sun-sun. You hold the picnic basket, Robert."

We went by trolley across the bridge, and rode—the farthest I had ever ridden it—to the south end of the line, a place of a few stables built upon hillsides, and some cow sheds. Professor Peacock asked my aunt Olivia if she wanted to go to Eagle Rock.

"You are the master today, Robert. It's a beautiful day, and Den and Ming-Sno and Sun-sun and I will accompany you wherever you wish, provided our poor, weak legs will bear us thither."

The Professor laughed at her. "You could walk the legs off me if you wanted to, Vi, and you know it. But there's a spot I've been wanting to look at."

And so we walked by strange, bent little paths, the dogs romping around us, and my aunt Olivia pointing out wild flowers and coining, quite straight-faced, fantastic names for them, so that the dogtooth violet and the lady's-slipper found themselves mingled, for that passing instant (as though they had attended an enchanted ball by mistake), with empress's tears, duchess's hat, and lavender star of George Sand.

"That's phlox," Professor Peacock said.

"Robert, how hopelessly mundane you are. Of course it is. It is also star of George Sand—I just renamed it, and you should know that the folk names of flowers aren't scientific, and that some of them have three or four. *Marguerite*, poor lady, is also the oxeye daisy, not to mention the white-swan and the memorial daisy."

"Vi, you—"

"And so when this darling boy is grown and someone asks him what a certain flower is, he will tell them; and eventually the name will pass into general use, and eventually some idiot will be writing something like, 'The name "star of George Sand," by which this flower is often popularly known, cannot have originated much before 1804, the year in which Miss Sand (nee Dupin) was born.'"

"Now you're talking like a book, which is what you always tell me I do, Vi. I was going to say that you also make up most of your Chinoiserie—you do, you know. But when you talk about George Sand you sound like that fellow Blaine."

"Stewart? Oh, no. He's all for General Wallace, and that kind of book. That hamper isn't getting too heavy for you, is it, Robert? Den and I could carry it between us for a bit."

"No, I'm fine. But the rest of the way is going to be steep. Up this hill and then down the other side, which is worse, then around the next and up. Think you can make it?"

"Of course. Anyway, we're nearly to the top already."

"How about you, Alden?"

"I thought we just came out to look at the flowers."

My aunt Olivia said, "Robert never asks me to come out here unless he has something to show me—do you, Robert? He comes here by himself and prowls about, and has all the fun of finding something, and then comes to get me to admire it. The last time it was a dinosaur's skull."

"A sloth," Professor Peacock said. "Manville, at the university, has identified it now. A giant sloth."

"At any rate, I thought it was going to be very frightening, but it was only a big piece of bone and a tooth—you are a deceiver, Robert."

"Only an enthusiast," Professor Peacock said.

· 51 ·

I asked him what the sloth was doing here. "Eating leaves," he replied shortly. "That's what they did, mostly." The ascent was sufficiently steep for him to be a little out of breath, as indeed all of us were except Sun-sun and Ming-Sno, who panted constantly whether the way was easy or abrupt, but never seemed to lack for wind.

I pointed out that the sloth could have gotten those anywhere, and my aunt Olivia told me to be quiet; but nonetheless it seemed to me that my objection was just, that no animal would have had to come to this remote and rugged area just for leaves. Not knowing what any sort of sloth was, much less a giant one, which sounded both clumsier and more exciting, I pictured an immense cow, and then Babe, Paul Bunyan's blue ox, of which I had read somewhere, and then the giant himself, ax in hand, a giant who almost immediately became myself magnified, stalking across the hills by stepping from hilltop to hilltop, and I thought of the fun it would be to fell the trees, sending them crashing down into the gorges, into the narrow valleys, so that more could grow where they had stood.

"When I grow up," I said, "I'm going to have a ax, and I'm going to come here and chop down a bunch of these trees."

Professor Peacock said, "Take my advice, Alden—when you're grown up, a pretty woman is a more pleasant companion than an ax."

"Oh, Robert!"

"Aunt Olivia, if Ming-Sno dies, or Sun-sun, can we bury them here?"

"What a thing to say, Den. They're not going to die."

"When they get real old." Actually I would gladly have killed them on the spot for the fun of the funeral. Sun-sun, who had been sniffing at a woodchuck hole, had dirt on his nose already.

"Why do you want them to be buried here?"

"So somebody a long time from now will find their heads and be surprised."

Professor Peacock said, "He's right, Vi. Look at their skulls

—no one would think that they were dogs."

My aunt Olivia said, "Don't be silly, Den, nobody would find them."

"Years from now," the professor said, laughing.

"Years from now they would know what they were: big Pekinese."

"You misunderstand me, Vi. I am on Alden's side, and we mean thousands and thousands of years."

"There won't be anyone then," my aunt Olivia said. She was pulling herself up the slope, and Professor Peacock stopped to give her a hand. We were nearly at the top.

"You don't know that," he said.

"It's not difficult to guess. You know the history of species. Each starts as an obscure new animal, inhabiting a small area, and rare even in that. Then, for some reason, conditions become favorable for it—it spreads and spreads and spreads and becomes the most common creature of all. If it is a grazing animal like us, it will increase until the plains are black with its kind."

"Men aren't grazing animals, Vi," the professor objected.

"The bread in that basket you're carrying was ground from the seed of a grass, Robert, and the turkey was fattened on grain. The Chinese, who constitute a quarter or more of the world's population, exist almost entirely on the seeds of a swamp grass."

A moment later we were at the top; while the professor and I sat down to rest, my aunt, facing into the wind, took off her wide hat and loosed the jet-headed pins that held her hair. It was very long, and as black as a starling's wing. Professor Peacock took a pair of binoculars from a leather case on his belt and said, "Do you know how to use these, Alden? Just turn this knob until whatever you're looking at becomes clear. I want to show you something. Where I'm pointing."

"A dragon," my aunt Olivia said. "The claws of a dragon, imprisoned in an antediluvian lava flow. When Robert cracks the rock, he will be free and alive again; but don't worry, Den, he is a relative of Sun-sun's."

"A cave," the professor said. "See the dark spot on the side of that bluff?"

I was still looking for it when my aunt took the glasses, saying, "Let me see, Den."

"Only about fifteen or twenty feet down from the top. I think they reached it by a trail from the other side, but part of that's fallen away now. Look off to the left."

My aunt nodded. "I saw Altamira while I was in Spain, Robert. I told you about it, didn't I—yes, I know I did. The name means 'to view from a high place,' I think, and you go down into a cave."

"I don't imagine we're going to discover another Altamira four miles from Cassionsville," the professor said, "but I thought it might be interesting. I'm going to let myself down from the top with this rope."

My aunt looked at him speculatively.

We made our way down the farther side of the hill we had just climbed, and splashed across a small, stony stream edged with moss-trunked trees whose limbs, stretching across the noisy water, muted it within a few feet to music, a sound that might have been the notes of a syrinx played to one who, by turns, laughed and wept.

Through smaller and more closely set trees, through blackberry brambles and thickets, the five of us passed around the shoulder of the hill; then, over grass now drying in the first summer sun, to its top. This was a higher hill than the first, though the ascent (on the side we had chosen) was easier, and I recall that when I looked from its summit toward the hill from which we had seen the cave, I was surprised at how low and easy it appeared. I asked the professor where the town lay, and he pointed out a distant scrap of road to me, and a smoke which he said came from the brick kilns; not a single house of any sort was visible from where we stood. While my aunt and I were still admiring the view, he tied a large knot—which he told me later, when I asked, was called a "monkey's fist"—in one end of his rope and wedged it between two solidly set stones. Then, with a sliding loop around his waist, he lowered himself from the edge, fending off the stones of the bluff with his legs much as though he were walking.

"Well," my aunt said, standing at the edge to watch him, with the toes of her boots (this I remember vividly) extending an inch or more into space, "he's gone, Den. Shall we cut the rope?"

I was not certain that she was joking, and shook my head.

"Vi, what are you two chattering about up there?" The professor's voice was still loud, but somehow sounded far away.

"I'm trying to persuade Den to murder you. He has a lovely scout knife—I've seen it."

"And he won't do it?"

"He says not."

"Good for you, lad."

"Well, really, Robert, why shouldn't he? There you hang like a great, ugly spider, and all he has to do is cut the rope. It would change his whole life like a religious conversion—haven't you ever read Dostoyevsky? And if he doesn't do it he'll always wonder if it wasn't partly because he was afraid."

"If you do cut it, Alden, push her over afterward, won't you? No witnesses."

"That's right," my aunt Olivia told me, "you could say we made a suicide pact."

Frightened, I shook my head again, and heard Professor Peacock call, "There is a cave here, Vi!"

"Do you see anything?"

He did not answer, and I, determined to be at least as daring as my aunt, walked to the edge and looked over; the rope hung slack, moving when my foot touched it. Trying to sound completely grown up, I asked, "Did he fall?"

"No, silly, he's in the cave, and we'll have to wait up here forever and ever before he'll come up and tell us what he found."

She had lowered her voice, and I followed suit. "You didn't really want me to cut the rope, did you, Aunt Olivia?"

"I don't suppose I really cared a great deal whether you did or not, Den, but I would have stopped you if you'd tried—or didn't you know that?"

If I had been older, I would have told her I did, and I would —after the fashion of older people—have been telling the truth. I had sensed that cutting the rope was only a joke; I had also sensed that beneath the joke there was a strain of earnestness, and I was not mature enough yet to subscribe fully to that convention by which such underlying, embarrassing thoughts are ignored—as we ignore the dead trees in a garden because they have been overgrown with morning-glories or climbing roses at the urging of the clever gardener. I continued to wait thus, embarrassed and silent, until the professor's head appeared above the edge of the bluff and he scrambled up to stand with us.

He said, "It was inhabited at one time all right, Vi. There's signs of a fire, and even some scratches on rocks. Not Altamira, of course."

My aunt walked to the edge—she had stepped back from it while we had been waiting—and looked over. "I could do that, I think," she said.

"Vi, don't be insane!"

In the end Professor Peacock made a sort of sling seat for her and lowered her over the edge. I asked him if she was not heavy, and he said, "Vi? Lord, no. She's all bird bones and petticoats. Her clothes probably weigh more than she does." I asked how I was going to get down (having assumed that since my aunt was going I would go, too); while the professor was looking surprised, my aunt, who must have had excellent hearing, called, "Put Den in the seat, Robert. I'll catch him when he comes down. All you have to do is hang on, Den, and keep yourself from scraping."

The way down was shorter than I had imagined, and at the bottom, standing on a narrow but apparently quite secure ledge, was my aunt, who took me in her arms and drew me into the cave. After a moment the empty rope rose again, and after another it returned, this time with the picnic basket slung by the handles. "Now," Aunt Olivia said, "even if cruel Robert abandons us we won't starve, Den; at least not for a while."

I asked if he was coming down.

"Of course, or he won't get any lunch."

He was there in a moment, his presence backing us slightly into the small cave behind the ledge. "See," he said, "how black the soil is here? That's charcoal." He squatted, sifting it between his fingers until he had a fragment of carbonized wood to show us; a tiny fleck of mica caught the sunlight for an instant and gleamed like a dying spark. "There were hundreds of fires here," he said, "perhaps thousands."

My aunt was already unpacking the lunch. "It's going to get the underside of my tablecloth black," she said, "but I daresay Mrs. Doherty will restore it for a price." She stopped for a moment to examine an unintelligible pattern of lines someone had scratched on the wall of the cave. "Could I make a rubbing of that, do you think?"

Professor Peacock said, "I'll do it for you. I want one for myself, too. Do you think Alden here realizes that this is the oldest house he has ever been in? Probably the oldest he will ever be in, even if he lives to be a hundred."

Aunt Olivia, having untied the blue thread that had held it shut in the basket, peered into a small milk-glass dish with a lid shaped like a setting hen. "Ah, olives," she said. "Ripe olives. I'd forgotten what I put in there. Den may realize that, Robert, but it won't mean anything to him. Not yet. Are you finding treasures in that dirt?"

"A bone." He held it up—a blackened twig. "My guess is wild turkey."

I said, "The Indians lived here, didn't they?"

"Pre-Indians," Professor Peacock said.

My aunt snorted.

"The aboriginal people," the professor continued, "who—

about ten thousand years ago, according to Hrdlicka—crossed the Bering Strait and eventually settled at Indianola, Indian Lake, Indianapolis, and various other places, at which points they were forced to become Indians in order to justify the place-names. That turkey may have gobbled his last gobble before the pyramids were built." My aunt handed him a sandwich; he put it down until he could dust his black fingers on the legs of his trousers. She said, "This may be the last meal ever eaten here, Robert—that's what I've been thinking while I got the food out. It's probably the first time anyone has eaten here in at least five hundred years, and it may be the last time anyone ever does. What are you looking at back there, Den?"

"Nothing," I said. It was a skull, a human skull lying amid a clutter of other bones, but I remembered a time several years before when I had found the skull of some animal—perhaps a rabbit or a squirrel—under the dense rose hedge in the garden, and carried it in to my mother, who had been horrified; I said nothing and took my place at the tablecloth. We had sandwiches and olives, and celery still wet from the spigot at the sink in my aunt Olivia's kitchen, and lemonade—no longer very cool. And cookies: hard gingersnaps I recognized as coming from the bakery. After the meal, my aunt and Professor Peacock made rubbings of the scratches on the rocks, and I watched each of them find the bones and decide—my aunt Olivia very quickly, Professor Peacock, I think, more slowly—to say nothing.

Then the professor climbed to the top of the hill again, and I sat in the sling seat and was pulled up. I expected him to lower the rope for my aunt then, but he climbed down again instead, saying that he had something to discuss with her and telling me to wait. I whistled up Ming-Sno and Sun-sun, but had only a minute or two of play with them on the hilltop before he returned and, letting down the rope for the last time, slowly drew up my aunt, with the empty picnic basket in her lap. As we were going home, while Professor Peacock was paying the conductor, I told my aunt that he had wanted me to cut the rope, too—when she was coming up. (He had not said so, but I had felt it.) But that I would not do it. She squeezed my hand, and after a moment whispered in my ear that she had left her little dish with the hen on top in the cave. "For me. Because I had olives in it—do you see, Den? And besides, it's china."

I pointed out that it was milk glass.

"The bottom," she said firmly as Professor Peacock took his seat, "was china."

The second of my aunt's three suitors was James Macafee. To me, at the time, he seemed somewhat set apart from the others —he always brought gifts, and his gifts were never flowers (which I loathed) or candy (which I favored, since my aunt seldom ate more than one piece, leaving the rest, the vanilla opera creams and chewy chocolate-covered caramels, for me) but something substantial, a music stand or a set of ivory-yellow coolies who would press my aunt's books together, one pushing hard with both his hands while the other leaned back against the last book, almost upsetting his wide hat. Mr. Macafee came less often than either of the others, came earlier, and left earlier. He regularly gave me coins (which neither of the others did) and once brought me a Marine Band harmonica.

I think that it was some time before I connected him with Macafee's Department Store, which he owned. He was short, somewhat stout, and going bald young; he dressed well, in a fashion I admired more at the time than Stewart Blaine's, the other suitor. He was, I think, genuinely kindly and genuinely fond of music, and always looked pleased when my aunt played for him and disappointed when she stopped. About forty years after the time of which I am writing, when the control of Macafee's (no longer under that name) had more or less passed to me as a result of certain financial transactions on the part of the company, I spent the better part of an afternoon searching the store's records for some trace of James Macafee's administration. Eventually I unearthed a few documents, but there were far fewer associated with him than with his father (Donald Macafee, the founder)—this despite the fact that those that might have been expected to bear his name were more recent, and that he had actually controlled the store for a longer period of time. He was a shrewd bargainer; but he must have disliked signing papers, and detested any form of personal publicity.

He entertained my aunt with walks, and with rides in his Studebaker, rides that often turned into antique-hunting expeditions, for he was as ardent a collector of antiques as my aunt was of Chinese, and Chinese-related, objets d'art. On summer Sunday evenings they went to the band concerts in Wallingford Park, to which, during the time I lived with my aunt, I was forced to accompany them, she sitting between Mr. Macafee and myself, all of us on a narrow green park bench with an iron frame and wooden-slat seat and back, applauding politely at the conclusion of each selection. The bandstand stood just in front of the Civil War Memorial (a gray stone statue of a man in a forage cap and what was intended to be the baggy blue uniform of the Union Army, a soldier who held, idly now, a Springfield musket while he stood—like a workman at the margin of an excavation —on the edge of an abyss of time whose farther side was the bandstand, and whose nearer side was his own pedestal, with its granite tablet carved with the names of the town's dead, and not, as I had supposed a few years earlier, of the men he had killed); the band was somehow a branch of the volunteer fire company.

Without rules or enforcement, seating was strictly regulated: the best dressed occupied the benches closest to the bandstand. The worst dressed of all, the very poor children and a few town loafers, did not sit in the park, but used as their bench the curb on the opposite side of Main Street. Since there was no traffic, even on Main Street, on Sunday evening, they heard the music as well as we (Mr. Macafee and my aunt Olivia always sat in the first row of benches) and missed only my fascinating close-up view of the trombonist.

The affair of the Chinese egg began, I suppose, about three

weeks after I had come to live with my aunt, when, having been sent to bed, I had my reading interrupted after two hours or so by her whirlwind entrance. "Den!" she said. "Jimmy Macafee's just gone."

I asked if I could get up.

"Don't be silly, it's after bedtime for you. But guess what— I'm going to have a shop! I'm going to give demonstrations and lessons! All in Jimmy's store. We can go down tomorrow and look at the place."

I don't believe I understood at all that night—mostly because I did not greatly care—just what this shop was to be or what lessons my aunt was to give there. As soon as she had left the room, I returned to my story, which concerned a princess whose lone tower stood upon a sea-washed rock, out of sight of any land. She was tended every day—on the order of her father, the king—by servants in a boat; a rowing boat, according to the picture facing the appropriate page, which supplemented its oars by mounting a very small mast carrying a single square sail painted with the royal arms. (This sail, I was happy to see, attempted to overcome the disadvantage of its diminutive size by hard work. It bellied out more enthusiastically than ever Titania's votaress did, and this despite the wind's blowing—as was shown by the pennant a foot above it—across its surface rather than from behind it.) It seemed rather a long way for the servants to come—the picture showed no land at all astern of the boat—yet such was their devotion to their lovely princess that they did it.

At night the princess lived all alone in her seagirt tower.

This was (of course) the result of a prophecy made at the queen's bedside by a certain bent and crooked and hairy wizard who had come hobbling up out of the night just when the rejoicings were loudest. This wizard, who dressed in wolfskins and was said to live exclusively upon tea, had chanted:

> "The little maiden you toast here
> Shall live alone full many a year;

And many a wight shall seek her hand,
  Though she not own a foot of land;
Earth, sea, and air
  Will woo the fair,
But fire will win her.

And though her sire be a king by birth
Greater, the groom will gin gold from the earth."

Naturally the king, though he would have liked to have a wealthy son-in-law, did not care for the sound of the word "greater," and thus the tower on the rock. This cloistered girl's fame spread far and wide, as was no doubt inevitable; and doubtless it occurred to a good many people that although there was no way of really knowing what was meant by "fire" in the rhyme—after the wedding it could doubtless be explained in a good many ways—it seemed quite clear that whoever won her would be a king (or better) and very rich. However, there was no place to anchor a ship within miles of the rock, and nearly everyone who tried to pay court to the unfortunate princess (whose name was Elaia) drowned.

At last (just when I was getting sleepy) the first serious lover arrived on the scene. He was extremely wellborn, being the youngest son of the king of the gnomes, and so handsome that he was entitled to a picture of his own, which showed him standing rather languidly on the rock outside the tower door—he having just that moment leaped from the stern of the king's departing boat where he had been concealed in the bilges in the form of a mouse. He had a sword, and a shield with a big spike in the center and divisions like those on the face of a sundial marked off around the rim. Whether he indeed entered through that door or was forced, out of deference to maidenly modesty, to climb the tower and come in through a window, I no longer remember. I do recall, however, that the princess set him a number of exceedingly difficult tasks—including such things as recovering the ring of a bell from the bottom of the sea—all of which he performed with what to me was astonishing but gratifying ease. In time, of course, word of this young man's fame reached the king, and he sailed out to pay a second visit to his daughter. He found her alone, but when he asked the whereabouts of that paragon of paladins, the youngest son of the king of the gnomes, she would say nothing but that his kisses had tasted too strongly of fresh-turned earth.

The second lover, whom I had expected to be a merman, was nothing of the sort, but an adventurous young merchant whose seamanship was such that he was able to bring his ship to the very rim of the rock (as the picture showed) and leap off dry-shod. He was not only deficient in supernatural abilities but rather short (again judging by his picture) as well, but he made up for these inadequacies with curly blond hair and a marvelous degree of cunning. At the princess's urging he traded that well-known shrewd bargainer the fox out of his ox, leaving him a mere "f," then exchanged the ox for a giant's shadow, with which he so terrified the people of a seaside town that they made him their king, whereupon he went back to the giant and exchanged the shadow (now more valuable than ever, since it was the shadow of a famous conqueror) for a magical bird of ruby and amethyst, which he presented to the princess. This bird sang in such a way as to calm the sea itself and charm every hearer, though to hear its most beautiful song its owner had to set it free; this the princess did, and then charmed it back into its cage again by singing herself. When her father asked what had become of the enterprising merchant lad, she said that she had sent him away because the heavy purse hanging from his belt bruised her each time they embraced.

The third lover was, to my mind, the most impressive, and hailed from that high country we see on certain summer days, from the flying islands that sail above our shaded and murky bottomlands with an invincible serenity, so that they are to us like swans that part the surface of a pool with their snowy breasts and never think of the worms and snails living in the mud below. Getting to the island was no problem for him, and his arrival was the most impressive of all, for he landed on the roof with a bodyguard of aerial spirits, of whom those closest to him could be but faintly seen, like ghosts, men and women in form, ugly and beautiful and strange, some with long flowing beards, some in fantastic clothes, while still others, farther away, hung silhouetted in the sunlight, winged like angels. The princess required of him the heaviest tasks of all, for she made him do every kind of filthy work about her tower, clean fish in the scullery and wash dishes, empty slops and even clean her servants' boots; but when the king asked what had become of him she would only say, "His kingdom was too insubstantial for me, all emptiness and moaning wind."

At which point, unfortunately, my aunt called, "Den, darling, are you awake in there?"—the signal that she had come up to bed and I must put out my light and go to sleep. I do not recall that I ever finished that particular story, and it is quite likely I did not, because I felt at that time—a feeling I retained until I was old enough to study books seriously—that it was a sort of desecration to begin an evening's reading in the middle of a story. I started fresh when I sat down to read, and if I was not held to the end, never reached it.

The next day I learned what it was my aunt had been so excited about the night before. We visited Macafee's, and most particularly that part of the store—the Morgan Street side of the second floor—which dealt in china and silver and glassware. Here a small alcove was being remodeled, and in it, my aunt told me, she would, on Tuesday and Thursday afternoons between the hours of three and five, decorate china and teach others to do so.

At once all her other hobbies fell into contemptuous neglect, so much so that I—when it had been established that all the women who came to clean for her positively refused to do it— had to rake out the dog runs and feed their inhabitants. The carved and gilded piano in the parlor and the harp in the solarium fell mute as stones, and the scientific periodicals the mailman brought piled up, still virginal in their brown wrappers, on the foyer table. My aunt Olivia, in other words, began to paint china as she had never before in her life painted china. And she was quite good at it.

Her favorites, of course, were Chinese scenes, executed largely or entirely in a pretty shade of pale blue. She reproduced the famous willow pattern, not only in its more or less pure state (which is English), but in variations of her own—of which I particularly remember one that included a crocodile in the river. (It may be in the house somewhere; I should look for it.) Dragons were another favorite: not only blue dragons on plates and bowls and cups and vases, all incredibly sinuous and sinister, but blue and red dragons *inside* bowls and cups and dishes as well, some lurking in the bottom where they would not be seen until the contents were consumed, others peeking playfully over the rim, sometimes with one frightening claw braced on the handle of a teacup. These dragons, with their rococo spit curls and bandits' mustaches, appeared, when finished, to have been extremely difficult subjects; but my aunt had so mastered her brushwork that she could execute a dragon of ordinary size (that is to say, about three inches long) in less than ten minutes.

One day—I believe it was a day or two before the breathlessly awaited Tuesday when her shop was to open—when I had spent an hour or so in watching her paint (mostly dragons), I asked her how she had learned to do them so well. After swearing me to secrecy (and I was, naturally, happy enough to swear, and would even more gladly have sworn in my own blood than on the old, falling-apart, black-letter, unreadable family Bible upon which she demanded my oath) she showed me her collection, which, so she said, she had been assembling since her girlhood. She had them pasted in a leather scrapbook whose cover writhed with yet more painted dragons, all executed by herself, and I very well remember the pause as she held the closed book on her knees, reviewing at the last possible second the advisability of making me a party to her secret.

When she opened the book, I saw colors so bright that it was as though an explosion of parrots had been released into the room. Quickly, almost as though she were ashamed, she turned the pages, giving me time only to glance at each. Mounted on the dull cream scrapbook leaves were the labels from packages of fireworks, scores and perhaps hundreds of them: tigers, zebras, brilliant apes, and fierce warriors, and, of course, dragons in myriads, twisting and flowing like gaudy smokes, lashing red Chinese characters with their begemmed tails, licking scarlet Roman letters with serpentine tongues: "KWONGYUEN HANGKEE FIRECRACKER FACTORY, MACAU." And similar names.

But as I have said, my aunt did not restrict herself to dragons, or even to dragons and willowware. Roundheaded, white-faced, humpbacked Chinese children with grotesquely merry smiles crowded some of her pieces, and serene court personages in clothes that were themselves painted with elaborate scenes. She pointed out the emperor to me once, on a vase, and informed me that the dragon throne was vacant now—but prophesied that it would someday be filled again; this was, I suppose, at the height of the warlord period, when the death of Yuan Shih-k'ai left the Middle Kingdom leaderless. The quaint costumes and stylized faces reminded me of a gramophone record of my father's, and I began to sing, " 'If you want to know who we are/We are gentlemen of Japan/Seen on many a vase and jar/Seen on many a screen and fan,' " marching up and down in time to the music.

"Oh, no," my aunt said, "these are Chinese gentlemen—they're quite different."

I asked if there were any Chinese "close to here." My aunt said, "Much closer than you think, Den," and putting down her brush, she smiled prettily at me and tapped her forehead with one finger. "There is a whole empire here—rice fields and wastelands and gardens. Pagodas and glass chimes that ring in the wind, and gentle water buffaloes and thousands of millions of people."

It is very hard for me to remember sometimes that my aunt
Olivia is dead. I once heard some sort of religious—or perhaps
they would call it philosophical—argument between Aaron Gold
and Ted Singer in which Ted said that something was "contrary
to everyday experience." This was what we used to call "a set-
tler." It was intended to terminate the argument, an irrefutable
and all-destroying assertion. I have thought of it since, often,
and of the things that are "contrary to everyday experience."

The most obvious one, surely, is the birth of children, or indeed of any living thing. New human beings—or, for that matter,
cats or calves—simply do not appear every day; they do not
spring from the ground. Perhaps only once in a lifetime an in-
fant comes into a life as though he or she had been dropped
from the sky. Most of us either have no younger brothers and
sisters (I had none, and no older ones either) or are ourselves
too young at the time of their birth to remember and understand.

Possibly because I have never married, I am more conscious
than most that marriage is "contrary to everyday experience,"
though sex is not. Male-female coupling is everyday: mature
men and women in hotel rooms and motel rooms and their own
apartments and homes, and apartments and homes that do not
belong to them, "have intercourse"; and immature ones, too, in
those places and every other conceivable and inconceivable
place—on the seats of automobiles and on blankets (and no
blankets) thrown on the ground, in shower stalls and in the back
rows of theater balconies, on stage, in sleeping bags and, for all
I know, hollow trees. But, very rarely, Melissa (who worked
last summer in Woolworth's, who wanted to be drum majorette
this year—but it was Heather Trimble—Melissa whom I used to
see waiting with her textbooks and notebook propped on one hip
when I drove my cold-natured, reluctant old Plymouth to the
plant in the mornings, waiting for the school bus that never
seemed to come early or even on time) and Ted (who never got

into the game unless Consolidated was fourteen points ahead; Ted ran the four-forty but who cares about the four-forty?) leave Melissa's father's brick ranch-style and Ted's mother's Apt. 14 and become four-legged two-backed four-armed (oh, be forewarned!) two-headed Ted and Lisa into which each less-than-half had vanished more or less utterly, and (though the monster is not completely indissoluble still) never to reappear. And this does not happen every day.

Nor death, but only once. We talk of strong personalities, and they are strong, until the not-every-day when we see them as we might see one woman alone in a desert, and know that all the strength we thought we knew was only courage, only her lone song echoing among the stones; and then at last when we have understood this and made up our minds to hear the song and admire its courage and its sweetness, we wait for the next note and it does not come. The last word, with its pure tone, echoes and fades and is gone, and we realize—only then—that we do not know what it was, that we have been too intent on the melody to hear even one word. We go then to find the singer, thinking she will be standing where we last saw her. There are only bones and sand and a few faded rags.

I wrote last night, before I went to sleep, about my aunt Olivia's painting, and her scrapbook, things I saw when I was only a boy. And last night in my bed here at the edge of this empty house (I have realized only now that I sleep and eat—when I eat—only at the edge; I had never thought of it before) I dreamed that I clambered over a wall. Where I had been, what was on the side of that wall I was leaving, I do not know. It was late evening, I think, of a winter day; the wall was before me, perhaps ten feet high, of stone plastered with stucco (or perhaps it was only mud) that was now falling away in great patches. The coping was of tile, and overhung the wall slightly, making it difficult to climb.

I dropped down on the other side. I was in a garden, I think, at any rate in a very picturesque landscape, in which there was or seemed to be so much arrangement of tree and stone and water that it could be called beautiful but not natural—though it may be that in a few places nature achieves by chance that air of orderly disorder and symmetrical unbalance. To either side of me the wall extended as far as I could see; but it seemed to me that at its extremities it curved slightly toward me, and this increased my sense of having entered an enclosure or sanctuary.

I walked over hills that were nearer and smaller than they seemed, and found between them a river of stones—stones with no water in them or through them or over them or under them at all, only the smooth, rounded, somewhat flattened bright cold stones, with here and there between them a weed, and once, floating on their surface, a dead bird. I reached a crooked little humpbacked footbridge, and found beneath it—crouched in the shadow, where he was nearly invisible—an earthenware troll with a fierce, sad face and stumpy limbs, fallen from his little pedestal. I climbed the bank of the dry river then, and took the footpath served by the bridge. I was beginning, as I walked, to be aware of myself, as I had not been earlier, and found that I was again a young man of twenty-five or so, and this was such a pleasant discovery that I congratulated myself, and thought, as I walked, What an excellent dream I am having—try not to wake up—probably never have this dream again, so make the most of it.

I did not know how old I was when I was awake, but I sensed at a level below the "conscious" thought of the dream that to wake would be a horror, that it was best to remain twenty-five and happy, walking the wandering little sanded path under the cypresses and cedars for as long as I could.

It grew steadily darker and colder, and a wind rose. I saw something bright, the only colorful thing I had seen in the garden except for the breast feathers of the dead bird, blowing across the path. I ran and caught it, and found that it was a broken paper lantern.

We now visited Macafee's every day. If Mr. Macafee was not engaged, my aunt would go to his office for a chat, leaving me free to wander the store; because of this, my memories of it at that period begin not at the wide Main Street doors, but at the third-floor offices, offices that were at that time all of dark wood, the floors very solidly built of wide boards cemented with innumerable layers of bright varnish and laid with carpet—a plain green carpet in the outer offices, where girls in white shirtwaists worked at wooden desks, a beautiful Oriental carpet in Mr. Macafee's own office. The doors, too, were of wood and shaped like picture frames, holding a magical glass that transformed whatever might be seen through it to a misty translucence. The rooms were paneled to a height above my head, and there was white-painted plaster above that.

Outside the office doors everything was changed, and this floor, the third floor, holding both the toy and furniture departments, was my favorite. The carpeting here was gray, but all the walls between the high windows were hung with bright carpets like the one in Mr. Macafee's office, and more were piled in heaps as high as tables. Between them, bed jostled bed and table crowded table, giving me a vivid impression of the bustling numbers of people there were in the world, people who would in a short time require all these oak and walnut and mahogany tables, all these brass beds. Men, I noticed, always pressed the mattresses with the flat of their hands, always sat in the chairs, often pulled them up to the table and crossed their legs to see if they could, often turned them upside down to see if they were well made. Women polished the surfaces of the tables with their hands and told the clerk about their old tables or their mother's; they only looked at the curls and furbelows of the beds, the brass morning-glories and sunflowers.

But the furniture was only the scenery on the road to the toys —there I loved and lingered. I never knew what to look at first, and this uncertainty remains, possibly the only part of my childhood still intact; I do not know now of which to write. There were soldiers, each kneeling or standing or lying on his own tiny patch of leaden grass. I was gradually acquiring an army; it included not only the living and marching, but the wounded and dead, snipers, frantic men who charged the enemies of their nation (and they were of several nations) with the bayonet, masked figures who lobbed gas grenades, artillerymen and Indian scouts, one a chief in full war bonnet who stood with folded arms, each hand grasping a hunting knife. These were five cents each; more elaborate figures, such as mounted cavalrymen, were ten.

And this was the age of the chemistry set, when all that was not glass or metal was wood, including little barrel-like wooden vials for the dry chemicals. I had a set, and longed for a larger one. The smell of new pine, or of burning sulphur, has invoked that small, stained bedroom-floor laboratory so often that I have sometimes wondered if I have not poisoned myself with its fumes, and now, when I think myself to have lived, if I do not in actuality lie still sprawled beside my candle and tiny smoking dish.

Of wooden swords and rubber daggers, guns that fired corks or water, I will say nothing; nor of the coin banks that performed so spectacularly for their pennies, or counted your money as they received it, or duplicated, with mysterious clickings and tickings, the black and beflowered safe in Mr. Macafee's office. But I remember the ball bats, with their taped handles; all of them were, I think, branded "Louisville Slugger." They were brand new, and so was I.

No doubt it should have been an intolerable imposition and restriction of freedom to be forced, at the sublime age of eight or early nine, to thus accompany my aunt, every day for nearly two weeks, and then often to be forced to spend a weary hour or more amusing myself among the counters. Since I did not know how children were supposed to act and feel, which is only to say that to me at that time childhood was a condition rather than a concept, I not only did not mind it but actually enjoyed it. The summer days were growing warm by then, and it was cool in the store under the big slow-turning ceiling fans, where nothing moved quickly but the dimes and quarters and receipts in their whizzing pneumatic tubes. When my aunt Olivia was finished and we had walked home again, I would change clothes and run down the street to find another boy who wanted to go to the river and swim.

The Tuesday and Thursday Nankeen Nook, when it opened, was small and interestingly crowded. There was (to begin at the end) a cashbox, into which my aunt put the money when she made sales, and which I was supposed to watch when I was present. There were two folding chairs, one for my aunt set up in front of her little worktable, and one for a student. And, of course, a large number of undecorated pieces of china, and (it having been transported from my aunt's house at the store's expense) my aunt's electric kiln—then, I think, a very recent development. This last enabled my aunt to show the difference between "overglaze" and "underglaze" decoration.

And there were showcases in which to display the finished work. On the first day, my aunt brought some of her best pieces, and Mr. Macafee contributed a selection of antiques. As time progressed, all these were returned to their accustomed cabinets and cupboards, and work done in the store substituted for them. These newer pieces were signed and priced, and though —especially as the prices were rather high—my aunt sold only a few of them, they afforded her a certain amount of money (which perhaps she needed more than I realized) and a considerable amount of satisfaction.

Often customers brought their own family treasures to show her, and she, after dutifully admiring them, would demonstrate that they could, if they were willing to learn, do decorations of the type they had been taught to value. For her art was by no means limited to the Chinese scenes she favored; she could paint Redoute roses with the best, and chains of dark violets twined together by the stem to circle the rim of a soup tureen, or even to form an initial "B" or "W" on the side of a tall pitcher. (Her Chinese pictures were signed in almost invisibly small letters with her full name; but these floral designs bore, as her device, a few dusky olive leaves circumscribed by the letter "O.")

Lessons were free, save that the student was expected to pay for her practice pieces, and after the first two or three weeks a handful of women came regularly, practicing at home between "Tuesdays and Thursdays" with materials they bought from my aunt, and carrying their best pieces back to the store with infinite care.

It was from one of these students—a Mrs. Brice—that my aunt, and Mr. Macafee, who as chance would have it was in the Nankeen Nook at the time chatting with the two women, that my aunt learned of the existence of the Chinese egg. It was, according to Mrs. Brice, an egg of very large size, and though it was possible that it was a natural egg, "from an ostrich, or one of those big-like birds," Mrs. Brice doubted it, and the bird on her hat swayed from side to side.

"You say it's quite old?" Mr. Macafee inquired.

"From the seventeen-hundreds is what they say. Now what there is is where somebody wrote on the bottom where you can't see it, where it goes in the little stand. That isn't painted on or anything, just written like with a school pen. It says, 'Easter, Hangchow, 1799.' Now, I didn't say it *is* from American Revolution times like that, but they say it's been in the family a long while, and that has always been wrote on the bottom."

"There's a story behind it," my aunt Olivia said. "I know there is."

Mrs. Brice said, "Well, you would have to ask Em about that. I said to her, 'Where in heaven's name'd you ever *get* that egg like that, Em?' and she said to me it was—I don't know, some relative of her mother's—and he was a missionary and with the government, I think she said he was with the government, and he did some kind of business there with this Russian. Don't ask me what a Russian was doing in China." She paused and looked at my aunt and Mr. Macafee to see if they believed her. "And he gave him this egg. He had it made there, or anyway the decorations put on. It's real pretty, but it sounds awfully mixed up to me. I told her I'd like to borrow it and try to copy it, but she won't let it out of the house."

"Do you think she'd sell it?" Mr. Macafee asked.

"I think she'd want a lot," Mrs. Brice said firmly. She radiated the fact that though she was annoyed with Em for refusing to lend her the egg, still Em was a friend and friends stuck together, particularly when somebody wanted to buy something.

My aunt said, "I've just got to see it, Jimmy; will you take me out there?" Mrs. Brice looked properly scandalized at having heard her call Mr. Macafee "Jimmy" *to his face*, and *in front of everybody*.

I supposed, from having heard this conversation, which terminated shortly after the point at which my aunt Olivia called Mr. Macafee "Jimmy," that they—perhaps accompanied by myself —would shortly go to view the Chinese egg. Possibly that same afternoon, after my aunt closed the Nankeen Nook; certainly within the next few days. I was, of course, mistaken.

Eager though they both were to see that rare object, it was quite impossible for them to simply "go barging out" to the owner's farm and demand to be shown it. It would have been possible if the egg had been advertised for sale, but it had not. It would have been possible to go in a somewhat more diplomatic fashion had Mrs. Lorn, who owned it, been a friend of either. And it might even have been possible had the Lorns been utter and complete strangers (my aunt's unfailing description of anyone she did not know and felt she could never wish to know). But the Lorns stood in the worst possible relationship: they were known by name only. They were reputed to be "nice." They were rather remote friends of rather remote friends of my own family, and of remote friends of the Macafees as well. Guarded inquiries were made. Much information was received, a great deal of it redundant, and some of it contradictory. To summarize these intelligence reports:

The thing was the property of Mrs. Emerald Lorn, a woman somewhat, though not a great deal, older than my aunt. Mrs. Lorn was the wife of the minister of a country church—the Reverend Carl Lorn. Like many country ministers, the Reverend Lorn preached on Sunday and farmed six days a week; the Lorn farm was north and slightly west of town at a distance of nearly twelve miles, which was far enough that the Lorns, although they occasionally came to Cassionsville to shop, visited other towns almost as often and did most of their buying at a crossroads store much nearer them. Mrs. Green, whose husband rented his farm from my father, knew Mrs. Lorn, but only slightly; the Greens did not attend the Reverend Lorn's church and, in any event, were shy of pressing their friendship upon those whom they felt to be above them. My own dear Hannah (who now, with my parents gone and the house closed, was "resting," but who had become one of the women who sometimes came for a day or two to "help" my aunt) divulged that her half-sister Mary knew Em Lorn; but Hannah herself did not "except to see." Stewart Blaine knew Carl Lorn quite well, having attended school with him; but the acquaintances of a husband are of little weight.

Reports of the egg itself were glowing. It was said to be not of a pure white color, but faintly and richly creamy, a detail which led Mr. Macafee to suggest that it might not be ceramic after all, but ivory and therefore (by implication) outside my aunt's province; so that she was forced to remind him that she collected Chinese art of all kinds. And it was painted with a variety of scenes illustrating—though with a Chinese cast, as it were, and in Chinese dress—certain of the less dramatic occurrences connected with the Resurrection, including Mary Magdalen's encounter with the risen Christ, and the final meal on the shore of Lake Tiberias. No two witnesses agreed precisely about either the number of scenes or their exact content. All coincided in saying that the artist's rendering of Jesus and the apostles as Chinese philosophers, and His mother and Mary of Cleophas and other New Testament women as Chinese ladies with bound feet, and his running together the various scenes (so that one of the guards before the tomb—armed, as Stewart Blaine told my aunt, with a quaintly curved bow and a Manchurian headsman's sword—was elbowing someone who might or might not be an awed native of Patmos) resulted in a confusion that, though charming, was nearly impenetrable.

For several weeks my aunt and Mr. Macafee collected these hearsay depositions, meeting frequently to exchange news and to speculate concerning the best means of securing an introduction to Mrs. Lorn. During this time I became aware, in the slow and only half-conscious way in which children recognize the existence of adult problems, of an unspoken and unresolved question which had sprung up between Mr. Macafee and my aunt. Should they bid against one another? Or should he, as a gentleman, stand aside and allow her to buy the egg at her own price if she could? Or, indeed, should she, with ladylike modesty, retire and leave the field of business to someone who undeniably was (as she was not) a businessman?

On twilit summer evenings they sat, with a good two feet of space separating them, on my aunt's porch glider, and talked of the egg (my aunt had convinced herself that it must be one of a pair, the other of which would show the Ascension, and had written a museum in New York about it), and doubt hung in the air like a ghost between them. Were they rivals? Were they allies?

So things remained until one evening when Eleanor Bold paid my aunt a late call, arriving perhaps five minutes after Mr. Macafee had left. That Miss Bold—who was, after all, Barbara Black's sister—should pay a call on my aunt, particularly while I was in the house, came as a considerable surprise to me; although in retrospect I can understand the dilemma into which the accident, and, later, Bobby's death, put the Blacks—and of course to a lesser extent Eleanor and her father, the judge. For them to have held no rancor toward me and my family would have been thought unnatural by the whole town, and "told against" them. On the other hand, I had been a mere child of five, and though my aunt had been present, so had Eleanor herself and Bobby's mother. To cut the social bonds irrevocably and irretrievably, forever, would seem rancorous, "unchristian," and unforgiving. The accident itself was four years now in the past; and at the time Eleanor came to call on my aunt, Bobby must have been at least four months in his grave, if not more.

Eleanor and my aunt Olivia had always been particular friends, in any event—perhaps partly because their good looks (they were strikingly attractive women) so complemented each other; and partly, too, from a similarity of temperament, for Eleanor, though she was several years younger than my aunt and kept house for her father, was as outspoken as the judge's favorite author could have wished, and not least in her admiration for Olivia Weer and Olivia's independence.

None of this, naturally, went through my mind as I crept downstairs and concealed myself in an alcove within easy hearing of the parlor. From my seat by the sill of my bedroom window I had watched Miss Bold come up the walk, and I supposed that I was to be arrested—at the very least—and perhaps that my aunt's house was to be taken away. Any knowledge, I felt, would be better than an awful ignorance, but I was prepared to hear the worst.

Ten minutes or more were spent in the usual feminine greetings, the inquiries after friends and relations (though in this case certain parties were diplomatically omitted), the admiration for each other's clothes, and the criticism of each's own. Then: "I have" (I heard Miss Bold say) "a surprise for you." I could not see her, but I feel certain that at this point she leaned forward to touch my aunt's knee. "You asked Sophie

Singer if she knew Em Lorn, the minister's wife at the Approved Methodists out toward Milton."

My aunt must have nodded.

"Well, she doesn't, but I do now; Saturday I went to the Approved Methodists' July picnic."

"Eleanor, you didn't!"

"Yes, I did. Sophie mentioned it to me, and I've been keeping it in the back of my mind—you know the way you do? So then Dick Porter asked if I didn't want to go, because he had to. Because of his mother. I know he thought I was going to say I wouldn't—I hate those churchy things, and I wouldn't know anyone there—so when I said I would just love to he nearly fell over and now he thinks I'm sweet on him—"

"Eleanor, you are a *minx!* You don't know how I've missed you this summer."

"So we went, and it was as bad as I expected, or worse, with everyone drinking lemonade and playing horseshoes, and Dick picking up mine for me—every blessed time—and wiping them off with this handkerchief; but Em Lorn was there, and I must say I was exceedingly charming to her and extremely sweet. By the time the mosquitoes made us want to go home—mosquitoes are all Baptists—well, I had her to where I don't think she was able to sleep that night, for wanting you and Mr. Macafee to come out and see her."

"She knows what we want to come for?"

"Indeed she does, and she's ready to sell it, too, if she can get what she thinks is a good price. By the time Dick Porter took me back, we were talking about the things she might be getting with the money."

There was a pause; then I heard my aunt say, "What kinds of things?"

"Oh, a lot of things; a sewing machine was one. She wants a new sewing machine—she sews a lot for the missions."

"Eleanor!"

"But I haven't told you the best part yet: you won't have to pay for it; Mr. Macafee's going to buy it and give it to you for your birthday. He told us."

"He told you?"

"Poppa and I. He comes to our house, too, sometimes, you know. To have dinner and play chess with Poppa and talk about Dickens and Anthony Trollope. And the last time, at dinner— Clara had just served the sweet potatoes, I remember—he mentioned the egg, and my father said, 'Oh, yes, the famous egg; Eleanor heard about it from Sophie Singer,' and he—I mean Mr. Macafee—looked right at me and said he intended to buy it and give it to Olivia Weer. For your birthday."

Another pause. Then, "Please tell Mr. Macafee—I mean—you know—"

"Just let it slip," Eleanor suggested helpfully.

"That's right. Just let it slip that I want the egg for *his* birthday."

"Vi! You're not serious."

"Tell him that. When did he say he wanted it for mine?"

"I told you, just—"

"Not that; what day?"

"Thursday."

"We'll go out Sunday afternoon. Is he coming to dinner again this week? Well, tell him then, if you can."

"Vi, I thought you wanted it yourself."

"I do. He *wanted* you to tell me—you said yourself he looked right at you."

"But—"

"My birthday isn't until November; he knows that, and he gave me a brooch last time. Don't you see what he's thinking? I'll let him buy it and he won't have to pay a lot because I won't be trying to get it, too. Then, when the time comes to give it to me, he can very easily give me something else that costs twice as much, and I'll have to forgive him; anyway, he'll say I have to marry him now to get it—I can just hear him. Jimmy is a very sharp trader."

"Well, I don't see what good it will do you to buy it and give it to him. When is his birthday, anyway?"

"Next month—August third. You're a goose, Eleanor."

"Aren't you going to buy it?"

"Of course not. But if he thinks I really want it for him and I would have paid a lot for it, then he'll *have* to give it to me— don't you see that? He'll see how badly I want it, and besides it won't be easy then to give me something that costs more."

There was another pause, during which I could hear someone pouring tea, the delicate splashing and the click of the cup the only sounds against the background noises of my own breathing and the sighing of the wind in the big elms outside. I ventured a peek around the corner, keeping my head very close to the floor, and saw my aunt Olivia just in the act of setting down the cozy-wrapped pot. Eleanor Bold said, "This is good, what is it?" and I withdrew.

"Formosa oolong," my aunt told her. "I'll have to have money. I'll go down Friday and draw some out. Then I can go by the store and tell Jimmy I've just come from the bank."

The next day, Wednesday, Stewart Blaine called upon my aunt. I have sometimes wondered if he was in fact the richest of my aunt's suitors (of that period) as he seemed to be, or if it was only his atmosphere of gentility which conveyed that impression, as Professor Peacock's carelessness, for example, and his coming by train so that he had no car in Cassionsville unless he rented one (though he owned one, as I learned much later), gave an exaggerated impression of scholarly poverty.

Mr. Blaine's car was British, and he treated it, or at least seemed to treat it, like a horse. Not that he pulled backward on the wheel (as old farmers sometimes did, *who*aing their Model T's) when it went too fast, or kept it in a barn, so that you found bits of hay on the seats; but he talked to it, using a kind of low, gentlemanly, side-of-the-mouth voice, as though he were telling it that it could jump a fence. The steering wheel was on the wrong side, and was all of the most beautiful wood, with no iron or brass at all, and the dashboard, which ought to have been wood, was Russian leather.

Thinking about that Russian leather, I can remember the smell of it, the odor that tickled my nose when I sat between Mr. Blaine and my aunt Olivia and reached out to stroke the leather with the tips of my fingers while the gearshift banged against my knees. I remember it, but I do not know why I have chosen here to write about Blaine—save that he was one of the three men who at that period called on my aunt, so that to omit him would be to tell only a part of the story.

He was a rich man—richer, I think, than Mr. Macafee—and like most rich men he had nothing distinctive about him, the money having assumed for him the task of self-expression that, in poorer men, is assumed by the personality; so that as we remember one man as witty, another as kind, and a third, perhaps, as athletic or at least energetic or handsome, one remembered Blaine, on parting from him, as wealthy. He was tall rather than short, but not very tall; his face was long without being Lincolnesque. His hair was of that lusterless yellow brown which is called sandy, and his money was in and of the Cassionsville & Kanakessee Valley State Bank, which he had inherited from his father, and a dozen or more farms.

We went to his house that night, which was a daring thing for my aunt to have done, at that time and in that place, although she had me with her and Blaine's housekeeper and cook would be present. I have always remembered it as a pretentious house, though it was much smaller than this one I have built for myself —pretentious because it had a sort of round portico, with columns, instead of a porch; it was the type of house that is painted white because that is the color that makes it most closely resemble marble. Mr. Ricepie, the manager of the bank, was waiting for us as we drove up, and I could see that Blaine was not happy to see him, though he introduced him courteously to my aunt, who smiled and explained that she and Mr. Ricepie had already met.

Mr. Ricepie said, "Miss Weer is a good depositor of ours." And Blaine: "Really, this is rather embarrassing—as you see, I have guests."

Mr. Ricepie said that he would be happy to return tomorrow.

"No, I don't want to wait around for you tomorrow. I know I told you to come out tonight, but I thought you would be much earlier."

"It took quite a bit of work to get everything together," Mr. Ricepie said. "Harper and Doyle stayed late to help me with it."

"You see what it is having employees," Mr. Blaine told my aunt. "I asked for a few figures, and thought I would be able to have everything done before I went to pick you up. When Ricepie didn't come, I supposed he had forgotten about it, or fallen into a pit or some such. Now here he is with his briefcase —though why Ricepie should have a briefcase, I don't know; he certainly isn't an attorney—full of enough arithmetic to give me a headache for a week, and at the worst possible time."

"You needn't worry, Stewart," my aunt told him. "Den and I can amuse ourselves quite happily for an hour or two. I'll show him your library—he's mad about books—and your stereopticon slides."

"Nonsense; you are my guest, and I wouldn't dream of keeping you waiting. Besides, I have to have Ricepie to dinner now, anyway. I'll look at his papers afterward."

My aunt giggled at the phrase "Ricepie to dinner," but Mr. Ricepie said, "You needn't do that, Mr. Blaine; my wife is waiting dinner for me at home."

"Don't be silly." Blaine drew out his watch. It was such a thin one I thought it might not be a real watch at all, but only a saucer of bright metal—perhaps the cover of an old watch—that

Mr. Blaine carried now because his real one had broken. Save for the smoothly rounded edges it could have been a gold coin. "It's nearly half after six. I can't send you away from my door now, Ricepie. Come in. Everybody come in. Vi, darling?"

He started to open the door for us himself, but his housekeeper had been standing, apparently, just inside with her hand on the knob, and Blaine had no sooner reached for it than it opened with a swift, smooth motion that (possibly because the door, too, was white-painted) for some reason reminded me of the wing of a bird; and we trooped in, my aunt Olivia first and Mr. Ricepie and I last. We bumped together as we went through the doorway.

When I designed the entranceway of this house, I tried to recreate the foyer of Blaine's—not its actuality in a tape-measure sense, but its actuality as I remembered it; why should not my memory, which still exists, which still "lives and breathes and has its being," be less actual, less real, than a physical entity now demolished and irrecoverable?

Between this paragraph and the last, I went to look for that foyer, and for my knife, too. (Have you never thought as you read that months may lie between any pair of words?) Unfortunately I made the mistake of trying to reach it by going through the house, rather than going outside and around. I knew that that was what I should have done, but it is raining, a gentle spring rain; and though I would not mind getting wet I had a horror of looking behind me and seeing the uneven trail of my crippled leg sinking into the soft grass. As it is, I feel I have been disobeyed.

There is a Persian room, with divans and carpets and wall hangings of embroidered silk, and scimitars on the walls, and huge stone jars. I know because I have been in it, but I am certain I never told Barry Meade I wanted any such thing, and if he (or anyone) were alive to hear me I would be in a rage—as it is, why should I rage, and how can I? Barry's dead bones will not shake because I stamp on his grave, though my own would. I have a Persian room: hookahs and curtains of beads before latticed windows overlooking—could it be Shiraz? I may as well enjoy it. I am sure I can find it again if need be. The door to the corridor opposite the picture of Dan French giving me the box (whatever it was, a silver cigar lighter or something) when I was fifty, on behalf of the employees. Down the corridor and through my aunt Olivia's solarium, with the smell of thinner and the little glasses of brushes and the drying palette; the fourth or fifth door, I think, on the right.

But I need not find Blaine's foyer to remember it: it was a narrow room, the ceiling very high; and though the walls, which one felt Blaine would have liked to be of marble, were wooden, yet the top of the hall table, and a low pedestal supporting a showy vase of cut fern, and the umbrella stand were all of white stone. My aunt said, "I love this hall of yours, Stewart. It always looks so cool."

"It's nice in summer, but rather a cold place in the winter, I'm afraid."

"Nonsense, Mrs. Perkins always has a fire going then, don't you, Mrs. Perkins?"

The housekeeper smiled and said, "It is not my duty to lay fires, but I see that one is kept there. Yes, I do."

I looked at the marble fireplace and wondered who had cleaned it; only deep in the wall, where the marble gave way to sandstone, could I see any traces of fire, and these were slight black stains so light they appeared brownish. Blaine said, "I don't know what I'd do without Mrs. Perkins, Vi. You know what I am, the typical impractical man, with money I never made. If I had to clean my own silver, I think I'd starve."

"You could eat with it yellow," my aunt said. "That's what I do. I *won't* use that tin stuff they sell that gets all rusty if you leave it in the sink."

The doorway through which we passed had an immense fan-light.

"Dinner at eight," Blaine said, waving toward chairs. "It doesn't suit my country ways, but meantime we might as well make ourselves comfortable."

I sat with the others, very miserable at the thought of having to listen to more than an hour of parlor conversation; but after a moment Blaine turned to me and said, "Wouldn't you like to see the stock, Alden? Queenie's had a family." He turned back to my aunt. "All children like puppies, don't they, Vi? You ought to know. And Alden could ride Lady. I'll have Mrs. Perkins turn him over to Doherty."

Doherty, gardener and hostler, wore an old soft cap from which his carroty hair (even then, I think, beginning to gray) stuck out all around; he had a wide mouth and smelled of a strange, strong smell I did not then know was veterinary lini-ment. Queenie was a Dalmatian who seemed to understand Doherty perfectly when he talked like a chicken—a talent of his —but who looked rather puzzled when he said to me, "You must only brush 'em the right way, if you understand me, for that spreads the spots apart farther and it's that the judges crave. But if you run your hand against their hair you'll drive every spot on the dog up to his ears, and that's as good as to drown him. Have you a cur or two yourself? I see you're not afraid of them."

I told him I did not, but that my aunt had two in the house and nine more in a kennel in the back yard.

"In the house, does she. My own mother's mother, the old Kate, she did that and never trained them to go outside at all, so she said. Friends would pay a call and see it in piles all over the floor, and the old creature would explain she had to let all the mess sit three days before it was hard enough to pick up— ah, you think that's funny, do you?"

I nodded, sitting in the straw in a mixture of my best and worst clothes (my aunt Olivia paid no attention to the way I dressed, leaving that to my own taste, which was shaky to say the least) with a pair of spotted puppies cuddled to my heart.

"Well, and I believed it myself until I was about as old as you. Then, as the devil would have it, I ran ahead of my mother one day and saw the old Kate out in the garden pickin' it up for us. It give people something to talk of, she said; besides that she rode on the ice wagon with Pat O'Connell. But wouldn't you yourself like to be riding Lady now?"

Lady was a steady old mare, and I, no horseman, rode her at a walk until it was time for dinner, then went into the house again—this time through the kitchen rather than by the narrow side door through which I had been led out—to sit between my aunt and Mr. Ricepie at a table on which every inedible thing not silver was the color of snow or of ice. We had a spicy soup that looked like tea, and a green salad threaded with little strips of salty fish. My aunt Olivia admired the chandelier, and Mr. Blaine told her that it was supposed to be the first crystal chandelier ever taken west of the Alleghenies, and that it had been made in Venice to order.

"Your family has lived here a long time," I said.

"So has yours," he told me. "There is properly no history, Alden, only biography. When your—what would it be, great-great-grandfather?—came here, he bought land to build a mill from an ancestor of mine. Do you know what he paid? A barrel of whiskey, three rifles he'd brought with him from Pennsylvania, and twenty dollars. And he promised to grind free for my ancestor for three years. You can see that the old boy—his name was Determination Blaine—drove a hard bargain. Today that land is probably worth a hundred times more, but I'd've given it to him for the whiskey alone if Ricepie didn't stop me—wouldn't I, Ricepie? And yet a man is only the bundle of his relations, a knot of roots."

My aunt said, "You don't drink to excess, Stewart; you know you don't. In fact, come to think of it, I don't think I've ever seen you drink anything stronger than port."

"Yes, but you must admit that I'm forever demanding madder music and stronger wine. Bacchant Blaine, I was called in college."

"You weren't!"

"That's right, I wasn't, actually. The truth is that I was disgustingly studious and failed to make the soccer squad. I still remember the emotion I felt one fine spring day toward the end of my senior year when I realized that I knew more about Emerson than my professor did. My feelings were a mixture of horror and triumph, and that mixture has been the dominating emotion of my life since. You went to Radcliffe, didn't you, Vi?"

My aunt shook her head. "Adelphi. What do you mean when you say horror and triumph, Stewart?"

"I suppose only the feeling that what I could do I cannot, and what I might do finds me unable. I cannot teach Emerson, which I should do very well, because I must oversee Mr. Ricepie's bank, about which I know nothing. They say that money, though it represents the prose of life, and is hardly spoken of without apology in drawing rooms, is in its effects and laws as beautiful as roses—yet I find I much prefer the roses, particularly Marechal Niel, which I grow in the hothouse here."

"It is scarcely my bank, sir," Mr. Ricepie said.

"You see," Blaine continued to my aunt Olivia, "there is always a certain meanness in the arguments of conservatism, joined with a certain superiority in its facts. Ricepie is correct, and though he is far better suited to managing the enterprise than I, and does manage it, yet I must take the responsibility. In a better-ordered world I should be able to shed the whole wretched affair by signing it over to him, but if I were to try that here I should be put away."

"If you would look at the reports—" Mr. Ricepie said, and added, "I can get them in a moment. I left my briefcase in the hall."

Blaine frowned. "Please, Ricepie, we are at table. Dinner lubricates business, or so it is said, though I own I have often wished it drowned it."

We had fish and roast beef, and I think I remember green beans cooked with mushrooms. After the pie I was sent away again, but Doherty had unsaddled Lady, and he said it was too dark for me to ride anymore. I suppose I whined at that, as small boys will, because after showing me the puppies a second time he began to tell me a story he said he had from his grandmother, "the old Kate."

"It was when there was kings in Ireland. There was a man then named Finn M'Cool that was the strongest man in Ireland; he worked for the High King at Tara, and he had a dog and a cat. The dog's name was Strongheart and the cat's was Pussy."

I laughed at that, causing Doherty to shake his head over the unseemly merriment of the young generation. He was sitting cross-legged on top of an empty apple barrel. "Why and from where do you think the name come, for all of that?" he said. "Did you ever know a cat in your life that hadn't a sister of the name?

"Well, upon a day it happened that Finn M'Cool was bringing in the cows, and the High King at Tara said to him, 'Finn, there's a job of work I have for you,' and Finn answered him, 'It's done already, Your Majesty, and what is it?' 'It's the king of the rats, that's aboard St. Brandon's boat gnawing at the hull of it and doing every kind of mischief.' 'I've heard of that boat and it's stone,' says Finn, 'he'll not get far gnawing that.' ''Tis wicker,' says the king, 'like any proper boat, and if you'll not be moving those lazy feet of yours soon Brandon'll never be reaching the Earthly Paradise at all.' 'Well, and why should he, now,' says Finn, 'and where is it, anyhow?' 'That's not for you to ask,' says the High King at Tara, 'and it's to the west of us, as you'd know if you weren't a fool, for the other's England.'

"So Finn walked every mile of it to Bantry Bay where Brandon's boat was, and the boat was that large that he could see it for five days before he could smell the sea, for it was so long it looked like Ireland might be leavin' it, and the mast so tall there was no top to it at all, it just went up forever, and they say while Brandon's boat was docked there an albatross hit the top of it in a storm and broke her neck, though that was all right, for the fall would have killed her anyway, for she fell three days before she hit the deck, and the deck so high above the water she fell three more after Brandon kicked her overboard.

"But when he could get sight of the water around her, Finn said, 'That's the good man's boat as I breathe, and she's about to sail, too, for there's a rat as big as a cow gnawing the anchor cable, do you see.' And the dog agreed with him, for dogs is always an agreeable sort of animal, and that one would have had this tale if you hadn't laughed at the cat. Then the dog drew his sword (and a big one it was, too, and the blade as bright as the road home) and lit his pipe and pushed his hat back on his head and said, 'And would you like that rat dead now, Finn?' And Finn said, 'I would,' and they fought until the moon come up, and then the dog brought Finn the rat's head on the end of a piece of stick about this long, and never told that it was because the cat had come up from behind and tripped him, for the dog's the most honest animal there is or ever was except when it comes to sharing credit, but Finn had seen it. Finn winked at the cat then, but she was cleaning her knife and wouldn't look. The next day they went out to be seeing the boat again, and sure there was two old men on the deck, each of them with a beard as white as a swan's wing and leaning on a stick taller than he was, alike as two peas. Then Finn scratched his head and said to the cat, 'As sure as it rains in Ireland, I've looked at one and the other until I'm that dizzy, and the devil take me if there's a hair of difference between them; how can you tell which is Brandon?' And the cat said, 'Faith, I've never met him, but the other one is the king of the rats.' 'Which?' says Finn, to make sure. 'The one on the right,' says the cat. 'The ugly one.' 'Then that's settled,' says Finn, 'and you're the girl for me.' And he picked up the cat and threw her aboard and went back to the High King at Tara and told him the thing was done.

"But the cat lit on deck on her feet as cats do, but when she stood up the king of the rats was gone. Then Brandon said, 'Welcome aboard. Now we've captain, cat, and rat, all three, and can sail.' So the cat signed the ship's papers, and when she did she noticed the king of the rats was down for quartermaster. 'What's this,' she said, 'and is that one drawing rations?' 'And don't you know,' says Brandon, 'that the wicked do His will as well as the just? Only they don't like it. How do you think I could have weighed anchor, a sick man like me, without the rat gnawed the rope? But don't worry, I'm putting you down for CAT, and the cat's above everyone but the captain.' 'When do we sail?' says the cat. 'That we've done already,' says Brandon, 'for the cable parted yesterday and our boat's so long the bow's in Boston Bay already, but there's an Irish wind ahead and astern of us—that blows every way at once, but mostly up and down—and whether our end will ever make it is more than I could say.' 'Then we'd best go for'rd,' says the cat.

"And they did, and took a lantern (like this one) with them, and it was a good thing they did, for when they got to the Earthly Paradise it was as black as the inside of a cow. 'What's this?' says the cat, holding up the lantern though she could see in the dark as well as any. 'If this is the Earthly Paradise, where's the cream? Devil a thing do I see but a big pine tree with a sign on it.' The king of the rats, that had joined them on the way for'rd, says, 'And what does it say?' thinking the cat couldn't read and wanting to embarrass her. 'No hiring today,' says the cat. 'Well, no cream either,' says the rat, and Brandon said, 'It's two o'clock in the morning in the Earthly Paradise. You don't expect the cows milked at two o'clock, do you?'

"Then the cat jumped off the boat and sat on a stone and thought about what time the cows *would* be milked, and at last she said, 'How long until five?' and the rat laughed, but Brandon said, 'Twenty thousand years.' 'Then I'm going back to Ireland where it's light,' says the cat. 'You are that,' says Brandon, 'but not for some time,' and *he* jumped off the boat and set up a cross on the beach. Then the boat sank and the king of the rats swam ashore. ' 'Twas stone all along,' said he. 'That it was,' says Brandon, 'in places.' 'Shall I kill the cat now?' says the king of the rats, and the cat says, 'Here, now, what's this?' 'It's death to you,' says the rat, 'for all you cats are fey heathen creatures, as all the world knows, and it's the duty of a Christian rat to take you off the board as may be, particularly as it was for that purpose I was sent by the High King at Tara.' Then the two began to fight, all up and down the beach, and just then an angel—or somebody—come out of the woods and asked Brandon what was going on. ' 'Tis a good brawl, isn't it,' says the saint. 'Yes, but who are they?' 'Well, the one is wickedness,' says Brandon, 'and the other a fairy cat; and I brought the both of them out from Ireland with me, and now I'm watchin' to see which wins.' Then the angel says, 'Watch away, but it appears to me they're tearin' one another to pieces, and the pieces runnin' off into the woods.'

"And now here's your aunt come for you."

It was now quite dark, and my aunt was escorted by Mrs. Perkins, who carried a light. Doherty picked up his lantern and accompanied us back to the house, so that we made quite a party; but he and Mrs. Perkins left us at the kitchen.

Blaine and Mr. Ricepie were talking in the parlor when we came in, and we entered very quietly, like tardy scholars in school. I remember Mr. Blaine's saying, "I'm not going to argue figures with you—I know what that bank has produced in the past and what it is producing now, and either I get it or we have the examiners in again. Your job is to make the bank yield what I think it ought to, and if you can't do it you're not doing your job and I'll have to find someone who can."

When Mr. Macafee came to take my aunt Olivia to Mrs. Lorn's, I begged to go with them. This surprised him, and I remember that he said he would have thought I would enjoy playing baseball more than collecting china, and promised to bring me a fielder's mitt from his store. I suppose he had been looking forward to putting his arm about my aunt's shoulders on the drive out, and now feared that I might spy on them from my position in the rumble seat. My aunt interceded for me and I went anyway.

It was a lovely midsummer day, though the sky had a hard quality to its blue that made men say it was going to be a scorcher, waving their straw hats before their faces in a kind of agonized anticipation; while their wives, who had slept in more clothing and had lost, from the perspiration at their temples, the curl an iron had given their hair, sponged themselves from shoulder to hip with Paris Bon-Beau Cologne from Macafee's and (when there were no males present) made sly little jokes about putting their underclothes in the Frigidaire. I rode rejoicing in the wind—twisting, sometimes, to kneel on the leather seat and look back at the twin lines of dust we raised after the asphalt ended. We had passed the run-down old farm that still offered to board horses for the townspeople, and the sign that announced that ours was the thirty-fifth largest town in the state, and rolled now on the powdery grayness that spelled country roads, with columns of fence posts whizzing along to either side.

I wanted to ask my aunt how much farther it would be, but in the closed cabin of the roadster she was as isolated as if I were left behind at home. I tapped (I suppose somewhat timidly) at the small rear window, but neither head turned. I tried to lean forward far enough to look into one of the side windows, without success. As I slumped back into my seat, I noticed that directly ahead of us—rising over the cabin, which otherwise blocked my view—was a lone pillar of white cloud that seemed as summitless as the mast of Brandon's ship. I thought it was singularly beautiful, and for a time it distracted me from my formerly urgent concern with distance, and I stared at it with the contemplation a saint might have lavished on some object in which he saw, or felt he saw, a clear manifestation of God. To me it was Brandon's mast and at the same time the princess's tower rising from the sea, so that the Irish holy man captained a wicker vessel with sails the size of continents bent to that enchanted edifice of stone.

There is no wonder, no amazement, quite like that felt when something supposed for amusement's sake to be magical and mysterious actually manifests the properties imagination has assigned it in jest—when the toy pistol shoots real bullets, the wishing well grants actual wishes, lovers from down the street fling themselves into Death's bright arms from Lovers' Leap. I was deep in my reverie, as serene and enchanted of mind as any little swan-prince despite the jolting of the Studebaker, when I observed that my tower of cloud was no longer of the pearly-pink white whose lustrousness had originally suggested to my mind the princess of my beloved green-jacketed book; it was now touched everywhere with a dusky black shot with purple that, even while I looked, deepened and deepened until the entire insubstantial spire might have been carved of night.

In the name of Allah, the Compassionating, the Compassionate! There is no god but God. . . . And when he drew forth the stopper there appeared a great son of the jinn with teeth like to the trunks of palms and with five eyes, each like to a pool. Then said he to the jinni: "Dost honor thy covenant with me, and art thou my slave?" And the jinni replied (as the poet hath it):

> "He that lord it with little ruth,
> Never he be lord in truth.

"But for the time I am bound and thine."

"Then tell me some tale, for the care of men weighs upon me and I would broaden my breast."

Then the jinni sat beside him on the sand, and the sweat that streamed from him fought the tide and poisoned the sea. And he said: "Prince of fishermen, it hath come to my ears that there was once a marid, Naranj hight, who had a man to serve him. This man's name was ben Yahya, and the marid kept him to his toil by day and by night, with never a moment without its task.

"Now, it chanced upon a certain day that ben Yahya carried a burden for the marid down a certain alley in Damascus. Often had he walked there, for it was the marid's custom to turn stones to kine, and then to have his slave butcher the kine and sell the carcasses, which were of such a weight as to bring him to his knees, and also to make his slave grub from the fields such roots as beasts eat, and by his magic make sherbet of these, which ben Yahya was then forced to sell from a great jar slung upon his back. On this day he carried this jar, and it chanced that as he plodded beneath the load a scorpion stung his foot. He killed the creature and for a moment set down the jar to rub his wound. Thus he saw what he had been too bowed beneath his burden to see previously, a branch that overhung the wall that walled the alley, and upon that branch a fine pear. Being hungry, he thought to pluck it, and to that end placed his jar against the wall and climbed upon it, standing on the cover. No sooner had his hand closed upon the pear than he beheld a beautiful maiden, with tresses like night and richly bedight, with eyes large as sloes and crimson-pink toes, seated in a garden on the other side of the wall, playing a lyre.

"No sooner had he clapped eyes upon her than he fell from the jar and violently in love; but as he fell, his heel struck the jar, knocking it over, and it dashed against a stone and burst to pieces. Then he was awash in the sherbet it had contained, and had no more means of beholding the maiden, and had lost the sherbet he was to sell, and the pear to the bargain.

"When he returned to the marid's cave, he was beaten for having lost the sherbet as he had often been beaten before, but he remained afterward so desolate that at last the marid asked him whyfor he was ever so downcast and weighed with cark and care. Then ben Yahya replied: 'Know that when I burst thy jar, Master, and lost thy sherbet, I saw at that same time also a maiden exceeding fair; and the sight of her drew my heart out through my eyes, and it will not come back to me.' So ben Yahya.

"And then the marid: 'It comes to me that this was when thou wouldst have stolen the pear.'

"Then was ben Yahya struck dumb with amaze; but after a time he said: 'And how comes it that thou knowest even that, Master? For I know you to be wise, but none but Allah knowest all things.'

"Then said the marid: 'Understand that the wall over which you peered is mine, and the garden into which you peeped mine also. And the maid you saw belongs to me, and that even as you looked upon her I watched you from the upper window of my house. Now, thou sayest that thou art sick for love of her; so be it, but I make a condition. Hear it: serve me thirty years more and she shall be thine, and both free.'

"Then ben Yahya fell to his knees and praised the marid, but when he had emptied the cup of his heart he said: 'O best of masters, why art thou so generous to me? For you know I am thy slave, and must serve thee rewarded or no, and for as long as thou sayest, though it be until I die.'

"And the marid: 'As thou sayest, but slaves sometimes flee their masters, and did thou not stop thy task, but a few days gone, to rub the place where the scorpion stung thee? Not so do I desire to be served. For all the days until thy time be done, I will have thee serve me as the windlass serves the well or the oar the ship; for the windlass looks not up or down but does its task only and that with a whole heart, though it drinks not of the water; and the oar ne'er stops nor slacks, but stirs the sea to the beat of the drum, though it be all the day and all the night —yet when the ship makes port it has no profit in the voyage. So wilt thou labor for me for thy thirty years—nor wilt thou see thy love until that time be gone.'

"Now, Prince, it hath reached my ears that in the fullness of time the years all were gone past, and the dust of their camels had left ben Yahya everywhere gray, so that he stood as old men stand, and coughed much, and was even as him for whom the poet speaks when he sayeth:

> 'Time gars me tremble Ah, how sore the baulk!
> While Time in pride of strength doth ever stalk:
> Time was I walked nor ever felt I tired,
> Now am I tired albe I never walk!'

"Then upon the day when the thirty years were past, ben Yahya made suit to the marid, saying: 'O Master, thou knowest I have served thee these thirty years, and now by thy word I am free, and am to have the maid.'

"Then the marid snatched him up, and with him flew over seas perilous and deserts dangerous too many to count, and at last came to a land of great mountains, all of marble and jasper and lapis lazuli, with lions about their feet, and black apes upon their slopes, and snow upon their summits; and in the midst of these there abode a great metropolis, and at its gate he set ben Yahya upright, slapped him, and said: 'Thy love is within, and by Allah thou art free of me and I of thee.' Then said ben Yahya: 'What is the name of this place? For I find myself in foreign parts wherein my feet have never trod.' And the marid replied, 'It is called the Haunted City,' then vanished he like smoke."

And Shahrazad perceived the dawn of day and ceased to say her permitted say.

A raindrop struck my face, and then another and another, and lightning cracked the sky just ahead of the car. I beat upon the flat glass of the rear window until Mr. Macafee stopped and allowed me to sit—already somewhat damped—in the narrow space between my aunt Olivia and himself. I remember that it was just as the Studebaker started to move forward again that the rain began in earnest, furious waves of water driven horizontally by the storm until they hammered the windshield like hail. Mr. Macafee said to my aunt, "We'll have to try to get there before the road gets soft—we could be stuck out here."

Several times the Studebaker's engine seemed to hesitate and almost to die as water drove under the hood. Each time my aunt would grasp my arm tightly; and Mr. Macafee, shaking his head, would say, "Don't worry—the rain's shorting out the spark plugs, but the block's hot and it will dry us out again."

Suddenly my aunt threw out her arm (impelled by what magic I have never known) and shouted, "Here! Here!"

"Where?" Mr. Macafee asked, then realized, as I did, that she was pointing toward a gate in a wire fence that ran alongside the road. Two very narrow ruts led away from it, into the gray rain. Mr. Macafee twisted the steering wheel sharply and said, "I hope this is really it; we could get struck in there, Vi."

My aunt, who had regained all her composure, said confidently, "Oh, we could always make a run for the house, Jimmy."

"If there is a house."

The rain slacked a bit and we saw it, a massive brick-and-fieldstone farmhouse whose solid masonry walls had probably been standing since before the Civil War. Beside the front door a white June rosebush as big as a laurel still displayed the year's last three blossoms, now being flailed to ruin by the rain; under the spreading, thorny gray-green branches a lonely hen sheltered herself; there was no porch but the bush, and only a single high stone step, to which Mr. Macafee drove as close as he could before tooting the horn. I could see a kerosene lamp burning in the parlor window. Mr. Macafee tooted again, and as he did so the door opened; a woman in a long, old-fashioned calico dress stood there, with a little girl behind her who watched us from the shelter, as it seemed, of her mother's skirts. The woman made a gesture I did not understand and disappeared into the house, followed by the little girl, who had pigtails. My aunt Olivia said, "She's gone to get an umbrella—we don't need that, and she'll get wet. Why don't you make a run for it, Jimmy?"

Mr. Macafee opened the door and dashed out. I followed him, and in the three jumps it took me to reach the door got as wet as if I had fallen into the river. "Get out of Vi's way," Mr. Macafee said, and drew me aside. My aunt, of course, was wet, too, and we were all three standing in the doorway laughing about it when the woman in calico and the little girl returned with an umbrella like a black bird, and a huge old slicker of the kind favored by farmers.

"I'm Em Lorn," the woman said. "I suppose you're Eleanor's friend Olivia Weer?"

My aunt acknowledged that she was, and introduced Mr. Macafee and me.

"Well, I'm glad you brought the boy," the woman in calico said. "Those roads won't be fit for a car before tomorrow afternoon earliest; you'll have to stay the night with us, and you'd be troubled to think of him home alone. Where'd you say his mother and father was?"

"In Europe," my aunt said. "In Italy now, I suppose, if they've stuck to their itinerary—I haven't had a card from them, though, since Paris."

"I've never been there. You know, we're a real traveled family, and I've heard about all those places for so long I think I've been to them until I stop for a minute and remember I haven't. I'd like to go someday and so would Carl. He's been trying to get somebody to put some money behind the work of God so he could be a missionary in foreign lands, but so far we haven't found anybody that would do it."

My aunt said, "I should think you'd hate to leave this lovely farm," and the woman answered, "Well, I suppose anybody always hates to leave home, but I guess fifty years from now it's going to look just about like it does now, and we've seen it." She gestured toward the back of the house (reached by a dark and narrow hallway). "It's not polite to hustle your company into the kitchen, but the cookstove's going there and you can dry out a little. Margie, did you put the kettle on like I told you?"

The girl did not reply—she was already skipping down the hall ahead of us—and I suddenly realized, with that shock which children feel when they gain some insight into feelings other than their own, that our coming—an automobile—strangers —my aunt in her beautiful clothes—even myself, a new playmate—were for this little girl a fearsome and yet thrilling experience.

"There's doughnuts," Mrs. Lorn said. "I made doughnuts today after church."

I could smell them, the fresh, spicy odor fighting the musty air of the hall. I was wet, and already very much aware that the Lorn farmhouse (like my maternal grandfather's house, which I had already, until then, nearly forgotten) lacked the cellar-ruling octopus of a coal furnace my father had installed in my grandmother's house when I was almost too young to remember.

"And we can have tea," Mrs. Lorn was saying behind me. "Us Murchisons picked up the tea habit in China and never let it go—that's what my mother used to say. I'm a Murchison on my mother's side and my father's both; they was second cousins and could marry according to the rule. Look at this picture." (I sensed that she had halted my aunt and Mr. Macafee, and I stopped, too, looking back to see why.) "This is the oldest Cardiff Brethren church that ever was in China—that's a store on the other side of it with the card with the Chinese writing in the window. That store used to sell opium, is what my grandmother used to tell. My grandfather—Eli Murchison was his name—was the first pastor of that church and established it. He's not in the picture, because he took it. I was born and raised in the Cardiff Brethren myself, but I go to the Approved Methodists now, because of Carl's ministry there; but they aren't generous about sending out them that would do God's work among the heathen like the Cardiff Brethren are."

My aunt Olivia said, "It's a lovely Chinese street scene—look at the peddler with his cart, Jimmy; I'll bet that's ginseng root. And the old woman."

The small girl was beckoning me from the kitchen; I left the adults and joined her in front of a huge cast-iron range. "There's buttermilk," she said, "if you don't want tea." It was the first time I had heard her speak, and I was suprised to find that she did not sound shy. Her hair was nearly as dark as my aunt Olivia's, but her face was very pale. I had never been permitted to drink tea at home, but I had it regularly since coming to stay with my aunt, so I was able to say, "No, tea is all right," with considerable sophistication, and even to add, "I like a lot of sugar in mine."

"There's white sugar for company," the girl said. "But we use tree sugar."

I told her I liked tree sugar better.

"I guess I ought to go ahead and set the tea to steeping, then. They're going to talk out there a long time." I nodded, and the girl, quite gracefully, and as matter-of-factly as a matron fetching an ashtray from the mantel, climbed upon her mother's kitchen table to lift down a squat Chinese teapot from a high shelf. "We don't use a tea ball," she said. "Papa brought one from town once and mother said it spoiled the flavor and threw it out. It was real copper, too." She spooned black tea into the pot and added boiling water from the kettle on the range. "Now it'll be ready when they come. Wait a minute and I'll get the cups."

The pot, I noticed, was painted with hundreds of tiny faces done in orange and black; I was certain my aunt would be attracted to it, and studied it with interest, ready to call her attention to it as soon as she entered the room, so as to be able to claim exclusively that glory which is the just property of a discoverer. "It doesn't go with the cups," the girl said, "it's real old. My name's Margie."

I mumbled that my name was Den, and pointed to one of the faces. "This one's smiling."

"It was all white when it was first made," the girl said, "and whenever anybody that owns it dies their face goes onto it. My aunt Sarah had it before my mother—want to see her?"

Of course I said I did, and she indicated a tiny, rather grim-looking (and, I thought, also rather Oriental) face near the tip of the spout. "It was all white to begin with, and the first ones were around the little leg part—see? Those are the oldest. Then they came here around the main part, and now the room is almost used up; when it's all gone, the pot will break."

From the doorway my aunt Olivia said, "And this is your kitchen, Mrs. Lorn! Why, this is delightful—I love a country kitchen, I always have. I'll bet that you have shelves and shelves of preserves and home pickles hidden away somewhere."

"We don't gamble in the Approved Methodists," Mrs. Lorn said, smiling, "or in the Cardiff Brethren either—which is handy for me, because you'd win. I'll give you some of my home-bottled corn relish at supper. Do you like corn relish?"

Mr. Macafee exclaimed, "I love it!" He perhaps felt my aunt was ingratiating herself too successfully with Mrs. Lorn, and wanted to catch up.

Mrs. Lorn turned her smile toward him. "You know," she said, "it's real funny having you in my house like this, Mr. Macafee. I shop at your store—we have for years, and Carl and I go into town about every month except just after Christmas, when it's usually real bad weather—and I see you walking around in there and you've always got that flower in your coat just like now."

"I remember you, too, Mrs. Lorn," Mr. Macafee said. "It took me awhile to place you and your husband after Miss Weer mentioned your name, but we keep track of our good customers. We sold you folks a Maytag washer two years ago—I trust it's working out all right?"

"I have to get Carl to start the engine for me," Mrs. Lorn said, "but it don't never give trouble and it's a sight easier than using the board was, believe me.

"Margaret, is that tea steeped yet?"

"They're wonderful for farm families," Mr. Macafee told my aunt Olivia. "I wish someone would make a gas engine for an automobile that would run as well as the ones they put in those washing machines."

My aunt said, "They would, Jimmy, if you sold cars."

"Here, Miss Weer, let me give you some tea. Margie, get down the good sugar. I'm going to have to apologize to you folks if you're expecting a big supper; dinner's our main meal, and I set the table—Sundays—soon as we're back from church. Naturally it takes us longer there than some people because Carl has to shake everybody by the hand and talk and then lock up when they're all gone. When we get home, he goes out for a minute to look after the stock, and then we eat."

"I have only a *very* light meal in the evening, Mrs. Lorn, and Jimmy will just have to suffer. But I hope your husband isn't caught out in this rain."

"Oh, Carl'll make himself comfortable wherever he is—he was going down to the south pasture; there's a curing shed close by there for the tobacco, and I suppose that's where he fetched up. We don't either of us smoke—the church is against it—but there isn't anything that says you can't grow it, though it's hard on the land."

I asked if I might have a doughnut, and found they possessed a deliciously hard and greasy crust. Under the table Margie handed me a small, gritty, sticky lump I soon managed to smuggle into my tea, which rendered it ambrosial.

"If it's all the same to you folks, though," Mrs. Lorn was saying, "I'd like to hold up eating a bit—if this rain ever lets up Carl'll come in, and he may do it even if it don't. Do you like those doughnuts, child?"

I nodded vigorously, and she added, "I put bee honey in them."

My aunt said, "We've heard so much about this wonderful Chinese egg you own, Mrs. Lorn. Would it be possible—"

The woman in calico waved the suggestion away with an impatient gesture. "Not before you've finished your tea and got dry. Now, you've waited all your life up to this minute to see that thing, and you can wait another five minutes; I don't know what all you've been told, but it's not that much."

"But I think Mr. Macafee would like it—I mean, like to see it. Wouldn't you, Jimmy?"

"From the descriptions it must be fascinating," Mr. Macafee said. He had gotten a doughnut, too, and seemed to be hesitating over whether or not to dip it into his tea. "That sort of thing is —well, you know, Mrs. Lorn, more a woman's business than a man's; but I'm very interested in it."

"Heaven help us, I used to play with it when I was a child. Of course I had to be careful—Mother made me set in the middle of the bed to look at it. But you know what those old beds was: so high you had to put foot to a stool to get up on them, and then all lumps and slopes. How old are you, Miss Weer?"

"Twenty-six," my aunt said after a barely perceptible hesitation. "But can't we be a little less formal? Call me Vi."

"You know, you do have the sweetest smile, Vi," Mrs. Lorn told her with an embarrassed laugh. "And I confess you're the prettiest thing altogether—no wonder Mr. Macafee here's sweet on you. I'm thirty-five myself and proud of it; I was twenty-six already when Margie was born; she's my only chick-nor-child. She had a brother—Samuel, we called him—that never lived to christening. *He'd* be fourteen and a rising young man now if the Lord had willed it so. There was a time when Carl and I thought we saw the Lord's purpose in Samuel's dying; they don't like to send couples that has children to the missions much; but we didn't get to go then anyway, and then Margie come along, so that wasn't it at all."

Margaret said, "I'm sorry, Momma."

"Didn't you hear me say we didn't go even when you wasn't born? If the Lord wills us to go, we'll go."

"You'd like to go to China, of course," my aunt said, leaning forward in her eagerness. "I've wanted to for years, but travel is so difficult for a single woman."

Mrs. Lorn shook her head. "The South Seas is what I'd like," she said, "but Carl, he wants Africa. We talked about it all one night—must have been eleven o'clock before we went to bed—and what we decided was we'd put in for everything, and whatever they give us we'd go to unless it was Eskimos."

"What about you, Jimmy?" my aunt said suddenly. "Have you ever thought of where you'd like to go if you were a missionary? I confess I hadn't, but I find it an easy question now that I have. I can picture myself aboard a junk on the Yellow River, letting the sailors teach me mah-jongg on the back of a big Bible."

From the parlor a clock struck, and everyone fell silent, counting strokes that were nearly inaudible against the roar of the rain outside. Six. "Well, it ain't letting up," Mrs. Lorn said, "and I don't guess Carl'll come home in this, and the children ought to eat—something besides doughnuts, anyway. If you folks are about dried off now, I'll get some supper out for us, and if Carl's not here time we set down, he'll have to take potluck."

"You weren't planning to have supper in your dining room, were you, Em?" my aunt asked, having divined more from some motion of our hostess's eyes than I ever could. "You don't mind if I call you Em—I feel we're such old friends already."

"Well, you are company," Mrs. Lorn said weakly.

I shivered (and no doubt Mr. Macafee did, too) at the thought of that icy, clammy "company" dining room.

"We'd *much* prefer to eat here, by the stove—and it would be so much handier for you."

And so we did. As Mrs. Lorn was setting the table, I saw my aunt—and Mr. Macafee as well—cast several longing glances toward the parlor; but both seemed to feel it would be impolite for them to suggest again (at least before the meal was over) that the Chinese egg be brought in. The tension, the desire to see what was so close and yet could not be named, affected them in different ways, and I have thought since that this same emotion—and perhaps even the response the individual makes to it, its visible manifestations—is more common than we suppose, as when, particularly before marriage, or carnal knowledge, or indeed intimacy of any sort, we wish to see and touch and even to smell the body of a woman to whom we are attracted, someone now near us, aware of us, perhaps even attracted to us, but whose reality is hidden from us by clothing and the iron conventions that govern us as long as other people are present—and even when they are absent, as long as their intrusion is, or at least is feared to be, imminent.

Mr. Macafee was silent, and kept his eyes cast down. On the few occasions when he attempted to assist in the preparations for the meal—moving chairs and suchlike—he was slow and clumsy. And yet this—this silence, this ineptitude—was clearly not caused by bad temper but rather by a species of shy desire that, occupying the center of his thought, left him a kind of idiot, and could not be dismissed (as he may have imagined) at will.

My aunt's reaction, though it proceeded from the same cause, was quite different. She was high-spirited, talkative, and exceedingly efficient. She set Mrs. Lorn's table for her, and did it so quickly that it seemed as if she moved by magic, actually tossing the plates and cups into place, but so dexterously that hardly a piece needed to be adjusted from the point at which it came to rest. She was the spring from which there flowed a constant stream of little sallies more remarkable for gaiety than wit but made very acceptable by the infectious good will that accompanied them, and at which she laughed more loudly than anyone: louder than Margaret, who went off into giggles when her cheeks were pinched and she was asked about boyfriends at school and promised a sample of my aunt's perfume; louder than I when she called Mr. Macafee "Jimmy-wimmy" and pretended to feel in the pockets of his vest to see if he kept marbles there; louder even than Mrs. Lorn, who was losing her nervousness at having strange company, and beginning already to store her head with tales of that company and the way they had behaved, the storm, the car, the supper eaten without her husband, "with everybody cracking jokes and carrying on like we was all children again, though there wasn't a drop of liquor served and no one wanted it," the praise she knew would come to her food, and the talk afterward "about China, where my family used to live and everything, and going-ons in Cassionsville, too—that Mr. Macafee, that's *the* Macafee that owns the store, and don't he know who owes what."

We suppered on the cold biscuits left from dinner, with honey and farm butter, tea, the promised corn relish, homemade vegetable soup, and more doughnuts. My aunt fell into conversation with Margaret, asking her where she went to school, what she studied, what she did to help her mother, and so on. "She's a bright one," Mrs. Lorn said. "She'll be a better cook than me soon's she understands the management of the stove. She can play, too, and sings a bit."

"The piano? Why, we'll have to play a duet, Margie—later this evening if your mother will let us."

"It's sad how out of tune it is now. That parlor's too wet for it, is what I tell Carl, but you can't have it nowhere else. Carl plays a bit—he taught Margie—and I try to get him to tune it, but he says his ears isn't good enough."

"You have to use a tuning fork and listen very carefully. I watch when the man from Jimmy's store does mine. But I never could do it—I don't understand about all the little wrenches and things."

"Well, if we're going to go into the parlor by and by," Mrs.

Lorn practically, "we ought to have a fire started in there now—it'll be as cold as a frog in a clabber crock." She looked at me. "Margie could do it, child, but it's more a boy's work and you look antsy. She'll show you where the things is."

"Oh, Den lays fires for me all the time," my aunt said. I could see she felt that having me as her representative in the parlor brought her in some mystical way a step closer to the egg. Under Margie's supervision I collected an armload of kindling from the smaller division of the woodbox by the stove, and we made our way back down the narrow hall to the parlor door.

It was a small room—no more, I think, than ten by twelve feet—much smaller than the parlor at my grandmother's or my aunt Olivia's. The fireplace was at one end of the room, the piano at the other; while I busied myself at the grate and brought in more wood from the box in the kitchen, Margie lit a kerosene lamp for me, showed me where the matches were, played a swift chorus of "Jingle Bells," and ran out of the room —I suppose to tell her mother the fire was laid, or to get another doughnut. I used the opportunity provided by her absence to look for the egg, first along the mantelpiece, then peering, with the aid of the lamp, through the somewhat dusty glass doors of a bookcase full of framed photographs and mementos. For a moment I stood in the middle of the room and held the lamp as high as I could, turning slowly about: the kindling in the grate was blazing brightly, and the larger pieces of wood were beginning to catch; the rain beat insistently on windows and walls and sent a thin trickle of water over one sill to form a small pool on the floor beneath; the yellow lamplight seemed to bathe the entire room; and yet I could not see the famous object. I returned to the kitchen dejected, and when my aunt sent me a piercing look I could only shake my head. Mr. Macafee was telling Mrs. Lorn about the Tuesday and Thursday Nankeen Nook, and Mrs. Lorn said, "Why, that's wonderful! I wouldn't have thought, Mr. Macafee, that a big store like yours would think about people like that at all."

Mr. Macafee said, "You don't understand, Mrs. Lorn; thinking about people is good business—it really is."

"Well, I'm glad to hear you say that," Mrs. Lorn said, "because I've always felt it was real important."

My aunt touched her arm. "Now that there's a fire in the parlor, Em, why don't we go in and have a look at that wonderful egg of yours; and then your daughter and I can play that duet."

Mrs. Lorn looked embarrassed. "I hope you won't mind," she said. "I wasn't going to say anything about it—Carl says I'm foolish, and you folks drove so far out here to see it in all this rain. . . ."

"We don't want to put you to any trouble, Em," my aunt said. I saw her knuckles tighten, and knew that she feared the egg had been broken; I thought so myself.

"It's the Lord's day," Mrs. Lorn said. "I do want to sell it—that is, if you folks are willing to give as much for it as that nice Miss Bold said you might—but it's the Lord's day. I was always taught it was a sin to buy or sell on the Lord's day, and particularly something like that that has his picture on it, or a Bible or a prayer book. Simony is what my father would of called it. So I thought the Lord sent the rain so you'd stay over —and then it will be the day after, you know. Just to relieve my feelings."

"Macafee's is never open on Sunday," Mr. Macafee said.

My aunt put an arm about Mrs. Lorn's shoulders, and I noticed how odd the lace at the end of her sleeve looked against the older woman's worn face. "We certainly don't have to talk about *price*," she said. "Indeed, I *wouldn't*, not if you felt the least scruple about it, Em. Why don't we just *look* at it today— you show it to company, don't you? Mr. Macafee and I are so eager to see it—we love that sort of thing."

"It's in the parlor," Mrs. Lorn said, "on the mantel."

I knew that it was not, but I followed them into the parlor nonetheless; my fire was crackling on the grate now, and the lamp Margaret had lit still illuminated the room. Mrs. Lorn walked to the mantel and picked up a squat three-legged wooden stand I had noticed there earlier. "Why, it's gone," she said. "It was right here."

My aunt and Mr. Macafee looked at one another.

"It's gone," Mrs. Lorn said again. "Why, you don't suppose that boy—"

My aunt's mouth tightened. "I'm sure Den wouldn't do anything like that," she said. "Or if he did, it would be just to play a harmless joke on us—just for a moment. You wouldn't, would you, Den?"

"No, ma'am."

"Could your girl—"

"Margie, dear, did you take it? You were in there with Den."

Margaret shook her head, then ran to her mother's side and, drawing her down, whispered in her ear. "That man!" Mrs. Lorn said.

"Could your husband have done something with it?"

"That's what the child says—I guess it could be true. I'll send her out, though I hate to on a night like this."

"It's outside?"

Mrs. Lorn nodded grimly. "It could be—that's what the child said.

"Margie, you go out and look, and if it's there, fetch it."

My aunt and Mr. Macafee protested.

"I'm not sending her out there on your account," Mrs. Lorn said, "I wouldn't do that. But I want to know myself, and the rain won't hurt her—she's a healthy girl."

"Den," my aunt said suddenly, "you go with her."

"There's no need of that," Mrs. Lorn protested.

"She should have somebody with her if she's going out in that storm—it's not far, is it?"

Mrs. Lorn shook her head. "Just out back. You children come with me, I'll get you a light."

There was a roofed porch with rusty, sagging screens behind

the kitchen; dimly I could see a table upon which tomatoes were stacked like cannon balls, and from under it Mrs. Lorn took a huge old-fashioned lantern, which she lit and gave to Margie. To me she said, "That's big enough for both of you. You, Den —that your name?—watch she don't set the henhouse afire with it. That coat fit you?" I was wearing her slicker; it did not, but I nodded. "Well, don't trip over the hem. And don't step on it neither if you can help it. And don't push your hat back like that—it'll rain on your face and run down through the neck; wear it way forward." She pulled the too large sou'wester hat over my eyes and Margie laughed, a laugh that, at the time, cut to the quick. "Go on, now."

We did not have to leave the porch to enter the rain; it splashed through the screens at us. But when Mrs. Lorn (getting wet herself, no doubt, in doing it) unhooked the door for us, it was as though we had stepped beneath a waterfall. I was still unsure of where we were going, and the noise of the rain was now too loud to permit me to ask; but the girl gestured imperiously for me to follow and we set out across what I knew must be the farmyard.

We skirted what looked like a woodshed and, splashing through puddles higher than the tops of our ankle-high shoes, made our way around the wreck of an old hay wagon. A moment later I saw that Margie was pulling at a low, crooked door set in a building hardly higher than my head, and I took the lantern from her. The door opened, and I heard, much muted by the roar of the rain, the sleepy protests of disturbed fowl. "This is the laying house," Margie said as soon as we had stepped inside.

The significance of the location escaped me, and I fear I stared at her.

"When one of the hens won't lay, Daddy puts a china egg under her—sometimes that starts them. Only it broke; last week that was. He said something about using the one off our mantel until he got another one at the store, only Daddy never gets nothing at the store if he can find something else that'll do. I thought he was funning, because he wouldn't set something with Jesus' picture on it under a hen. But it's gone, so I told Mother. He don't want her to sell it."

"Your father?"

The girl nodded. She had enormous eyes, wide and solemn; they seemed to glow in the lamplight. "He can be funny. Do you think he'd put a egg with Jesus on it underneath a common hen like that? Suppose it was to hatch?"

I said, "I don't think it's a real egg, is it?"

"Suppose it was. It'd be blasphemy to put it under a ordinary hen like that. It might hatch something little and squirmy, with a hundred little teeth as sharp as needles, and when it got big it would be one of those things that live in the woods and at night when it's raining like this come out and kill the cows and sheep, and even people if they get too close."

I shrugged, endeavoring to show that it made no difference to me whether the Chinese egg hatched into such a creature or not.

"So we'd better get it out," the girl continued, "before it does. Stick your hand under the hens and feel if there's any eggs—it's bigger than the other kind. You start on that side and I'll start over here and we'll meet in the middle."

I did, with a nervousness compounded of a town boy's fear of hens, and the unpleasant image the girl had just introduced into my mind—the whole multiplied by the fact that she had taken the lantern, so that I worked in near darkness, with my own magnified shadow bobbing on the unpainted boards of the wall before me. I found two eggs, both of the ordinary, dirty sort laid by chickens.

When we met (she had examined about twice as many nests, I noticed, as I had), she said, "Didn't you find it?"

I shook my head.

"Let me look," she said, and she quickly rechecked the nests I had already searched. When she had finished, she said, "It's not here."

I readily agreed, and without saying anything more she threw open the door and stepped out into the rain again, leaving me to close it behind her. After a wild dash—I was afraid that she would get so far in advance of me that I would be left in total darkness, which in that rain would have required a distance of only a few yards—I found myself in a cavernous building filled with the odors of cattle and cow dung. I asked if we were not going back to the house.

"This is our barn. I thought you might like to see the animals."

"I've seen lots of cows."

"We've got some real good ones. See that red one over there? That's Belle, she's a Jersey; and that one next to her—Bessy—she's half Jersey."

I showed my courage by stroking Bessy, very gently, on the nose.

"Some of them will hook you. That Bessy'd hook anybody, and there's a billy goat in one of these stalls."

"Which one?"

"This one." She walked across the barn to an apparently empty stall and looked inside. "He's lying down now."

"Can I see?" I began to follow her, but she laid her free hand on the latch menacingly.

"What I do," she said slowly, "is just open it here, and pull it back on me so I'm behind it and he can't get at me. He comes straight out like a bullet, then goes for whatever moves. Then while he's busy I give a jump for that ladder over there and get up in the haymow."

I backed away from the stall and said, "I don't think there's really a goat in there at all," and as I did, I caught my heel on the handle of a hayrake and, putting out a hand to steady myself, put it purely by accident into the feedbox of an empty stall. Under musty hay it met something smooth, round, and cool.

My face must have told Margie that something extraordinary had happened. The goat (who had been purely imaginary, in any case) was forgotten as she came rushing to see what I had found; it was too large for me to grasp securely with one hand, and I was rooting in the box with both. When I drew it up at last, my first impression, still not totally erased, was that I had found a pearl.

It was cream white and gleaming, and the light of the lantern seemed to penetrate it slightly. I had imagined that it would be nearly spherical, with one tapering (but only slightly tapering) end like the chicken eggs with which I was familiar. In fact its length was somewhat more than twice its diameter, so that it resembled, at least in shape, the eggs of certain wild birds. It was white, as I have said, with the pictures that decorated its surface executed in a brown so dark that I then, in the lantern light, believed them black.

"You've got it!" Margie said. "We found it."

I wanted to look at it, but she stopped me by depriving me of the light. "Come *on*," she said, "let's show everybody. Only don't drop it."

I was careful not to: ignorant though I was, I had already seen that the egg was not ivory (as had sometimes been reported) but porcelain.

3

THE ALCHEMIST

I saw Margaret Lorn only rarely after my aunt Olivia bought the egg. Only rarely, that is, until we were of high school age and found ourselves (who had so often, it seemed, been kept apart by destiny) now thrust together. The mobility furnished —or, rather, dropped raw and unfurnished—into the hands of young people by the invention of the automobile has often been commented upon. The mobility conferred at a much earlier age by the bicycle has been wholly neglected. Margaret and I wheeled ours down narrow footpaths, threading the woods lining the banks of the Kanakessee below Cassionsville, threading the banks in early spring, when the black willows were dabbed with green, and birds called through a forest littered with the wind-fallen branches of the winter past, coming out at last on stony banks, with sand farther down, sand where the high winter water had cast it in making its wide turn: a beach that would grow cockleburs later, but was fine sifted sand now, dotted with driftwood. Bass in the clear river water dodging in and out; brown moccasins without venom swimming upstream like sea serpents in long lashing esses, their heads above the ripples; minnows with theirs in a circle, their bodies radiating out like the petals of the memorial daisy.

"Now, Mr. Weer, if you will just sit down. . . ."

"I thought we were finished with you, a long time ago."

"In a moment. You promised to look at these cards for me, remember?"

"Ink-blot cards? I've heard of those."

"No, these are TAT cards, Mr. Weer. Thematic Apperception Test cards. You stood very straight in front of the mirror, Mr. Weer, but I notice that you are slumping in your chair now. Are you ill?"

"Just tired."

"Very well—"

"The fool. One of the greater trumps—some say second only to the juggler."

"I haven't even shown you the first card yet, Mr. Weer. Or explained how the test works. I'd like you to answer a very important question very honestly for me, Mr. Weer. Do you use drugs? Drugs of any kind?"

"No. Oh, I smoke an occasional cigar, drink coffee, sometimes a highball."

"Do you enjoy your work?"

"I'm afraid I couldn't say. I'm usually too busy to notice."

"You are the president of your company, are you not? As well as its board chairman and chief stockholder?"

"Yes."

"I had a professor in medical school who used to say, 'Happy is the man who has found his work—but of course the addict who has found a quart jar of heroin is happy, too.' One kind of addiction is approved by society, Mr. Weer, and the other is not, but both destroy their victims."

"You're telling me that I would be better off disliking what I do."

"Work was meant to be work, Mr. Weer. Toil. Now I'd like you to cooperate with me. Look at this card. Will you describe it for me?"

"There's a woman—at least I think it's a woman, it might be a boy, an adolescent. She's handing that other one something."

"Very good. Now you are to make up a little story for me— a story for which this picture is to be one of the illustrations."

In the days of Ch'in a certain young man of military family was summoned to Peking on a matter having to do with a heavy fine that had been levied against his dead father. You are to think of him as tall, handsome, and strong, riding a dappled stallion in the rain. His clothing is quilted and rough; his saddle-bag holds only a ball of boiled rice, and a few cash. Very well, then.

When he had ridden all day and his horse stumbled with every second step, he stopped at a certain hostel to sleep; and there he found that because of the bad weather there were few travelers—indeed, only one beside himself, and that one a venerable old man of long white beard and piercing eyes. "Welcome," the old man said. "For a time I feared I would have to stay the night alone in this deserted place. But see, I have built a fire for us, and I have some tea. Will you be my guest?"

The young man was pleased by this friendly reception and, though he had nothing to share with the old man but his rice, made himself as useful as he could, tending the fire and spreading their garments before it to dry; and in time he came to tell the old man the story of his plight. When he was finished, the old man said, "You do not know how fortunate you are. You possess a healthy body, warm clothing, and a valuable horse. The reputation of your family assures you of a commission in the imperial army for so long as you consent to wear a sword. Your only difficulty is this debt, which is but a matter of money and need worry you no more than you allow it."

"Everything that you have said is true," replied the youth after a moment's thought. "But another, equally truthful, might state the matter otherwise, saying, 'This young man is without friends or family or funds, and bears so heavy a debt that should he win a fortune it would all be forfeit. If things go ill for him in the capital, he will find himself in the hands of the torturers; if they go well, the best he can hope for is a life of drill and skirmishes spent at the frontiers of the empire, and in the company of men not much more civilized than the barbarians from whom they defend it.' "

When he heard this, the old man rose stiffly from his mat and, hobbling to the doorway, stood there for a long time looking out into the darkness and the rain, and the young man was bruised in heart with fear that he had offended him, for he was of that antique cast of mind that fears most displeasing those who are powerless. And at length he said, "Grandfather, if I have disturbed the tranquillity of your wisdom with my thoughtless remarks I beg ten thousand pardons. Sit once more before this fire and drink this excellent tea, and I pledge upon my honor as a soldier that you will hear no more foolish complaints from my lips."

"Do not think you have cast this poor one into confusion," the old man said, turning to face him. "I was but meditating. The road outside this hut is empty, but if all those who would change their place for yours were to pass by tonight the clamor of their feet should allow us no rest."

"There are many who are poor and miserable—" the young man began.

"Many also," the old man said, "of wealth and fame. Rich palanquins would enliven the concourse of beggars, like bits of fish in a bowl of poor rice. Young man, you doubtless think me a person of no consequence, and in that you are correct. But I have one precious possession." And with that he unrolled the bundle of rags that served him for luggage and showed the young man an elegant night-rest for the head, of green ceramic.

"*A china pillow, Vi?* Come, now."

My aunt regarded Stewart Blaine with assumed hauteur. "Certainly. They are curved to fit the contours of the head, and are much cooler than the feather things we sleep on."

Professor Peacock's friend Julius Smart (whom my aunt had insisted on inviting to the party) said, "I've seen them in curio shops. There's a wide foot, then a sort of stubby little pedestal, and on top a thing for your head shaped like a banana."

"That's one kind. This one—remember this, all of you, it's important—was the older sort, like a dented tube. If you'll think of the potter rolling his clay out flat like pie dough, and then rolling it up like a carpet, and *then* laying his head on the middle while it's still soft to get the right shape, and then firing it, you'll have the right idea."

The young man said, "That looks very comfortable, Grand-father."

"It is more than that," the old man told him, "it is magical, for it possesses the peculiar property of fulfilling the wishes of anyone who sleeps upon it. Each night for fifty years I have slept there, but for tonight I will lend it to you."

Now, the young man did not in the least believe what the old man had told him, but he was much too polite to say so, and laid himself down with his head on the green rest as the old man had directed. There was no sound but the dancing of the raindrops on the rice straw overhead, and the snapping of the fire, and soon he went to sleep.

When he woke, day had already broken. His head lay not on the green china pillow but upon his own rolled-up coat, and the old man was gone. The rain had stopped, so after eating what remained of his rice he mounted his horse and continued his journey to Peking.

"Aunt Vi, did anything else happen before he got there?"
My aunt Olivia shook her head.

When he reached the city, he laid his case before one of the leading mandarins, casting himself upon his mercy.

"Who said, 'Take my lovely daughter and my fortune as well'
—right, Vi?"

"Shut up, Jimmy. Just because it's your birthday you don't
have the right to interrupt."

Naturally the mandarin did nothing of the kind—he had a
heart as hard as jade. But he cared a great deal about the emperor's treasury, which was his responsibility. So, seeing that
the young man had no money, and no relatives who might pay
the debt if he was subjected to the position of "monkey with a
peach," but had the training and temperament of a soldier, he
told him that in the future nine-tenths of his pay would be withheld until the debt was discharged, and ordered him to report
to a certain garrison town in the north. Then (reckoning that
as the army required a certain number of high officers in any
case, it was best to have at least one whose costly salary did not
desert the imperial coffers) he sent an order to the military
commander of the district, stating that the young man was to
be appointed colonel of that town.

Thus the young man had no sooner arrived at his new post
than he found himself the chief officer there, and as he was still
penniless and could afford neither the comforts of domesticity
nor such debaucheries as the town offered, he amused himself
by drilling his men and hunting boars, wolves, and even the
huge Siberian tigers with the bow and the spear, and in that way
gained a great reputation for courage, and the admiration of
the soldiers he commanded.

He had hardly been in his new position a year when a rebel-
lion against the emperor was fomented by the secret society
called Seven Bamboo. Immediately sending a pledge of his
loyalty to the imperial palace, the young officer led his troops
south and, during the three years that followed, fought in a
thousand and ninety-six battles and skirmishes, always with
distinction and success.

When the war was over, he was placed in charge of the entire northern military district, which included the city of Peking, and was the most important in the empire. He married four wives, all of whom were beautiful and the daughters of important mandarins. The fine was forgiven, and the emperor made him a gift of three palaces; and in this style of life he passed forty years in happiness and tranquillity, a period during which the Celestial Kingdom was untroubled by treason, treachery, or barbarian invasion. At the end of this time he begged the Dragon Throne that he be permitted to retire from its service, though his beard was not yet white and his carriage and strength were those of a young man. This was granted, and he celebrated his retirement by leading a hunting party of seventeen sons and grandsons into the northern mountains.

"*To me,*" Eleanor Bold said, "*your young officer sounds a lot like your brother John, Vi.*"

"Don't be silly. Actually, I don't care for hunting or the men who do it, but this is the story."

Spurring his horse in the pursuit of a savage wolf, he lost his way in fog and rain, and had reconciled himself to spending the night in the saddle when he saw a glimmer of light far off on the sheerest face of one of the most forbidding mountains. Then, after tying his mount to a bush when the beast could scale the rocky slope no farther, he climbed until he found himself in the shelter of a small cave, at the back of which sat an old man brewing tea over a fire of twigs. Politely the soldier asked if he might spend the night. The old man agreed, offered him tea, and then, when he saw how silently he stared into the fire, asked if he were troubled. The retired officer recounted his story, and ended by saying, "As I sat here, I was thinking of that night on the road to Peking; how I woke and found the rain gone and all of my life before me. If I could live only that one day again—"

"Fool!" the old man exclaimed. "Do you not recognize me? I have granted your heart's desire, and for it I receive your ingratitude!" And with that he picked up the teakettle and dashed the boiling contents into the face of the young man, who leaped up and ran out of the cave.

But as he left the cave he discovered that in place of the steep slope of the mountainside he stood upon a level plain of brownish gray, seemingly of infinite extent. He turned and looked behind him, and there, instead of the hermit's cave, he beheld a circular opening in a wall of glassy green. Even as he watched, it dwindled, and after a moment he realized that he himself was expanding; in the winking of an eye he was standing on the floor of the hostel, and the hermit's cave was only the hole in the end of the green headrest. He washed his face, saddled his horse, made his farewell to the elderly philosopher, and set off for Peking.

"That was very good, Vi," Stewart Blaine said, *"but I hope you're not expecting the rest of us to do that sort of thing."*

My aunt Olivia laughed. "Not Den, because he's too young. But everybody else ought to have at least one good story in them. I'm going to spin this bottle, and the one it points to has to tell the next one."

Julius Smart, as I have said, was a friend of Professor Peacock's. He was not—officially, as it were—a cripple, and did not seem to be in any way handicapped, but there was something wrong with his shoulders, one of which was noticeably larger than the other. Beyond that there was nothing remarkable in his appearance: he was of just under average height, and had a long nose, a pale complexion, and pale hair.

I remember quite clearly what Bledsoe's was like before he bought it: a dark, cluttered shop filled with everything imaginable to suggest sickness—not only medicines, but crutches and bedpans and those hideous walking sticks that seem to be made by the same factories that make handles for mops, and obscene contrivances of red rubber. Mr. Bledsoe (who was, of course, called "Doc" by my elders, as druggists always were in Cassionsville until much later) was an aging man who had early—doubtless in the expectation, justified later by the event, of a long life—adopted the principle of selling whatever no one else in town sold, but at a high price. Sooner or later (you could almost hear him muttering it as he worked behind his counter), somebody would want it badly enough to pay for it. Double trusses are not needed often, nor are catheters with genuine Bakelite tips, but when they are needed they are needed very badly indeed. When Julius Smart bought the store, he threw a great deal out, moved a great deal more into a back room Mr. Bledsoe had fitted up as a sitting room, and moved more still (so I learned when Smart married my aunt) into a building south of town—that is, on the other bank of the Kanakessee—only a few miles from the spot where, a long time afterward, Lois Arbuthnot and I searched for buried treasure.

Like the other changes Julius made, this clearing and rearranging was not done all at once, but bit by bit as he found time. The window displays of sickroom supplies, which had stood untouched and even undusted for years, gave way to fancifully shaped jars of colored water, and these were kept scrupulously clean. A showcase that had formerly held no one could remember what was one day discovered filled with Fatimahs, Camels, Chesterfields, Sweet Caporals, Prince Albert Smoking Tobacco, and Muriel Cigars.

Later, when he had become my Uncle Julius, I used to try (mostly, I think, while lying on my back in the little bedroom overlooking my aunt's front walk, for I was still living with her, my parents still in Europe, and cruising, at about that time, among the Greek Isles in a rented yacht) to remember the drugstore and Cassionsville itself as they were before he came. He was the first major change to take place within my memory, equivalent for me to the building of the new bridge at Oak Street. Julius Smart was an improvement, but I sometimes felt even then that he had improved my home out of existence. The first time I saw him, sitting in my aunt Olivia's parlor with a saucer of crumbs from Mr. Macafee's birthday cake at his feet and a teacup balanced on one knee, he did not strike me as a powerful —much less a symbolic—figure. Just a man rather smaller than most, with an amusing, mock-sincere way of speaking.

"This is a true story, but I don't expect you to believe it. It happened to me the year I graduated. Right in the middle of summer after graduation, as a matter of fact.

"I suppose everyone here realizes that when a young man comes out of college with a pharmacy degree it's not as though he was given a key to the bank. If he's lucky, his father already has his own business and he can go in with him; or his family has enough money to set him up in a place of his own. If he's not lucky—and I was one of the unlucky ones—he has to find a place that will take on another man, and since a drug business can be run pretty handily by one, those are few and far between.

"I had been looking for a place for about a year before I graduated and had all my relations looking for me in the usual way, but none of us had come up with anything, and I was just about ready to accept a position in a medicine show if one should be offered. I'd collect newspapers from every place that had them and sit around home a lot, reading them over and looking for something that might be in my line. And then I kept writing, of course, to all my teachers at school, reminding them to let me know if they should hear of anything—I figured that was my best bet. And my various aunts, you know, and cousins and in-laws and whatnot would come around to tell me about something they'd heard of two or three counties away. I'd always go, but it wouldn't be anything. At least it gave me a chance to get out of the house and buy more papers.

"This had been going on for quite a time when I finally decided that if I kept on the way I was, I wasn't going to get anything until the next class was graduated, and then there'd be more after the same jobs. So I made up a plan for a trip that would take me nearly all over the country except for the East and way out West. I used the cheapest way I could figure out to get everywhere; and that was mostly milk trains."

"You mean you just took those little trains from town to town looking for work?" my aunt asked.

"Not just for any kind of work—for a job in a pharmacy. But I told my mother and father—both of them were alive then, though they've gone to their reward now—that if I didn't get anything on that trip, when I came back I'd take any kind of work I could get. But what I was really thinking was that if I didn't get anything I wouldn't come back; I'd just stop off somewhere.

"Well, I won't tell you where it was I ended up, because everybody around here has the wrong ideas about that place. Let me just say that it was pretty far down South—south enough that there was palm trees and magnolias growing alongside the streets, and the house I stayed at—which was with the man I was working for, as I'll tell you in a minute—had two trees in the front yard and one of them was an orange tree and the other was a lemon. It was hot there most all the time, and the ground so sandy it seemed like it was almost ready to move around, and all the houses were wood or stucco—no brick at all.

"I got off the train there, like I did everywhere I went to, without expecting anything much of it. To tell the truth, I'd already been to a couple big places without getting anything, and this didn't look like it could have more than one drugstore in it—and as a matter of fact it didn't. I got a newspaper like I always did, and walked down the main street thinking to get breakfast there and then to try at whatever drugstore there was, and then to ask around of people before moving on.

"There was a drugstore all right, and the thing that surprised me was that it was already open, though it wasn't much after seven o'clock. I thought most likely someone had to have medicine in a hurry for a sick relative and had gone and got the pharmacist and made him open the shop; then maybe he'd figured since it was already light out and he was up and dressed, he'd just keep the place open. Well, you can believe I didn't wait to get any breakfast. I just went right direct in after I straightened my tie and brushed my suit a little.

"I guess probably most of us would say this room here of Miss Weer's has got a high ceiling, and I have to admit it looks mighty pretty with that fancy woodwork going around the corner of it, and then not flat but curved up like a courthouse, as you might say. But that place had a ceiling must have been close to twice as high as this—just up and up, with shelves, you know, all along the walls, and a ladder that you had to carry around to reach them. At the top was a good big electric fan, a six-blader, and he had it going already. All the lights were on—they were converted gas; you know the kind—and I could hear somebody moving around in back, but there was no one in front to be seen.

"Naturally I didn't want to go in back and bother him, figuring most likely he was compounding a prescription. I just took off my hat and found a good place to set it, and waited for him, and I must have waited half an hour, standing there and wondering if I wasn't making a big fool of myself. Finally he came out, and I wish I could describe him to you in a way to make you see him. He was one of the tallest men I ever saw, I guess, but most of the time he stood like he didn't have any chest at all, all hollowed out there, so he didn't look much taller than the average. Once in a while he'd reach up to get something, and it was like watching a tree grow. He had a long face, a very long jaw, and a high forehead like you see in pictures of Shakespeare. His hair was black, and he wore it long because it was getting thin, and combed over. He said, you know, 'What can I do for you?' the way you do, and I said, 'I'm a pharmacist, Mr. Tilly' (I had gotten his name, you see, off a framed certificate while I had been waiting), 'and I'd like to work for you. If you had another pharmacist here, you could stay open longer, and that would mean more business. And you could take holidays while the store made money for you.' That was what I always said.

"He said, 'You're a druggist.' Just like that, flat, and let it hang there.

"I said, 'Let me show you my credentials,' but he waved his hand in a vague kind of way to show that he believed me. After a minute I said, 'I could come back this afternoon if you'd like to think it over; and I don't smoke or drink, in case you're wondering, and I'm a regular churchgoer.'

"Just then I heard the little bell he had on a spring over the door. I turned around, and coming through the door—

"Well, I guess you've all seen a man with only one arm, and maybe some of you've seen one without any. But this wasn't a man, it was a woman, and she didn't have any arms but she had hands."

"I should think her hands would have fallen to the ground, Mr. Smart," Eleanor Bold said, giggling behind her napkin.

"Her hands sprouted right out of her shoulders, without arms to space them out. The thing I particularly remember about her was that she was smoking a cigarette—"

My aunt leaned forward with quickened interest. "On the street?"

"She'd just come in from the street when she made the bell ring, so I suppose she must have been smoking it out there."

Stewart Blaine said, "I imagine she was accustomed to being stared at."

"That's likely so. She held it like this—between her fingers, you see—and just sort of flipped it up to her mouth when she wanted some. She wasn't a bad-looking woman, either. Mr. Tilly sort of nodded at her when she came in—I could see he knew her—then he said to me, 'Pardon me a minute,' and got a little parcel wrapped in brown paper and gave it to her. I didn't see how she could pay him, because she wasn't carrying a purse or reticule, and she couldn't have reached her pockets if she had any. But she was way out in front of me, I'll tell you. She took that package in one hand, and put the cigarette in her mouth, and then flipped her free hand up into her hair and brought out a roll of bills. I couldn't tell how much it was when Mr. Tilly counted it, but I saw that one was a twenty, and there were a lot of them there."

"How could she have lit that cigarette you say she had, Julius?" Professor Peacock asked.

"I got to wondering about that, too, just about that time, and where she kept the pack. But then I looked outside through the glass in the door and saw a man waiting in a car out there, and looking in at us—a big man with big, wide shoulders and strong arms. He had one of his arms laying across the backs of the seats—you know how a man will when he's driving—and I noticed particularly how muscular it looked. While I was still watching him, the woman finished her business with Mr. Tilly and walked past me and got into the car with him."

"It would seem to me that a gentleman would have allowed that poor lady to remain in the car, and gone inside to get the medicine himself," my aunt Olivia said.

"That kind of struck me, too, but I didn't have much time to think about it, because Mr. T. was asking behind my back if I'd had any breakfast yet. I told him I hadn't, and explained I had just got off the train and was looking for some when I noticed he was open already.

" 'Then please accept my hospitality,' he said, and we locked up the store and went a couple of blocks down Main Street to a place that was called the Bluebird Cafe (like so many of them are) and sat down in a booth. It was plain that he intended to pay, and since my money was running a little short after all the journeying around I'd been doing, I ordered myself a good breakfast—pancakes with a slice of ham on the side, and a glass of milk. Mr. T. had waited for me to go first, and when I was done he said two eggs over easy for him, and biscuits and sausage and maybe a dish of grits. And coffee. Naturally I didn't think anything about it.

" 'Now, then,' he said, 'you are seeking a position.'

"I told him I was.

" 'I could use a man,' he said, and he named a figure. I won't tell you what it was, but it was just about twice the best I'd hoped to get. 'Have you a place to stay here?'

"I told him I hadn't, and I had just come there, without knowing anybody.

" 'I live alone,' he said. 'My wife passed on a number of years ago, and I have never remarried. You might stay with me, provided you are willing to undertake a certain amount of bachelor housekeeping. I will not bind myself to furnish your board, but there would be no charge for the room and I would be glad of your company.' Naturally I thanked him and told him I would.

"Just about that time the woman that ran the cafe—I got to know her a little bit later on, a heavyset woman with a gold tooth in front that had a girl that was a schoolteacher; her name was Mrs. Baum—came with our breakfasts. I was just about to pick up my fork and dig in when Mr. T. reached out and touched my hand to stop me. He had the longest fingers I have ever seen on a man, and believe it or not they were as cold as pieces of ice. 'Mr. Smart,' he said. I said, 'Yes, Mr. Tilly,' sharp and polite, like he had just asked me to pass him the quinine.

" 'Mr. Smart,' he said, 'I am bothered from time to time by digestive disorders—tell me, do you ever experience that problem?'

"I told him I didn't.

" 'You're a fortunate man, then. Your appetite is always good?'

" 'Yes, indeed.'

"He gave a big sigh then. 'Not so my own, I'm afraid. Mr. Smart, could you do me a very great favor?'

"I told him, of course, that I certainly would if I could.

" 'Then allow me to exchange breakfasts with you. I am badly underweight, as no doubt you have already noticed; yet very often just when I am prepared to eat I am overcome by a terrible revulsion at the thought of food. At this very moment I find I am completely unable to touch the breakfast I have ordered, while your own breakfast appears quite appetizing to me. Will you exchange? You have no objection to eggs?'

"So I gave him my pancakes and ham, and he gave me the eggs and biscuits and so on, and he even took my milk and gave me his coffee. And after that we pitched in. Now, if you had asked me I would have said that I was hungry. I hadn't eaten since dinner the day before, and had gone to bed without supper in order to conserve my money, of which, as I've said, there wasn't a whole lot left. But I hadn't hardly begun when Mr. T. was finished, and he ate everything except the plate, with the exception of one thing. Now we've got some smart men here— even a college teacher—and two clever ladies, and I've noticed a clever lady is cleverer than any man since Adam. So can any of you tell me what it was Mr. T. didn't eat?"

"*Let me see if I can remember what you told us you ordered,*" Stewart Blaine said. "Pancakes and ham, wasn't it?"

Eleanor Bold added, "And a glass of milk."

My aunt Olivia smiled in a way that managed to be both charming and superior. "I really don't think this is so difficult, Mr. Smart. It was the ham, of course."

"I would have said the milk," Mr. Macafee put in. "It disagrees with a great many people, you know."

Stewart Blaine shook his head. "The pancakes."

My aunt said, "Stewart, dear, it's perfectly obvious—isn't it, Eleanor? There are two great aberrations concerning food in this country: Orthodox Judaism and vegetarianism. And Mr. Smart's Mr. Tilly would not eat ham no matter which he belonged to."

Blaine still disagreed. "Julius is expecting to surprise us, Vi; and therefore I'm sure we'll find that the dish not eaten was the principal one of the meal."

"Besides," Eleanor Bold put in, "he said this drugstore man was finished before he had hardly begun. I'm with Stewart. The pancakes."

"Well, I'm not going to tell you right now, because it wouldn't make any sense to you. Later on maybe it will, and then I'll let you know.

"Anyway, Mr. T. waited for me to finish; then he paid for everything and we went back to his store. He showed me where things were in the pharmacy, and the more I looked, the more I came to think that by the purest kind of luck I had come into one of the best shops in the whole country, because he had just about everything I'd ever heard mentioned when I was in school, and a whole lot that I hadn't. And I already knew enough about the business to know that at a lot of pharmacies they don't keep the rarer things in stock—only order them if some doctor close by starts prescribing them.

"After about half an hour he asked me if I knew my way around well enough to keep the shop open without him. I said I did, and he said that in that case he was going home, and for me to keep the place open until eight, and then to come over to his house, and he'd show me where I could sleep. He wrote out the address for me on a slip of paper and gave me directions how to get there; it was only about five blocks away. I gave him about an hour to get off and be doing whatever it was he was going to do; then I locked the store for a minute—he had given me the keys so I could lock up at night—and nipped over to the depot to get my Gladstone, which I had left there and was worried about. After that I stayed right in the store.

"We didn't do much business, and I noticed that the people that did come in never asked about Mr. T., even though I could see they were surprised to find me there instead of him. One man did ask me if I'd taken over the business, but when I said no, that was the end of it—he just clammed up. By and by dinnertime rolled around, and I thought about locking up the shop and going down to that cafe again—the eggs and sausage had been good—but I remembered I had already gone out once to get my bag, and decided I would just stay there until suppertime, then go out and have a good one.

"It got to be about six o'clock and Mr. T. came back—not wearing his white coat like he had been, but one of those black suits and a little ribbon for a necktie, like so many of them do down there. He asked if I'd had any supper yet, and when I said I hadn't he asked if I would be willing to go by the grocery and pick up a few things for him so we could have supper at home. I said I would, and he gave me ten dollars and a little list he had written out; and he told me not to wait until eight because the grocery would be closed by then, but to go over now and get the things and meet him at his house. He said he'd close up the store for me.

"I found his house all right with no trouble, but he wasn't there when I came. They build their houses thin down there because it's so hot and they want the wind to get through them without being slowed down. Some of them are thin back to front—wide but not deep, if you know what I mean—and others are thin side to side. Mr. T.'s was one of the side-to-side kind, two stories, but so narrow you thought it wasn't any bigger than just a cottage when you looked at it from the front, but it went way back.

"The lot it stood on was narrow, too, and the front yard was deep, with a little walk not much wider than your shoes running right down the middle that had sea shells on it instead of gravel, and an orange tree on one side of it and a lemon tree on the other. There was a porch in front about big enough for three chairs, with screens around it to keep the mosquitoes out and eight or nine steps leading up to it. I set the groceries down on the porch and tried the door, but it was locked. That puzzled me, for I had already got the idea that there it was just about like it is here, and nobody hardly ever locked their doors unless they were going away for a long time. But that one was locked for sure, and no one answered when I knocked.

"I left the groceries there and went down the steps again to have a better look at the house. It was two stories, as I have said, and had a high-pitched roof on it that ran straight along, front to back. There was a little sloped roof over the porch in the regular way that ended under the second-floor front window. I walked around to the back, and like I have said, she was long. There had been flower beds along the sides, but they were gone to seed, and I said to myself, 'There's the work of poor dead Mrs. T. returning to nature.' In back was a doghouse, but no sign of a dog, and the grass was high everywhere.

"I had just got around to the front again and was looking up at the house trying to decide what to do next when I saw the curtains at that second-floor front window twitch, and I'm here to tell you it was a strange thing to see; it was just like somebody was standing in front of that window and pushing them to one side—you know the way you do—to see out. Only there wasn't any face."

"Is this a ghost story, Mr. Smart?" Stewart Blaine asked.

"I guess it is."

"Then my sister-in-law ought to be here," my aunt exclaimed. "She knows all the different kinds—revenants and poltergeists and goodness knows what else. Den's shaking his head. Den thinks it's the dog."

"So does Sun-sun," I said, trying to be clever. Actually Sun-sun was asleep.

"Well, you can believe I was puzzled. There wasn't a breath of air stirring, and it hadn't looked like wind anyway. I went up and pounded on the door again, but no one came. Then I heard feet on that shell walk—I had been listening at the door to see if I could hear anybody moving around in there—and I turned and looked, and saw Mr. T. coming. He got his key out and opened the door for us without saying anything, and I gave him the change from the money he had given me, and a receipt from the grocer showing it was right; then I carried them back to the kitchen and started putting them away. It was a great mess in there, very dirty, but before I get onto that I'd better give you some idea of how the house was laid out. . . .

"It was built for coolness, as I have told you. Parlor, dining room, and kitchen, all big rooms, were all that was downstairs, all of them running from wall to wall, so that all except the dining room had windows on three sides. They were all about twice as deep as wide. The front stairs came up out of one corner of the parlor, with a coat closet under them, and back steps came out of a corner of the kitchen, with a little toilet—if you ladies will excuse the expression—underneath.

"That kitchen was in a bad way, which I said before: dirty dishes and spoiled food lying about, and even a couple of full plates left out until what was in them had gone to mold. I looked at them and said to myself, 'I know *your* story—Mr. T. fixed you for himself, and then his stomach come over queer the way it does, and he left you lay.' Anyway, I pitched right in and started to clean up, and when Mr. T. came in I told him supper'd be in about an hour, as there were some things I wanted to tidy up first. He asked if I had objections to company while I worked, and when I said I did not, he brought a book in and sat himself in a corner to read and watch me. I washed up and threw out a lot of spoiled food, and all the time I was thinking of the way that curtain had moved when nobody had looked out, and about the woman with no arms. I kept listening for somebody moving around upstairs, but I couldn't hear anything. Finally I asked him if he lived alone here. He said he did, and I asked if he didn't have a cat or a dog, because it had struck me that a cat or dog walking under the window might have made the curtain move like that, though I didn't think so. He said no, he had bad luck with animals; but he didn't say what that meant. I fixed us a simple supper out of the food I had brought—corned-beef hash and canned tomatoes it was, as I remember, and coffee, and oranges afterward. Just plain oranges off the tree, not made into a salad or anything fancy like that. I had bought them because they were cheap, not having to be shipped any distance down there.

"I noticed that Mr. T. didn't salt what he ate, or pepper it neither, and he drank his coffee black. He ate slow, tasting everything, as it seemed to me, until he had all the taste out of it, but eating a lot. When we had finished up the hash and tomatoes, I brought out the oranges in a bowl and set them down on the table and started to peel one with my fingers. Mr. T. looked at me for a minute; then he started to smile, and before I had got most of that funny white stuff that's inside oranges off mine he had almost laughed. 'Smart,' he said, 'I wonder if you would do me a favor?'

"Naturally I said I would.

" 'The front bedroom upstairs is mine. If you'll look in the upper left drawer of the largest white cabinet, I believe you'll find some hypodermic syringes and some needles; bring me a ten-cc. syringe, please, and a fine needle.'

"I said, 'Right away,' and went into the parlor and up the stairs. The front bedroom was almost as big as the parlor, and about half of it had been fitted up as a pharmaceutical laboratory, with a regular bench, and racks and enameled cupboards to hold the preparations and equipment. You can bet I went over and had a look at that front window, but it was just an ordinary window, with long curtains that hung nearly to the floor. I got the syringe and needle just like he had told me, and slicked up my appearance a bit in his dresser mirror (for I found the kitchen work had rather wilted me, and I wanted to look sharp), and took them downstairs to him.

"He took them from me and put the needle onto the syringe, and then filled it from a glass of water I had poured for him when I had set the table. I told him that he shouldn't use it like I had given it to him, pointing out that I had handled the needle and it ought to be sterilized, and the water to be boiled if he hadn't got distilled. He laughed and said the patient wouldn't mind, and then picked up an orange from the bowl and injected about half a cc. into it. 'Look here,' he said, and he showed me the place where he'd pulled the needle out. There was a little drop of juice there, and he wiped it away.

"I couldn't divine what it was he was wanting me to see, so at a venture I said, 'It doesn't show much, does it?'

"'On the contrary, there is a distinct puncture mark in the skin. An alert observer, searching for it under a strong light, could hardly fail to find it.' He began to peel the orange, but after a minute he stopped (he seemed to be having trouble with his fingers) and asked me to do it for him. When I had got the peel off, he broke the sections apart and showed me the one that had got the water; it had a little blister, like.

"'Obvious, isn't it?' he said. He was smiling. 'Now that you have put me in mind of it, there are several other fruits of which the same thing must be true. And eggs. Just as I should have thought of oranges, I should have remembered eggs myself. A hard-boiled egg should be very difficult to tamper with.'

"Well, naturally I asked him questions and tried to find out what he was talking about, but I didn't get very far; and after a couple he started to get angry. The thing of it was—this is what I came to believe—that he was used to talking to himself, living alone like that, but when I asked questions he remembered someone else was really there and he didn't want to answer, so pretty soon we went up to bed.

"That night, I can tell you, was one I'll never forget. Remember that when I had come into town in the morning I had been broke and out of a job and not even in sight of getting one. Now I was fixed up, and it paid a lot more than I had ever thought of getting, and I was sure, even then, that Mr. T. was a brilliant man, a pharmacist I could learn a lot from. And at the same time I was wondering about that woman with her hands right up at her shoulders that kept her money in her hair, and about the orange. I'm telling you I must've speculated an hour just about the orange before I finally fell asleep, and to make it worse, when I was just about in dreamland, a big yellow moon started shining in at the window of my room, looking just like an orange. You may not credit it, but I still think of oranges most nights before I fall asleep, especially if I see the moon, and I've got some ideas about them that may make folks sit up and take notice one day.

"I don't believe I told about the top layout of rooms. There were three bedrooms up there, just like there were three rooms down below, only there was a little hall, too, that the stairs from the parlor and the kitchen led up to. It was on the south side of the house and didn't run the full length; just had Mr. T.'s bedroom at one end—that was the front one—and mine, the back one, at the other. On the side there was a door leading into another bedroom that was on the north wall of the house, if you understand me; but Mr. T., when we went up to bed, told me that he had some things stored in there he didn't want to clean out for me, and it was hotter than the other rooms, anyway, because of only having windows on one side. The back room was to be mine. It was pretty sparely furnished, I must say—and not good furniture, either. Mr. T. kind of apologized for that, and said he hadn't known I was coming. 'It was the cook's,' he said, 'when my wife was alive. The second bedroom —between mine and this—was my son's.'

"I said I took it that he was departed, too, and that I was real sorry to hear of it."

" 'I'm sure you must be thinking that you should be in there instead, and that it would be better furnished,' Mr. T. says, 'but that isn't really the case, Mr. Smart. I sold poor Rodney's little bed and table when he passed on. I couldn't bear to have them around, and the room is full of lumber from my store, as I told you.'

"So, as I said, my room was the one at the back of the house, which was large and a nice enough room, but hadn't much in it but a high bed, a rickety chair, an old dresser, and a chromo— I think it was 'The Stag at Bay'—and me. Well, I drifted off looking at that yellow moon and thinking about Mr. T.'s orange; and then I woke up.

"The moon wasn't shining right in at the window the way it had been, but was off at a slant, so just a little spot of light hit the floor in one corner. That made the rest of the room darker than it would have been otherwise. I sat up in bed, listening and trying to look around: there was someone besides me in that room, and I was as sure of it as I'm sure I'm sitting here in Miss Olivia's parlor. I'd had a dream, if you want to call it that, and in the dream I was lying in that bed like I was, and there was a terrible face, a horrible face, just within inches of mine. I swung my legs over the edge of the bed, and as I did my hand touched a spot of damp on the sheet that I knew was none of my doing."

"Why didn't you turn on the lights?" Eleanor Bold said. "It's such a simple thing, yet no one in these stories ever seems to think of it."

"I did. That's what I did right then—jumped out of bed and turned on the lights; but naturally in a strange room like that I had to do some feeling around before I could find them. You know the way you do.

"The door to my room was open; that was one thing I noticed right off, and I was sure I'd shut it before I went to bed. And the damp spot I told about was real, though it was already drying fast. Too fast, I thought, for it to be water, especially as it was so hot and muggy there that a man could hardly stand to wear a nightshirt when he slept. Where it dried, though, it didn't dry clean, but left a sort of a soil behind that was sticky when I touched it.

"I didn't fancy getting back into that bed right away, as you can imagine; so first of all I pretended to search the room, though I knew that now there wasn't anybody in it but me. There wasn't anywhere to hide anyway, but I looked under the bed and behind the old dresser. Then I decided to get myself a clean sheet, remembering that Mr. T. had fetched the one I had been on out of a linen closet in the hall right outside. I went out to get it; and what did I see but Mr. T. himself, standing there at the other end of the hall holding a candle. I don't mean to offend you ladies, but the truth of it was that he wasn't wearing a thing but a pair of drawers, which is going to be important in a minute, and I'll tell you he looked a regular skeleton, as tall as he was, and no flesh on him. I said, 'Hello,' and he said, 'Hello,' back, and then he asked me if I'd heard anything. I suppose I crawfished around a bit and didn't give him too straight an answer.

" 'I grant you,' he says, 'that innocent sounds are often magnified in dreams, but are you certain you heard no one walking in this house?'

"I said that if I had it wouldn't signify, because I could have been hearing him and he could have been hearing me. And naturally while I was talking to him I didn't want to do it from clear down at the end of that hall, so I walked up to him.

" 'I know your step,' is what he said then, 'and I should think that by now you would know mine. What you heard—if you had heard her—would be quite different.'

"Well, I didn't say anything to that, for I had noticed something while he was talking that was taking up all my mind. On Mr. T.'s right side, just here where the lower ribs are, was a big place where the flesh didn't look natural; and now that I could see up his arms I could tell that whatever was wrong with it was wrong with both his hands as well, so that it looked like he had on a pair of rough, scaly gloves of a kind of dirty-white color. 'You appear interested,' he says to me.

"I said yes, I was, deciding, you see, to take the bull by the horns. Then I said I wasn't aware before that he was unwell, and asked if he'd tried cocoa butter on it.

" 'Here,' he said, and before I could do anything to prevent him, he took my left hand in his and touched it to his side so I could feel the place. Some evening when you go out for a stroll, when it's a trifle damp and cold, and you wear a wrap and find yourself thinking of having a nice cup of coffee or cocoa when you get home, reach down and feel the walk. That was just what poor Mr. T.'s side felt like—cold, and gritty, and not quite dry."

"*I think I should have screamed,*" my aunt Olivia said. I could see, however, that this expression was intended merely as a conventional indication of excitement. What she would really have done was borrow a knife and whack off a piece to put under the little microscope in the conservatory.

" 'Now you are aware of my distemper, Mr. Smart,' Mr. T. says. 'If you were not already. I am dying, Mr. Smart. My living flesh is being turned to stone.'

" 'That's impossible, sir,' said I.

" 'Not at all. What are your bones, Mr. Smart, but limestone? Why, limestone itself, as it is dug from a quarry, is composed of the bodies of myriads of ancient sea creatures, as you must surely be aware. And your teeth, Mr. Smart. What are they but a species of white flint? Stones form in the kidneys and galls even of normal men.'

" 'Do you mean you're turning into a statue?' I asked. That was foolishness, of course, but there hadn't been time for my thoughts to catch up to what was being said. If you feel like laughing at me, think of how you'd feel being awakened in the middle of the night by someone in your room, and then having someone else come out with something like that just after you'd felt him and found him hard and cold as a rock pulled out of a pond.

" 'I will never achieve complete ossification,' he said, 'because I will die when the calcium compounds which are now permeating my epidermis invade my vital organs. Mr. Smart, I believe you told me today that you are not a drinking man.'

"I said, 'That's right, sir.'

" 'On such a night as this, I think even a teetotaler might be forgiven a pony of brandy, and I know I am going to have some. Will you join me?'

"I told him I wouldn't, it being against my principles, but that I'd be honored to have a wholesome beverage in his company while he treated himself to whatever he fancied; so we went downstairs—back to the dining room. Mr. T. got the brandy bottle and a glass out of the sideboard there, and I squeezed some of the oranges for myself and added a hunk of ice from the box, and I can tell you I wouldn't have traded *that* drink for just about anything, because it was nearly ninety degrees—that's what I saw on a thermometer somebody'd hung up in the kitchen—though it was past midnight.

" 'I am a haunted man, Mr. Smart,' Mr. T. says about five minutes after I sat down with him.

" 'You're joshing me,' I say.

" 'I only wish I were. This house in which we sit harbors a ghost, and it is intent upon my destruction.'

" 'Sir,' I said, 'that may be true, but I'd advise you to talk about it as little as you can. My grandmother, the late Rebecca

Appleby, was a very knowledgeable woman in these matters, if I do say so, and she always counseled me that ghosts and such dislike and avoid those that won't profess no belief in them, while clustering about them that does. I myself have never for one minute thought there was such things, and I'd advise you not to either.'

" 'And what do you call this?' he says, and holds out one of those cold hands for me to feel.

" 'Skin disease,' says I promptly, 'and you ought to be seeing a doctor for it.'

" 'What if I were to tell you, Mr. Smart, that this skin disease (as you call it—believe me, it is in no way limited to the epidermal tissues) was my own discovery? That it is induced by a preparation I have compounded, and in no other way?'

"Well, I couldn't think of a thing to say. I just stared at him openmouthed.

" 'The malignant spirit of which I told you, Smart, has been drugging my own food with it. It is by this means that it intends to bring me to my grave.'

" 'I noticed,' I says, not knowing what else to say, 'that you are what I might have called a peculiar eater.' "

"*Wait a minute, Julius,*" Professor Peacock interrupted. "I think it's high time you answered that riddle about the breakfasts. Are you trying to tell us that the reason this Mr. Tilly changed meals with you was that he thought the ghost might have doctored his food even though he was eating in a restaurant?"

Mr. Smart nodded.

"All right, you said there was one item in your breakfast—the breakfast he traded you for—that he didn't eat. But then when we named everything, you said none of that was right. I think you should explain yourself."

"And I think," my aunt Olivia said, "that you should be ashamed of yourself, Bob. Haven't you ever been below the Mason-Dixon line?"

Eleanor Bold said, "I have, Vi, but I still don't understand the riddle."

"When I was a small girl . . ." My aunt leaned back in her chair and looked dreamy, though she was careful not to spill her tea. "When I was a small girl, my father took Mother and John and I on a trip to Tallahassee. It was lovely. I have always remembered the snowy tablecloths in the dining car, and the flowers the waiter brought in a cut-glass vase, and eating with my parents—we children ate in the kitchen at home—with telegraph poles whizzing past the window."

Stewart Blaine cleared his throat. "Lovely lady, since you have obviously no more intention of unraveling Mr. Smart's conundrum than he has himself, I would like to pass along one observation that may be of use to the rest of us. The haunted Mr. Tilly, as described by our friend here, waited for him to order, then gave an order that had no item in common with his employee's. He wouldn't care what it was, I suppose, since he wasn't planning to eat it anyway."

"I noticed that, too," Eleanor Bold said. "Everything was different."

Mr. Smart nodded and continued.

" 'I endeavor to swallow as little of the drug as I can,' says Mr. T., 'and by my vigilance I have prolonged my life now for two years. I ask your assistance, Mr. Smart, in extending it further still.'

"I told him I would help in every way I could.

" 'I ask no more than that,' says he. 'Food prepared for me must not be left unattended for a moment, and it would be better if it were not known to be mine before it touched my lips. Do you understand me, Mr. Smart?'

"I said I did; then I ventured to suggest that if the house

was haunted like he said, it might be better for him to move away.

" 'It is not this house that is haunted, Mr. Smart,' he told me, 'but I.'

"We went up to bed after that, and you may believe I fetched out the old shaky chair and propped it against the door tight before I went to bed. And it was a long time, it seemed like, that I lay there listening to every little stir of that old house.

"Next morning came, though, and there hadn't anything happened. I fixed breakfast for us, but Mr. T. just sipped a bit of coffee and said that that was all he wanted. He took a little notebook out of the pocket of his black suit, and while I was eating he started writing in it. I looked—as well as I could—at what was there, upside down as it was, and I could see some of the symbols we use in writing prescriptions. I came close to asking him what it was he was studying so, when I got a glimpse of his face, and the pain there, and the concentration, and I knew then what it had to be. He was working on a cure for his condition; and after that I wouldn't of interrupted him for anything in the world.

"By and by, of course, I finished my breakfast and thought to get up and go; then it came to me that I would be certain to disturb him if I did, and it was better not to, so I just poured myself a bit more coffee, and there we sat, the two of us, for I suppose twenty minutes. Then he lay down his pencil—a pretty little gold pocket pencil, it was—and put his head in his hands. And there we sat. Then he moved a little—I suppose moved his elbow on the tablecloth—and that pencil started rolling. He didn't see it, and it rolled right off the table and onto the floor. He made a motion to pick it up, then stopped himself (as it seemed to me) and looked at me and said, 'Mr. Smart, I fear you'll have to get that for me.'

"Well, I shook my head at that. 'Mr. Tilly,' I said to him as bold as if I'd a thousand dollars in my pocket, 'I'm a pharmacist, and planning to be a licensed pharmacist soon. I don't mind cooking for both of us—it's the least I can do to pay for my room and board. But if you want somebody to pick up your toys for you, you'd better hire a maid.'

" 'You think I am being arrogant,' he said. 'I am not. My spine has become inflexible, Mr. Smart, and my hips will bend just enough to permit me to sit down.'

"I went and got his pencil for him after that, as you may imagine, and we went down to the store and opened up. It was pretty near to ten o'clock by that time, and I wondered for a bit why it was Mr. T. had been open so early the day before, but of course it was that woman—the one without arms. She hadn't just happened to come by then; that had been all arranged, and Mr. T.'d had her prescription ready and waiting for her, knowing she'd come by early like that. I thought about it some more and concluded she'd probably wanted it to be when there wasn't many people on the street to see her."

"Vi, you really must stop looking smug like that," Eleanor Bold said.

"Hominy grits." (They stared at her.)

"Hominy grits," my aunt Olivia said again. "They give them to you with *everything* down there, and they *always* give them to you with ham. Mr. T. forgot that for a minute when he was ordering, and asked for some himself. Then when both breakfasts came, he saw there were two dishes of grits, and didn't dare eat either for fear the drug had been put in one of them. He was quite mad, you understand, poor man."

Once, a long time afterward—I suppose it must have been thirty-five or forty years—I started to tell this story to Bill Batton, the agency man, when he flew down to show me a campaign they'd cooked up. The consumers soaked the labels off the jars, and the first person within a ten-mile radius to turn in sixty could have the circus, free, for a child's birthday or whatever.

"The whole thing fits inside one van," Bill said, "even the

elephant. The elephant's mechanical, and the girl works him with switches on the back." He set his projector up on my desk. "Nice office you have here."

"Thank you." It was a nice office; I had it duplicated here in this house, and if you will excuse me, I think I'll take my writing materials there and work at my desk again for old times' sake. It will be the first time I have written outside this room, but with spring coming now it will no longer be necessary for me to stay so close to the fire.

I found it! I must say—quite truthfully—that I hadn't much hope I would; with my notebook and pen I set off into this house as if I were entering a jungle. But it is close, quite close. Down the smaller of the halls, the crooked one, eight or ten doors and to the left. I must remember that.

It's cold in here. Winter has not left the interior of the house yet. The windows (as president, I have seven windows; Charlie Scudder and Dale Everitton, my executive vice-presidents, have six, other v.-p.'s five) look out onto the plant, and the calendar mechanism must still be operating: it is a cold, wet spring day out there, and I can see the water dripping from the handrail of the catwalk that winds its way up No. 3 spray tower. My desk is as it should be, with the telephones, and the mail Miss Birkhead has opened for me lies in the middle of the blotter. It cannot be read, however; concealed nails hold it in place.

"That's your founder, isn't it?" Batton was looking at the picture above the bar at one side of the room. "Formulated the original product and thought up the name? Good brand name, by the way."

"My aunt chose it," I said.

Their wedding was the largest—so everyone said—ever to take place in Cassionsville. I would have thought that my aunt would have preferred a small, private ceremony, which shows how little I really understood her. My father, who was in Istanbul at the time, paid for everything, having been instructed by his own

father's will, as I learned much later, to "do right by Olivia."
He must have given her a completely free hand. I heard that
ceremony discussed (always by women, of course) for most of
the rest of my life.

Margaret Lorn was one of the flower girls. (Perhaps my aunt
requested her services, at least in part, to show that she did not
hold her mother's religious and wholly unconscious part in Mr.
Macafee's victory against her.) Mrs. Lorn had, on that fatal
Sunday when my aunt had wished to make Mr. Macafee believe
that she was bidding against him, in the end refused his check
on the grounds that to accept it would be to trade on the Sab-
bath, and then had indicated that it would be quite allowable
for my aunt to leave her money (which she had carried in green-
backs in her purse) in the stoneware jar that served the Lorns
for a bank. It was the writing of her name on Mr. Macafee's
check, she had explained, that involved her directly in a viola-
tion of the Lord's commandment. It was not until it was much
too late that it occurred to my aunt that Mr. Macafee's check
might have been written to cash.

Like my aunt Olivia's other attendants, Margaret wore a
costume of pale green, embellished with daffodils. I remember
puzzling, as I sat uncomfortably in church, over what it was
about her that attracted me. I had already decided quite defi-
nitely and, as I thought, for life that girls were silly. It was not
her coloring. She had brown hair and brown eyes. Her hair was
pretty—I remember thinking at the wedding how lustrous it was
and how soft it must be—but not unusual. It may have been
her smile, and something in the way she held her head and
looked at me sidelong from those eyes, as though her soul were
staring at me out of narrow windows in a tower.

"Now look at the seal," Batton said. The seal was balancing
a dimpled orange ball that looked a great deal like a real orange.
"I know a story—" I began, but Batton wasn't listening. "Here,"
he said. "Here, by God, we've got a boxing kangaroo."

"*Now we must let Mr. Smart proceed,*" my aunt Olivia declared. "I confess I'm dying to find out what happened."

"We opened about ten, like I said. There weren't enough customers to keep one man busy, let alone two, so I started straightening up the store and so on. It wasn't as much of a mess as old Bledsoe's here, but bad enough, and I took things down and dusted them and washed the shelves and so on.

"About eleven-thirty Mr. T. told me, without giving any reason for it, that he was going home and would see me again in a few hours. Well, that was fine with me; to tell the truth, it made me a little nervous to have him about when I was working. It made me think of the ghost, and I got to noticing how he never bent or picked anything up that was down low, and how he turned his whole body, shuffling around his feet, when another person would have just turned his head.

"So with him gone I was happy as a clam, as they say. I quit straightening out the stock and went through the files instead, looking at the prescriptions; I had already caught on, you see, to the fact that Mr. T. knew more about medicines than I was ever likely to learn. I was doing that when I heard the little bell over the door chime. Naturally I hurried out to wait on the customer. Well, you won't believe who it was."

"*The woman with no arms,*" said Eleanor Bold.

"That's right. And she had a man with her—a man that—well, you can't imagine what he looked like. His face was gray, and the skin all wrinkled and hanging down. He was a big man, too, and with that face you didn't want to cross him, if you know what I mean. The woman—after I'd got used to her not having arms, I could see she wasn't much more than twenty—said to me, 'Where's Mr. Tilly?' And I told her I didn't know. 'We have to find him. Did he go home?'

"I told her I didn't know where he went—that I worked for Mr. T., and not him for me.

" 'Where does he live?' she says, and I gave her the address, thinking that they could get it from the telephone book anyway. They went running out, and through the door I saw them jump into that same car I had seen the woman with no arms get into before; a Pierce-Arrow, it was, a beautiful car.

"They were back in ten minutes or so. 'He's not there,' the woman said, and I reminded her I hadn't said he was. Then she said I had to come with them, and I told her I couldn't— that Mr. Tilly'd left me in charge, and there had to be somebody there to take care of customers.

" 'This is an emergency,' she said.

" 'Then what you need is a doctor,' I said, and I told her where the closest one was, having looked it up. Then, before I knew what was happening, my arms were clamped to my sides and I was lifted up in the air. The fellow with the gray skin, you see, had got behind me. Well, I'm no giant physically, but I like to think I'm a fighter, and I cussed and kicked and even did my darnedest to bite him (though I was glad afterward I hadn't been able to) and I wiggled like an eel. But he had me and he wouldn't let go. I found out afterward that the woman turned around our sign so that it said 'CLOSED' as she went out, and even punched the lock button so the door would lock behind her, but at the time I didn't know that, and I was worried about the store, as you can imagine.

"The man that had me threw me in the back seat and got in with me. The same man I had seen drive the woman the day before was driving now, and she got in front with him. Like I said, the car was a Pierce-Arrow sedan, and it was big but the man with the gray skin pushed me over into a corner of it and pulled down all the shades in back. I hit him in the nose while he was doing that, and he bled just like anybody else, but as soon as he let go of the shade-string he had me by both wrists, and he was too strong for me. He tried to butt me—hit me, you know, in the face with his big head—but I twisted off to one side, and then the woman stopped him. After that he just sat there with a handkerchief to his nose and every once in a while looked over sideways at me to show he hadn't forgotten.

"The woman said to me, 'You're a druggist, aren't you, Doc?' She didn't sound Southern like most of them down there. More like she might be from Ohio or maybe Pennsylvania. I told her I was a pharmacist.

" 'That's good,' she said.

"The man who was driving looked around at her and said, 'Maybe you ought to tell him about the kid now, Jan.'

"But she shook her head. 'Let him see him, and then he can ask whatever he wants.'

"I said, 'How far is it?'

" 'Just the edge of the next town. We're almost there now.'

" 'You're going to let me go after I see this child, aren't you? Anyway, I may have to go back to the store for medicine.' I didn't mean that last, of course, because if I were to be caught prescribing, that would be the end of my career; but I wanted them to let me loose.

"The woman said, 'You going to go to the police?'

" 'Not if you let me go.'

" 'Okay, then.'

" 'Is it all right if I put the shades up? I'm not going to yell now or anything like that.'

"The woman looked like she wanted to think about that for a while, but after a minute the man that was driving looked around at me and said, 'You do and Clarence is going to kill you; he's meditating on it now, and if we let him loose on you you're not going to come out of this car breathing.'

"I said, 'I told you I wasn't going to,' and put up the shade on my side. It didn't do me any good, but it made me feel better, and after a while I even rolled down the window so I could get some air. It was hot as housafire in there.

"Well, pretty soon the car went around a bend, and I saw

off a ways about eight or ten little tents, some with flags on them, pitched in a field, and in a bit more the man driving the car had pulled it right in among them, and we got out. Clarence —that was the man with the gray face—stuck close to me, but he didn't grab me, and that was good because I was all set to paste him another one if he did.

"When the driver got out, I can tell you I was never more surprised in my life. I saw the door open and him turn around in his seat and get two canes from off the floor, and I thought he was probably crippled or had the arthritis. Then he grabbed the crook of them in his hands and came out, and so help me, he didn't have any legs at all; he just swung himself along on the canes with his body hanging between them, and the legs of his trousers folded up in front and pinned to his shirt. He was a big, square-faced, gray-headed man, and when he saw me gawking at him he kind of grinned. Then he just leaned over and balanced himself on just one of those canes and used the other to point with. 'It's over there,' he said, and pointed the cane at one of the tents. 'Just a few steps.' Then he tapped me on the shoulder with the cane he had used to point. I found out later that he had the car fitted up special so he could drive it just using his hands.

"The carnival was small. That was the thing that struck me first about it, and the thing I remember most now. There were three rides, and I think two little shows in tents, and a booth where they sold lemonade and cotton candy, and that was all there was. The man with no legs owned it—that's what they told me. He'd worked in them for years and saved his money, and finally bought this one.

"The woman took me into a little tent that wasn't any bigger than from the sofa there over to the fireplace. There was plenty of light coming in through the door, but it seemed dark at first because it had been so bright outside. There was a little boy, about four years old, lying on a cot in there. He didn't move or say anything when we came in, and when I touched his arm

it was cold, so at first I thought he was dead; but I lifted him
up and saw his eyes roll, and then I could feel that he was still
breathing.

" 'It's the hair medicine,' the woman said. 'We're going to
have him a dog boy.'

"I asked if it was what she'd got from Mr. T. the morning
before, and she said yes, so I said I wanted to see it. She got it
out; it was an ordinary two-ounce brown bottle, and I noticed
that there was a good deal of it gone already, and asked how
much she had been giving him. She said she had started last
night—that was the only time she'd given him any—and she
gave him a spoonful then, which was what Mr. T. had said. I
pulled the cork and wet my finger with the medicine. There's a
certain bitter taste to tincture of opium, and it was there. I
suppose Mr. T. included it to keep the child from throwing the
medicine up; it's a good stomach-settler and used to be used
in colic cures a lot. I asked the mother then if Mr. T. had said
teaspoonful or tablespoonful, because it looked like there was a
good two tablespoonfuls gone, and it came out after I'd talked
to her awhile that, like a lot of other people, she thought that if
a little was good more would be better. (I've known of a man to
drink his whole prescription as soon as he got it, when the
doctor'd meant it to be taken over ten days.) I told her that was
the trouble, and to dose the child with cold coffee if she could,
and if he threw up that was so much the better. She ran off to
what she called the pie wagon and came back with coffee in a
cardboard carton, but it was hot and I told her to wait until
it was cool as wash water before she tried to get her boy to
swallow any. Then I said that I knew she'd paid a lot of money
to Mr. T. for the medicine, but that if I were her I'd think
twice about giving it to her child if it was going to make him
grow hair all over.

"She said, 'Everybody says he's the best. You don't know
what people do, sometimes. I've known of a mother and father
to feed their girl a plug of chewing tobacco every day cut up

fine in her food to make her be a midget. It didn't work, though —just gave her a bad stomach. They quit when she got to be forty inches tall, because a midget taller than that is just a small person. And a man will salt his food with gunpowder so he can eat fire.'

"I told her I'd heard people say chewing tobacco swallowed would expel worms, but I knew better ways.

"She said, 'I was hoping little Charlie could be a dog boy. While he's still small, he could be a puppy boy, and then a dog boy afterward when he was bigger. I've seen them, and it can be a good act if the person is willing to work at it a little. I saw one where the talker held out a hoop with paper in it, and the dog boy ran around—like a dog, you know, and pretended to bite him on the ankle—and then jumped through it. Then they let out a cat—like it had just happened to be under a tub the talker picked up for another trick. It went flying out of the top —the tent, you know?—and the dog boy chased it. Everybody said it was a great act, and they were right. Out on the midway you could hear the marks talking about it.'

" 'Don't you think it would be better just to leave little Charlie alone?'

" 'No.' She thought for a minute—I could see her thinking— then she shook her head. 'No, I don't. Only, mister, do you know what I just thought of? You don't know my name, and I don't know yours. I'm Cleopatra the Seal Girl, but really it's Janet Turner. You don't have to shake hands with me.'

" 'I'm Julius Smart, Mrs. Turner,' I said, 'and I don't mind shaking hands with you.' And I reached and took her right hand up by her shoulder just like it was the regular thing. I noticed she didn't have any wedding band on the other hand, but I didn't say anything about it.

" 'Well, it may be that your name's Smart, but you work for a mighty smart man, do you know that? That Mr. Tilly's famous all over. Everybody said that if that girl that her mother and father fed her tobacco had bought off of Mr. Tilly instead, she would have been a real midget. There's several now that owe it to him, and when I was with Rossi Brothers Combined Shows there was one there named Colonel Bolingbroke, and he told me three years ago he'd started to grow, and he said he didn't waste any time; as soon as he saw what was happening, he left the show and bought a ticket to come down here and get some stuff from Mr. Tilly, and it stopped him dead. He makes dwarfs, too —I guess you know? And pinheads and human skeletons, and the Great Litho owes it to him. . . .

" 'You think that coffee's cool enough now?'

"I dipped a finger in it and said it was, and she bent down and propped the boy up on some blankets and started spooning it into him. It was surprising how well she could bend around and do things with her hands, though she couldn't reach.

" 'See, Mr. Smart, it may be a lot of trouble, but I want little Charlie to have something. You look at me, now—I'm the only special person in my whole family, and I got two brothers and three sisters. When I was little, sometimes they made fun of me, but not so much, really, and Mother always looked after me specially because I was different. Then a show came through and they gave my family some money to take me with them, and sent half my pay home for me, too. My mother wanted to save it for me, but I told her the first time I got back to spend it, because I'd seen enough of tent shows by then to know that God had given me something that would always feed me, something that nobody could ever take away.

" 'My one brother was killed in France; the other one has got the farm now, and I still come and see him and his wife once about every two years. An old run-down farm where everything's been taken out of the land, and they can't move a step from it. My sisters are all married to men that work in the mills. What kind of a life would that be for little Charlie? Working like a slave all day and knowing that if he lost that one there wasn't no other jobs? And the growing up—'

"She got a good, big spoonful of coffee down Charlie's mouth just then, and stopped for a minute to kind of pat him and make little noises like mothers do.

" '—in shows like this ordinary. When you're a special person, everybody respects you; when you're not—I've seen it—you've got to work all the time, hustle and brag all the time, to make people see you're not just a Monday Man, to show you're pulling your weight with the outfit. I've seen it, and it wears them out.'

"After a while the little boy threw up, and I showed her how to hold him to make sure none of it went into his lungs. A man came in and sat down with us, and because it was kind of shadowy in the tent except for the bright spot where the sunlight came in at the door, I didn't notice until I'd spoken with him that one side of his face was all white and didn't move like a face naturally will; so I asked him what he did in the carnival.

"Charlie's mother said, 'This is Litho, Mr. Smart. The man of living stone.' And Litho took a big kitchen match out of his pocket, and scratched it on his cheek and lit a cigar with it."

"Mr. Smart, you're making this up," my aunt Olivia exclaimed. "I've thought so for ages, and now I'm sure of it."

Mr. Macafee said timidly, "I saw a man strike a match on the palm of his hand once. He was a gandy dancer on the railroad, and pounded in spikes with a sledgehammer all day."

"Don't be ridiculous, Jimmy. No one pounds spikes with his face."

Mr. Smart said, " 'Once a living man like you, now a living statue.' That's what he said, and then he blew cigar smoke in my face. You may not believe it, Miss Weer—"

"Call me Vi, Julius. Can't you see everyone else does?"

"You may not believe it, Miss Weer, but that's exactly what he did. Then he said, 'You think I got something on my face, don't you? That's what marks always think. I've heard them say I put on a thin glue mixed with powdered pumice. That's the way you can fix a wood floor so it still looks good but nobody'll slip, except you use varnish. Then I let them touch me, and they see my whole skin is hard—clear inside my mouth.'

"I told him I would like to touch him myself, and he leaned up closer to me and let me feel of his cheek. It felt just like Mr. T.'s side.

"The woman with no arms said, 'He works for Mr. Tilly; he knows all about it, Harry.'

"I said, 'I just started. You take the regular medicine for this, I guess.'

"He said he did, and that Mr. T. had told him that he had to be careful; so he watched how his spots grew (that was what he called them, his spots), and when they started getting too big he stopped taking it until they went down again."

"Don't you think, Den, that it's time you went to bed?"
My aunt Olivia was not serious. She belonged to that school which recognizes the just demands of duty by ritual observance, and had ordered me to bed in exactly the spirit in which she would later—when she was Mrs. Smart—repent three or four times a year of her casual connection with Professor Peacock and her occasional nights with Mr. Macafee. Much later, of course, I did go to bed, a bed haunted by armless women and galloping Chinese officers. I remember waking in the morning with a confused impression of terror, but I was not bothered again by Julius Smart's story until I recited it (by then I feel sure both faded and embroidered by time, as it is now) to Margaret Lorn.

We had gone among the sands and black willows of the lower Kanakessee on what was supposed to be a picnic, though I don't think either of us harbored any real desire for the sandwiches and thermos of iced tea Margaret had packed. For myself, what I felt was not hunger, but the tumbling feelings which have served, I think, at least in part, to give to virginity that magical connotation which it had not yet, at that remote date, entirely lost: the ability to entrap unicorns, descry the future, see the fair folk. In the same way that primitive people attributed supernatural powers to alcohol, calling it the water of life, or sought admittance to the world of spirits in suffocating sulphur fumes and decoctions of herbs, so the confusion of emotions characteristic of virginity seemed to them a state more than human. The experienced feel love or desire, or both. The inexperienced are sick with a thousand feelings, most of them unformed: fearful that they may be unable to love or to inspire love; fearful of what they may do if once they allow their emotions to carry them away; fearful that they may be unable to cut the cord that binds them still to the superficial affections of childhood; longing for adventure and yet unable to see that their adventure is in the present, that there will soon be nothing left but love and desire.

I cannot tell you all we did that day. Found a coin in the sand; saw a kingfisher; and on a shadowy beach not much larger than a small room, I told Margaret (inspired originally by some incident I have now forgotten, perhaps only the feel of a wet stone beneath my hand or the oranges she had packed for us, oranges whose peels we launched like cockleboats into the Kanakessee, soon to founder) the story of Mr. T. and his haunted house, the circus in the South, the drugstore and the dinners at the Bluebird Cafe, a story that had somehow retained for me its odor of oleanders and magnolias, its hum of mosquitoes.

And that night (when Margaret and I had long since gone to our beds) I dreamed again about them all: the long grass blowing in a field in Florida, blowing in the Gulf wind, tap, tap, tapping at the tires of the parked cars with its little sword points, square black cars, Fords with mohair upholstery, Duesenberg cabriolets with jump seats and steamer trunks and cutglass flower vases, men of stone stalking through the long grass like statues walking, like telamones on their way to assist Atlas, dead men become their own grave markers, their birth and death, their names and the names of their wives and children all written across their faces and all washed away, washed away by the rain, the Gulf storms out of Yucatan and Jamaica, washing away the Mayans, smelling of parrots like the living rooms of old women.

Then I woke and heard my parents (returned from Europe at last and strangers evermore) half snoring in another room, Hannah muttering prayers over and over against the night, praying to the ceiling of her room, painting there with the tip of her short tongue fat angels with harps and bows, and a God who loved old women.

The dog boy running, barking, snarling, piddling on the rug, hiding from a beating beneath the table, mounting my leg when I sat with Margaret on a sofa long since sold and never—never that I knew—in that room at all, yelping when I kicked, snarling and looking at me with human eyes, Margaret with his head in her lap while I explained that it did not matter, that my father would take him hunting the next day, that that would make him happy. He rises and begins to clean a gun.

"That isn't the end, Mr. Smart. It can't be the end!"

"You mean when Litho told me how he took the medicine? I'm not going to tell you about the rest of the time I spent out there at the tent show. Everybody was more or less friendly, but the man with the canes had gone off somewhere, and we had to wait for him to come back so he could drive me back to town. I sat up front with him when we went back, and got to see how he worked the car without having any legs. It was almost as good as watching the things he did on his canes—he could jump up in the air and wave both of them over his head, then catch himself on them; he showed me—and I told him so. I told him he ought to have a ring like a regular circus, and then he could drive around in it in the car, and back up and everything, and then get out and let everybody see how he walked. He said it was a good idea, but the show wasn't big enough for that yet.

"But all the time we were driving back I was thinking about Mr. T. . . . and the closer we got to town the more I thought about him, and having to sleep in that house of his again.

"He hadn't come back to the store yet when I got there, and I opened back up, so when he came it looked like I had been there all the time; but when we went down to the cafe for supper—he said we'd eat out that night, and made me lock up and come with him—I told him about it. Then I told him that when he'd said the ghost was putting that stuff in his food I hadn't believed him; I'd heard of them playing the piano and unlocking doors and all that—even pulling the covers off beds—but never of one putting something in someone's food before. I told him I'd thought he had a disease, and maybe worrying about it had affected his mind a little. But now that I'd talked to Litho I could see it was real. Then I asked if he couldn't just get rid of all that stuff. He said he had, but the ghost must have a bottle of it somewhere."

"Tell me, Mr. Smart, did you save him? Mr. Tilly?"

"No." Smart sighed and looked at the floor. Until then even I (though at that age I possessed a child's credulity in full measure) had been half convinced that he had been composing his story as he proceeded; but there was an expression of real grief in his face. He had felt, if not love for, at least loyalty to his Mr. T., had struggled to preserve him, and had failed. "No, he died. I thought maybe Bob had told you."

My aunt shook her head.

"He died. I came in his bedroom one morning when he didn't come down to breakfast, and found him dead in his bed. He didn't have any kin of his own, but he left the store to some relatives of his wife's—he had her picture on his dresser, not a pretty woman like you ladies here, but I suppose he loved her in his way—and they hired me to run the store for them until they could find a buyer. That's what I've been doing ever since he died. People down there were getting to think I owned it, but I didn't want to buy it, though I had enough saved to do it—for collateral, you know, on a loan from the bank, just like I'm doing here—but I wanted to get back closer to the farm."

It has suddenly struck me, after scribbling for days here, that Julius Smart, who will scarcely appear in it again, is actually the central character of this book. I recall him clearly only at three stages of his life:

When he was an elderly man and I myself was middle-aged, an unimportant employee of the corporation he had founded, he was a shrunken figure whom I saw perhaps once in two years when his inspection of our laboratory was the climax of weeks of preparation. His thin white hair was always tousled on these occasions, though I never saw him run his fingers through it; his clothes were neat, rather old-fashioned (he wore a vest, and a gold chain across the front of it during that period when it seemed that the vest had vanished never to return), and appeared expensive despite the rumor that he bought boys' shoes for his tiny feet. As I've said, we knew of the impending visit for weeks before he came, so that what he saw was not the real work carried out in the laboratory or anything like it, but an elaborate show produced for his benefit. I thought at the time that this was what he wished, that he desired to impress us—not only those of us who worked there, but our superiors, and their superiors, and theirs on up the line—with his importance. Miss Birkhead has told me since that several people at the top of the research department had learned to anticipate an inspection when he began to ask certain types of questions at the department heads' meetings. This would explain the long delays that sometimes occurred between the announcement of an inspection and its taking place, delays in which everyone was forbidden to carry out any sort of experiment for fear of disturbing the meticulously prepared stage set, and we all sat bored at our desks.

At my aunt Olivia's funeral he had been much younger; small, stocky (he was already beginning to make money, and my aunt had hired an excellent cook, a Latvian who subscribed to foreign-language newspapers and who had spent five years in Paris learning entrees and three in Vienna learning desserts, but who was unfitted for the hotel kitchen he had earned by a nervousness bordering on frenzy), dressed entirely in black. He might, except for his soft hands, have been a local farmer. He cried continually throughout the service, as did Mr. Macafee. Professor Peacock did not come, and I supposed at the time that he felt no grief; but he died only a few years afterward of a complicated series of disorders said to have been aggravated by hypertension, and it may be that—once she was no longer available—he had found that he had loved her more than he knew.

On the occasion of Mr. Macafee's party, Smart must have been absurdly young—he was at least five years younger than my aunt. To me he was a grownup, and I did not notice. A neat young man with hair the color of straw plastered flat across his head, and wearing clothing so new it must have been purchased especially for the occasion: a white shirt from Macafee's with pinholes still in the broadcloth; a crisp suit of a material the color of butterscotch, with yellow threads running through the weave. His face was rather long and thin, but smooth. His teeth were large, and so good that they looked false, as actors' teeth often do. His complexion was clear and high. He told his story so earnestly (at this point) that you might have thought him on trial for his life. . . .

"It's a mess when you find a dead person like that," he said. "Especially a dead person that nobody thought was sick. I've tried since to remember how many nights I spent in his house before he died. I think it was five. It was the fifth night. I got up like I usually did and went downstairs and started coffee, then came back up to my own room and shaved. The ghost had been walking the night before, and I had laid in bed listening to it. Up and down the hall, mostly; sometimes up and down the front and back steps. I had bought a lock for my room and locked myself in at night, so I wasn't too worried about it, and besides it had never shown any wish to harm me.

"That morning I got through shaving and made toast and got ready to fry some eggs as soon as Mr. T. should come down. Well, he didn't come, of course, and I sat down and had myself a piece of toast and some coffee while I waited for him, and then I thought perhaps he was oversleeping. I knew he had been taking something to help him sleep, for he was troubled by the noises the ghost made, walking up and down, so often outside his door, and—he said—whispering at the keyhole sometimes or scratching at the panels like a dog, sometimes climbing around outside, he said, and standing on the windowsills looking in at him.

"I went up to his bedroom door and knocked and called, but no one answered.

"Then I thought that perhaps he had been up early that morning and had already gone out; but the chain was still on the front door, and the back door stuck so bad I didn't think he could have opened it and closed it again without waking me. So he was still in there, and I went back up and knocked again, getting no answer as before."

"You should have kicked the door down, Mr. Smart."

"Well, it was a pretty solid-built door, and it would have taken a lot of kicking. What I did finally was to go outside and climb up on the top of the front porch. Standing on the roof there, I could look in the window. What I saw was him lying dead there on the bed. I knocked in the screen, and went inside and felt him and tried to take his pulse; but I think he'd been dead most of the night. Rigor had set in already. That's when they get stiff. There was only the one doctor in town, and I unlocked the door and went downstairs and telephoned him."

"And you continued to live in that house, Mr. Smart?"

Eleanor Bold said. "I don't believe I could have stood it."

"Yes. Well, for one thing I was getting used to it—a person gets used to anything, you know, except hanging. And for another, I didn't think the ghost would stay around much with Mr. T. gone. Then, too, his relatives, you see, wanted me to run the store for them until someone was willing to buy it, and I was to have my same salary there, and I thought while we were talking about it—there was three of them, all kin of his wife's, really, an uncle and two aunts—that they didn't really need that house, and free rent was something else I could get out of them."

"Why, Mr. Smart! Gouging them like that."

"If I hadn't, Miss Weer, I never would have been able to buy Bledsoe's here. I didn't think I owed them anything—if I owed anyone, it was Mr. T., and he had been giving me free rent and paying a very good salary, too."

"Call me Vi, Mr. Smart; everyone does."

"They took some kickshaws out, and the good silver and photograph albums and some letters of Mrs. T.'s, but I made them leave the rest of the furniture, and they never even tried to go in that third bedroom, the one between Mr. T.'s and mine. I found out afterward that the house had the reputation of being haunted all around town, and they were just as happy to have it not standing vacant. Besides, I told anyone that asked—when they came in the store, you know—that it wasn't, so I suppose they were able to sell it when I went away."

I—Alden—beg your pardon for breaking off this way. But I think I just heard a door close. That cannot be; or can it? I am in my house, and they are all dead—aren't they? Dale, even Charlie Scudder. Dead. Charlie used to stop at the roadhouse

on his way home and have a highball; mostly the shift workers
drank in there, fellows in denim shirts—or sport clothes if they'd
changed before going home. Some of them changed and took
showers. Charlie suggested we stop there one day, and we sat in
a booth with all of them looking covertly at us, and drank rye
and ginger ale. I kept thinking of Charlie's Chrysler outside
among the Fords and Chevies, and wondering if they would
slash the tires. I could hear someone talking, he telling the
others at the bar that one of us was the president of the company; and someone else saying no, the president is a little man
with white hair. Julius, of course. I have seen that roadhouse
tumbled down, the foundation overgrown with weeds.

But I did hear a door close. I know I did. I have been sitting
here ever since wondering if I should try to buzz Miss Birkhead
on the intercom. What if she should answer? But it might be
only a trick, like the view from the windows. I shuffle the papers
on my desk, and my finger touches the button and draws away.
What if she should answer? There is a can of film in my upper
left-hand drawer, and a projector, my private projector, at one
side of the room. My side hurts so much I do not want to leave
my chair. The label on the can says, "For Den—Merry Christmas and Happy Memories from Dad," and I have forgotten in
the pain what it contains.

"Yes, Mrs. Weer?"

"It's Den," my mother says. "He has a sore throat."

"Won't you please be seated?" We are seated. The chairs are
leather, and my feet will not touch the floor. There are broad
walnut arms, and on the wall opposite are two pictures in heavy
frames. In one a doctor sits at the bedside of Margaret Lorn
(though I do not know this at the time), a little girl with large
eyes and brown braids. In the other eight doctors are opening a
corpse. Why is it that there are so many physicians for the dead
and so few for the living? My mother is reading *Liberty*, and
tries to show me pictures.

"Mrs. Weer? Alden can go in now."

"Shouldn't I come in with him?"

"The doctor likes it better if he can see the little ones alone. He says it makes them braver. He'll ask you in after he examines Alden."

Dr. Black sits at a heavy mahogany table. To his left, against the wall, is a big rolltop desk. As I enter, he stands, says hello, musses my hair (which angers me), and lifts me to the top of a leather-covered examination table at one side of the room. "Open your mouth, son."

"Doctor, I have had a stroke."

He laughs, shaking his big belly, and smooths his vest afterward. There is a gleaming brass spittoon in one corner, and he expectorates into it, still smiling.

"Doctor, I am quite serious. Please, can I talk to you for a moment?"

"If it doesn't hurt your sore throat."

"My throat isn't sore. Doctor, have you studied metaphysics?"

"It isn't my field," Dr. Black says, "I know more about physic." But his eyes have opened a little wider—he did not think a boy of four would know the word.

"Matter and energy cannot be destroyed, Doctor. Only transformed into one another. Thus whatever exists can be transformed but not destroyed; but existence is not limited to bits of metal and rays of light—vistas and personalities and even memories all exist. I am an elderly man now, Doctor, and there is no one to advise me. I have cast myself back because I need you. I have had a stroke."

"I see." He smiles at me. "You are how old?"

"Sixty or more. I'm not sure."

"I see. You lost count?"

"Everyone died. There is no one to give birthday parties; no one cares. For a time I tried to forget."

"Sixty years into the future. I suppose I'll be dead by then."

"You have been dead a long, long time. Even while Dale

Everitton and Charlie Scudder and Miss Birkhead and Ted Singer and Sherry Gold were still living, you were almost forgotten. I think your grave is in the old burying ground, between the park and the Presbyterian church."

"What about Bobby? You know Bobby, Den, you play with him sometimes. Will he become a doctor, eh? Follow the family profession? Or a lawyer like his granddad?"

"He will die in a few years. You outlived him many years, but you had no more children."

"I see. Open your mouth, Den."

"You don't believe me."

"I think I do, but my business now is with your throat."

"I can tell you more. I can tell—"

"There." He wedges a big forefinger between my molars. "Don't bite or I'll slap you. I'm going to paint that throat with iodine."

4

❧

GOLD

"And now this card—a figure writes at a table, another peers over his shoulder. What do you make of this card, Mr. Weer? Can you tell me a story about it?"

The Golds were not native to Cassionsville, and it was seldom remembered that no family was. They had come in a rattling pickup truck and an old Buick on one of the fine autumn days, and moved into a commonplace brick house. They were supposed to be Jewish, but there was little about them to mark them as Jewish—no quick-witted, persuasive men; no curly-haired, clever, slant-eyed girls. The elder Mr. Gold, a machinist and tool and die maker, had an indeterminate accent that might have come from anywhere east of the English Channel. He took a job at the juice plant, terminated after a year, and opened a bookstore. His son Aaron took a similar position, applied after a few weeks to be rated as an engineering technician, and was assigned to me.

It was one of the peculiarities of the Golds that there was no family face. Aaron resembled neither his father, a stoop-shoul-dered man with weak blue eyes, nor his brisk, black-haired little mother. He was tall and gangling, red-headed and freckle-faced, with a large, straight woodpecker beak of a nose that always appeared to be testing the wind like a young hound's. He was a hard worker, but clearly had no future with the company—not only because he lacked a college degree, but because he was talkative, noisy, and fond of practical jokes; these were characteristics the middle management (who counted in these things, as Julius Smart did not) detested. He was so talkative, in fact, that it was two years and more, long after his father had left, before I realized that I knew almost nothing about him beyond his opinions of the movies he had seen, his favorite make of automobile (Mercury), and his thrilling adventures with women, most of them production workers he met while repairing bottling or case-packing machines, or assisting me in my occasionally successful attempts to improve them. These girls always seemed to dote on Aaron, whom they called Ron—even the ones he no longer took home at the end of the day, or reminisced with about Valley Beach, the amusement park that had sprung up on the opposite bank of the river just below town. He made them laugh, flattered them, and I suspect spent freely on them when he could afford to.

His father was so unlike him that, after visiting his shop, I concluded that my original impression of their relationship was mistaken. The elder Gold was a bookman—so much so that I, who have been considered bookish ever since receiving my first green-bound volume of fairy tales, was a trifle repelled by it. Louis A. Gold had his name lettered (in gold leaf, appropriately) in the window of a store that until a few months before had sold shoes; and the lettering had instantly gone from bright newness to an antique patina that might have graced the Great Chalice of Antioch. Dust settled on the glass, as bats in the tropics settle upon certain fruit trees, and half the fluorescent tubes in the light fixtures extinguished themselves at once, while the rest were obscured by tall stacks of books, books Gold brought from God knows where, many of them worthless outdated popular novels, though there were strange and interesting books as well: the technical works of little-known sciences; for-

gotten and eccentric tales; old books of verse; and the reminis-
cences of vanished circles of wits (of famous men who were
known largely to each other, and who met, when they met at all,
at enamel-topped tables in the cheap restaurants of New York,
and talked mostly about jokes played after midnight in the
corridors of second-rate hotels).

Louis Gold's clothing changed with his occupation, gray mole-
skin work pants and union-made "Top Production" shirt replaced by a dark and baggy suit that might have buried Charles
Curtis, and foggy gold-rimmed glasses; so that the only thing
that remained of the man I remembered (though only vaguely)
at a bench in the central machine shop was his calloused hands.
I dropped by his store whenever I was downtown and found him
open; but that was not often; he seemed to lock his door whenever he chose, and when the CLOSED sign, which hung on a nail in
the window and bore OPEN as its reverse, was in place, he never
answered my knock, though I could sometimes see a light at the
back of the store, and his bent figure moving like a spirit among
his stacks of books.

Aaron never spoke of him; nor of his mother; nor of his sister
Sherry, of whose existence I learned from a girl who, on her
hourly respite from the demands of a labeling machine, came
looking for Aaron.

"There was a young lady here asking about you," I told him
the next time he came into the office.

"She bother you? Sorry." Aaron extracted a sandwich from
one of his desk drawers and began to eat. It was about ten
o'clock in the morning, and I was trying to sketch up a star
wheel for a sanitary conveyor.

"Nice-looking girl," I said. "I wish you'd send more like her."

"I thought you were too old for that. Black hair?"

"Brown. She said she knew your sister."

"Just like that. *I* know his sister. Just dropped in to say 'Hi.' "

"She asked where you were, and when I said I didn't know,
she said she was a friend of Sherry's; so I had to ask who

Sherry was, and she said your sister. What's her real name?"

"Was it Emma?"

"Don't you know? I mean, your own sister."

"The girl who came. Sherry's name is Shirley, but nobody calls her that. She's younger than I am."

"She didn't say."

There was a pause, during which I thought our conversation had ended.

"Say, Den, you've lived around here a long time, haven't you?"

"All my life. I was born here—I can show you the house."

"You know a man named Stewart Blaine?"

I put down my pencil and swiveled my chair around to face Aaron. That had to be done carefully because one of the casters was broken. "He used to court my aunt Olivia," I said.

"I didn't even know you had an aunt." He was grinning, getting even for my asking about Sherry.

"I had two. My aunt Olivia's been dead a long time now—she used to be married to Mr. Smart. My aunt Arabella's still alive—she's an old lady. Aunt Bella was my mother's sister, Aunt Vi was my dad's."

"She was Mrs. Smart? Are you going to come into some stock when Uncle Julius kicks off?"

"He hasn't spoken to me since my aunt's funeral, and Aunt Vi has been dead now for twenty-five years. Do I look like a fair-haired boy?"

"Anyway, who is Stewart Blaine?"

"I told you—a man who used to court my aunt Vi. He owned the bank—the Cassionsville and Kanakessee Valley State Bank, not the First National. I suppose he still does."

"He's rich?"

"He was then."

Aaron stood up with a spurious air of aimlessness and shut the office door. "Tell me about him."

"I've been telling you stories about my family and our friends ever since you came into the department. I'd think you'd be sick of them."

"You haven't mentioned Blaine, or if you did I forgot him. This is serious, Den."

I told him what little I knew, and he nodded, looked thoughtful, and went out of the office. The next time I saw him he did not mention the incident.

About a week later, when I was straightening up my desk at quitting time, he said, "You read a lot, don't you?"

"I'd like to," I said. "I wish I had more time for it."

"How many books would you say you read in a month?"

It was raining outside, the drops sloshing down the thermopane window and puddling on the too flat concrete sill outside the glass, and I was in no hurry to leave. I sat down on the edge of my desk and said, "About five. More some months than others, of course."

"You ever go in Pop's store?"

"Is that your father? Louis Gold on Mulberry Street?"

Aaron nodded.

"Maybe once or twice a month."

"Has he ever offered to get books for you?"

"Usually he just lets me browse around. I suppose he'd get a book for me if I asked him for something particular. If he had it."

"That isn't what I meant."

I locked my desk and put my coat on, and found myself suddenly remembering that when my father and mother had returned from Europe and reopened the high, white house that had been my grandmother's, the change in my life that seemed to me most important was that I was no longer free to run outdoors in any weather dressed as I chose. My aunt Olivia never made a fuss about coats and hats and galoshes; my mother, perhaps partly because she felt guilty about having left me for so long, always did.

"Den, have you ever heard of a book called *The Lusty Lawyer?* By a woman named Amanda Ros?"

I shook my head.

"Pop sold it to a Mr. Stewart Blaine for two hundred dollars."

"It must be a rare book."

"I guess it is," Aaron said.

"Pornography?"

"I don't know. I don't think so. You never heard of it, though?"

I assured him I hadn't, picked up my umbrella, and went out into the hall and through the side door of the building into the muddy parking lot. I was living by myself, as I have ever since Mother died and I sold my grandmother's house, and I decided on God knows what impulse to stop by the library before getting my dinner. There were no books by Amanda Ros listed in the card catalogue, but there was a biography of her, *Oh, Rare Amanda.* I thumbed through it and found that Mrs. Ros had been an eccentric Victorian novelist with a penchant for alliteration. Her works were given as *Irene Iddesleigh, Delina Delaney,* and *Donald Dudley,* plus two books of verse—*Fumes of Formation,* and *Poems of Puncture.* No *Lusty Lawyer.*

"Can I help you with something, sir?"

"No," I said.

"You looked rather lost." The librarian smiled. "But I see you've found a book."

"I'm not going to read it," I said, and reshelved it.

The librarian was a rather pretty woman of thirty or thirty-five, quite slender. "If I can help you," she said, "I'll be at the main desk."

"I didn't mean to be rude," I said, "but I don't read much biography."

"What do you read?"

"Fiction and history, mostly."

"Then you should try biography. Someone said that it was

the only history, and I suspect most of it's more than half fiction. And it can be quite interesting."

"It depresses me, to tell the truth. I came in here looking for what I'm told is an old novel—*The Lusty Lawyer*."

"Sounds eighteenth century, though if it's a novel that isn't too likely—"

"Nineteenth century."

"Did you look in the card file?"

"It's not there."

"We can borrow books from other libraries for you, you know. There's a central clearing house that takes the requests and passes them on to a library that catalogues the book. It usually takes about two weeks. Would you like me to put that one on order for you?"

"Yes, please." I followed her to the desk, and she wrote, "*The Lusty Lawyer,*" on a card. I said, "By Amanda Ros."

"By Amanda Ros. And your name?"

"Alden Weer."

"You have a library card?"

I nodded.

"You don't come here often, do you, Mr. Weer? I don't think I've noticed you before."

"I usually prefer to own the books I read."

"Well, don't be such a stranger. We're small here in Cassionsville, but it's a lovely library. This used to be a private house, as I suppose you can tell by the way the rooms just wander into one another, although you might be fooled by the Greek cupola thing on the roof."

"I know," I said. I must have looked upward as I spoke, because she continued to talk about the cupola.

"I've never been up there, but it's the kind of thing I would have loved as a child. I don't even know if you can get into it from inside the building."

"There used to be a trapdoor in the attic; you pushed it up with a pole, and leaned an old ladder nailed together from flooring against the edge when you had it open. The upper side of the door—inside the temple—was higher than the rest of the roof by an inch or so, and covered with sheet copper so it didn't leak. I used to climb up there and dangle my legs over the coping and look at the endless sky."

And it has just struck me that that sky must be the only thing left unchanged since my childhood. There is an elevator somewhere in this house that will take me to the attic, if only I am in my house and this office in which I find myself is, as I hope it is not, Barry Meade's simulation of the real thing. In a moment I will press the intercom button and ask Miss Birkhead to bring me coffee.

"What are you thinking about, Mr. Weer? You looked very abstracted there for a moment."

"Nothing. It doesn't matter."

"I need your telephone number. So we can call you when your book comes in."

"Five six two, seven oh four one."

"Your telephone number."

"That was—"

"Telephone numbers are supposed to have exchanges—you know. Our number here at the library is ELmwood four, five four five four." She had a large mouth, bright teeth, and a wide, infectious smile.

"I'm sorry; it seems I drew the wrong number from my memory. The right one is TWinbrook five, four six seven oh. Would you like to have dinner with me?"

"That's very nice of you, Mr. Weer, but I'm afraid I couldn't."

"I just realized what a long time it's been since I've really talked to anyone except a friend at work, and it was very pleasant talking to you here."

"You live alone?"

"Yes, I have a small apartment now. Do you have to make

supper for someone? Your mother? You're not wearing a ring."

"I'm divorced, Mr. Weer. I have to stay here until six."

I looked at my watch, and discovered with some surprise that it was my old one. I said, "That's only forty-five minutes off. No problem."

"You won't be able to wait in here—we close at five-thirty."

"I'll be outside in my car."

What was her name? I can't remember it, I who pride myself upon remembering everything. And of course there will be no coffee. The drawers of this desk are nearly empty, but not completely so. A few stale cigarettes, a picture of a girl caracoling a clockwork elephant before the eighteen-foot-high orange in front of this building, the orange that shines like a sun by night. In a moment I will leave this place and find my way back to the room with the fire, where my bed is, and my cruiser ax leaning against the wall.

"There you are. Do you know, I didn't really think you'd be here." She was wearing a woman's tan trench coat, and had raindrops in her hair.

"It wasn't long. I was waiting at my desk."

"You mean you prop a book against the wheel of the car?"

"Something like that. Where would you like to eat?"

"That's up to you, isn't it? Besides, I don't know much about restaurants around here. I've only lived here for a couple of months."

"We'll go to Milewczyk's, then. The food is good—mostly French—and I know the owner slightly."

"You've lived here since you were a child, haven't you? I thought so because of what you said about our building."

"Yes, all my life."

"It's a funny town, isn't it? So mid-America. I'm a city girl myself."

"Chicago?"

· 174 ·

"You're guessing from my accent, aren't you? No, St. Louis."

"Is it polite to ask why you came to Cassionsville? I don't mean to pry."

"Very polite. I came here because I'm a librarian—I have a master's in Library Science. I'd been cataloguing—and not much else—in the St. Louis Public Library System ever since I graduated, so I answered an ad and came here, and now I'm a big froggy in a little puddle. I like that better."

"You enjoy the work here, then."

"We've got a good collection of early documents, and I'm sorting out our genealogical material. Then, too, I like our building, even though . . . Weer. I should have spotted that name. Are you—you have to be, you said you'd lived here all your life. I was just going to ask if you were one of the locally prominent family, but you must be; I didn't think there were any of you left." The wipers sponged generations of raindrops from the windshield as she spoke.

"I'm the only one."

"Your ancestors used to own most of this town—I suppose you know that."

"I know they bought land from the Blaines and built a gristmill on the Kanakessee."

"At least they bought it—the Blaines stole it from the Indians."

"I thought there was some sort of treaty."

"All right, they stole it by treaty. Only the treaty can't be found, and for that matter neither can the Indians. The thing they show the school kids was painted on buckskin by a group of local ladies about forty years ago."

"I know."

She was silent for a moment. In the library I had noticed that, as so many librarians seem to, she wore glasses that hung from a chain passed behind her neck; these were gone now, and from the way her eyes flashed when she looked at me, I suspected that they had been replaced by contact lenses. "Have you ever thought," she said, "of Indians inhabiting this land? People killing deer with stone-tipped arrows on this street? . . . Oh, I see Milewczyk's! Is that how you pronounce it?"

I told her it was, and swung the car into a parking place. It was early, but the lot was already more than half full.

"Now that I see it, I can remember having driven past it, but I've never been inside. . . . It's nice, isn't it. . . . Louis Fourteenth. I like Louis Fourteenth, particularly his carpets, and I feel I should be wearing a powdered wig."

"And I should be carrying a sword."

"Why, how gallant you are, Mr. Weer." A waiter—not Milewczyk—led us to a table. The wallpaper was gilded in a pattern of fleur-de-lis; a reproduction of Watteau's *Le Mezzetin* hung on the wall behind us in a velvet-covered frame. When we were seated, the librarian said, "I daresay you do have a sword, Mr. Weer—no, I'm not thinking of *Jurgen*. Have you read Chesterton? He said that a sword was the most romantic thing in the world, but that a pocketknife was more romantic than a sword, because it was a secret sword."

"Yes. I do have a pocketknife." I took it out and showed it to her.

"A Boy Scout knife—I think that's sweet. It looks old; have you had it for a long time, Mr. Weer?"

"I got it for Christmas when I was six."

"That's marvelous—you've carried your secret sword almost from the beginning."

"I'm afraid it hasn't slain many dragons."

"What do you do for a livelihood, Mr. Weer? I've told you what I do."

"That's very mid-American, isn't it? You are what you do."

She nodded. "Yes, we think that when someone loses his job he goes out like a match in the wind. That's the trouble with a lot of us women, I think; we don't have jobs, and so unconsciously we feel we're no one."

"I don't believe I've ever been unemployed, technically. I had accepted the job I have now while I was still in college. But I've felt I was no one for a long time now."

"Maybe being the last of the Weers has something to do with it."

"I think being the last human being is more important. Have you ever wondered how the last dinosaur felt? Or the last passenger pigeon?"

"Are you the last human being? I hadn't noticed."

"You were talking about the Indians—how do you think the last Indian felt? Indians have more feelings, I should think, than dinosaurs or pigeons."

"There are still Indians—perhaps not around Cassionsville."

"Don't you think we should call them Americans of Indian descent?"

"I see what you mean, but it makes them sound as though they came from Bombay. Is that what you feel like yourself? What do you call it?"

"Various things. Let's just say that I'm conscious from time to time that my skull is being turned up by an archaeologist's spade."

"You shouldn't feel dead before you are, Mr. Weer."

"That's the only time you can feel it. You're like the people who tell me I talk too much—but we're all going to be quiet such a long time."

"You don't seem to me like a talkative man. And you told me in the library that you never talked to anyone except a friend at work."

"Aaron Gold. That's why I was looking for *The Lusty Lawyer*. For Aaron."

"You're going to have to tell me about him." (The waiter came to take our order.) "I haven't even looked at this menu. What's good here?" (I told the waiter we would have champagne cocktails while we looked over the menu.) "Is your friend Aaron a reader? Why does he want to see *The Lusty Lawyer?* And why are you anxious to get it for him?"

"I don't know. I hardly know the Golds, except for Aaron, but they seem to be an odd family."

"It's not just for himself that he wants the book, then."

"It has something to do with his father—Louis Gold. He operates a used-book store on Mulberry."

She snapped her fingers. "I know him. I'm trying to buy a book from him: an old diary. I know his daughter, too. She comes to the library to do her schoolwork. A bobbysoxer—is that what they call them now? Very pretty; a bit plump yet, but she'll outgrow it; a nice girl with lots of bounce. Would you mind if I asked her why her father wants to see *The Lusty Lawyer?*"

"He doesn't want to see it; his son does. Mr. Gold sold a copy for quite a high price." I was beginning to feel that I had said too much, told more about Aaron's affairs than I should.

"He probably thinks his father is being cheated."

"Why do you say that?"

"Isn't that the way sons and daughters always think? They believe their parents are senile and that someone else is taking advantage of them. If Mr. Gold sold this book for fifty dollars, you can bet his son thinks it's worth five hundred. But I doubt that anyone is really robbing poor Mr. Gold blind. He wants enough for the Boyne diary."

I said, "Let's change the subject. I'm getting tired of *The Lusty Lawyer* already. What's this about a diary? There used to be a woman living around here named Katherine Boyne— it wouldn't be the same one, would it?"

"It's the same name. Or at least close. Mr. Gold says the diarist calls herself Kate Boyne."

"This woman was called Kate. I knew a grandson of hers when I was a boy. He called her 'the old Kate.' "

"This is fascinating—listen, do you mind if I have another of these? Did he ever talk about her?"

"He told some stories, yes. But I'm afraid I've forgotten most of them. I got the impression that the old Kate—I mean Doherty's grandmother, as distinguished from your Katherine Boyne—was illiterate, or nearly so."

"She was. You understand, Mr. Weer, I'm not committing the library to buying a pig in a poke—I've already read quite a bit of the diary. It's full of misspellings and so on, but nevertheless it sheds a great deal of light on the history of this region. From what Mr. Gold has told me and what I've read myself, Katherine Boyne was born in Boston of Irish immigrant parents —probably before 1850. That would have been the period of the potato blight, and it seems quite probable that the family had just arrived in the United States. Somehow or other, she became a kind of girl-of-all-work to a lady schoolteacher, and when the teacher left Boston to marry a man who had settled here she went with him. It—"

"His name was Mill," I said. "I've forgotten the first name."

"That's right—how did you know?"

"Our cook was his daughter by his first wife. The schoolteacher was her stepmother. She used to talk about Kate."

"You mean a cook you have now—"

"When I was a child. She was an old woman then; her name was Hannah Mill."

"She might be mentioned. I think there was a Mary Mill."

"You're trying to buy this for the library? From Louis Gold?"

She nodded. She had dark hair, curled (I suppose artificially) close about her head. The curls bobbed when she moved her head, as the bird on Mrs. Brice's hat used to long ago.

"How much does he want for it?"

"Seventy-five dollars. Now, don't smile; that may not be a great deal to you, but we only have two hundred and fifty to buy new books for the entire library for the year. If I were to spend seventy-five on one book, there would be some eyebrows raised at the next board meeting, believe me."

"Suppose I were to give the library a gift, specifying that it was to be used for the purchase of this book?"

"Could you? I mean, it's not too much? It won't inconvenience you?"

I wrote her a check.

"You wanted coffee, Mr. Weer?"

"Yes. Coffee, Mr. Batton?"

"Call me Bill. You know I'd expected I'd be drinking your juice when I was at your plant."

"It makes a good screwdriver—I'll show you at lunch. But I thought you might prefer coffee now."

"Thank you. Let me begin by saying, Mr. Weer, that there are two basic types of campaign—the institutional campaign and the selling campaign."

"We want a selling campaign."

"I know you do. What I was leading up to is that in an institutional campaign you want to reach everyone, but in a selling campaign you have to reach the buyers. The buyers of your product are housewives, Mr. Weer. Good coffee."

"What is it, Miss Birkhead?"

"Sir, there's someone outside who wants to see you."

"I'm sorry, Bill. Apparently this is an emergency."

"It isn't, Mr. Weer. Not really. It's just that I was hoping you'd either see him now or send him away. I don't like having him out there. It's a little man all covered with hair."

The next morning was Saturday, and I slept late. (My job required that I get up at six on weekdays; our early starting time was supposed to stagger traffic in the plant area—though by nine there was almost none, and a late start would have spaced things out better—but had actually been instituted, as I came to realize, because our section and department heads wanted the luxury of late arrival without the danger of being away from their desks when the main office called.) The telephone woke me. "Den? This is Lois."

"Who?"

"Lois Arbuthnot. Don't tell me you've forgotten me already."

"Sorry, I'm not awake yet." (Nor was I. When we are asleep, so it seems to me, we sleep surrounded by all the years. I have imagined, sleeping, that I heard the footsteps of the long-dead; I have held conversations with them, and with the blank-faced people I was yet to meet, conversations that seemed of unbearable poignancy, though when I woke I could remember only a few words, and those not words that possessed, waking, any emotional significance to me. It is said that this is because content is divorced from emotion in sleep, as though the sleeping mind read two books at once, one of tears and lust and laughter, the other of words and phrases picked up from old newspapers, from grimy handbills blowing along the street and conversations overheard in barbershops and bars, and the banalities of radio. I think rather that we have forgotten on waking what the words have meant to us, or have not learned as yet what they will mean. But the worst thing is to wake and remember that we have been talking to the dead, having never thought to hear that voice again, having never any expectation of hearing it again before we ourselves are gone.)

"Your book. Remember your book? I phoned in the request, and Marie—that's a friend of mine, we went to college together —says there's a man in their office who's a shark on the Victorian novelists, and he'll be able to tell you all about it, and where you can find a copy if it's rare."

"I think I already know that."

"I thought you were looking for one."

"I was. I just thought of something, that's all. Listen, I want you to keep on with your man for me if you will; my idea may not work out."

"He's not there now—that's the only thing. He's on vacation; but Marie promised to ask him as soon as he comes back."

"Fine."

"And I ordered the diary. We have to put a check through,

and it goes by mail, but I called Mr. Gold just a minute ago, and he says that as long as I'm willing to vouch for the fact that I've put it through, we can come by and pick it up anytime."

"Good."

There was a pause. I was conscious that I had failed her in some way—as I fail people so often in conversation—but too stupid to see in what way it was. In desperation I said, "You've been very active. And very successful."

"Don't you want to go by with me?"

"What?"

"Go by and pick up the Boyne book. I had the impression you were anxious to read it, and we could go past this afternoon and get it. The library closes at noon on Saturdays, and I'm through by one."

"I'm sorry. When you said 'we' could pick it up, I thought you were referring to some messenger from the library. I've told you I'm still asleep, Lois. Your call woke me up."

"I'm sorry."

"Yes, I'd like to see it. I'll meet you in front of the library."

"You're invited to dinner with me later. At my apartment."

What I had told Lois was perfectly true: I had remembered at last that someone I knew had a copy of *The Lusty Lawyer*, that someone being Stewart Blaine. The only question was whether or not to telephone him before driving over, and in the end I decided against it.

I bought a car during my third year at college, and brought it home with me when I graduated, and have since owned several others, but it has always seemed somewhat unreal to me to drive on the old brick streets of Cassionsville. So many of these streets are meant only for walking, streets that would be called courts in an English city, streets without sidewalks or curbs, the houses and their little plots of grass, their evergreens and rosebushes, at a level with the bricks, so that I might have driven unimpeded to their front doors, or parked beneath their windows. So many others retain clear traces of the Age of the

Horse, having limestone curbs with iron rings (still staunch, though I have heard children wonder aloud why the horses were not tied to the parking meters) set into the stone, and even faint narrow grooves in the brick from the iron rims of wagon wheels. As I drove to Stewart Blaine's, however, it seemed to me, doubtless because of some association awakened by the route, which was not one I normally had reason to take, that an automobile was the proper vehicle; but that it should be open, a thing of heavy steel and brass, with free-standing lamps and a brake handle (beloved of small boys) *outside* the car, sprouting from one running board, a handle whose operation required reaching across the top of the door.

Stewart Blaine's house was gone. When I reached the corner at which it had stood, it was no longer there—the U-shaped drive, the pillared portico, the stable and carriage house that had employed Doherty, all gone. Half a dozen smaller houses stood in its place. I went to one and knocked, and told the woman who answered that I was looking for Mr. Blaine, who had once lived there. She was a friendly woman, plump and not pretty, but smiling, wiping soapy hands on a checkered napkin, and she asked me in, and called to her husband. He lumbered out in trousers and a strap undershirt, and proved to be a man I knew slightly from work, a draftsman. He had never heard of Stewart Blaine, nor had his wife. They had lived in the house eight years.

I found Blaine's address (of course) in the telephone book, an address in an area that had been a farm when I was a boy, a farm I had passed, once, on my way to the Lorns', when Mr. Macafee and my aunt Olivia had gone to buy the wonderful egg which was to be Mr. Macafee's forty-first birthday present. The house was timber and plaster now, in the style that is called Tudor. Two stories and what appeared to be a finished attic, but nothing to the glory that had been Blaine's old house. I rang, and the door was opened by a stout, frowning woman who was not Mrs. Perkins. She told me that Mr. Blaine was ill, and seldom saw visitors, and asked me for my card. I gave it to her, writing on the back, "Olivia Weer's nephew. About *The Lusty Lawyer*." The woman asked me to wait in the hall.

It was an old house—that was the first thing that struck me. The woodwork had been painted several times, and in differing shades; the light fixtures and the switches looked worn, and so did the dimly patterned runner, worn by that heavy, frowning woman's going to the door to say that there would be no candy this Halloween, no oranges or apples, nickels or dimes, for carolers this Christmas, that no brushes, brooms, or cosmetics were wanted here, that there were no knives to sharpen, no pots to mend. There was a tarnished silver tray on a marble-topped table, and several minutes passed before I recognized the table as the same one that had stood in the hall of the old house, the white house, the house in which Doherty, that lax and lazy and doubtless drunken Irishman, had scrubbed the interiors of the fireplaces until the blacking of the smoke could scarcely be seen all summer long.

In an upstairs bedroom Stewart Blaine held court in a wheelchair. He no longer shaved—to conceal, he told me later, the scar left on his throat by an operation—and perhaps it was his beard, as much as his proud, cold eyes, that made me think of a mad king, of Lear lording it over a flock of rooks on a windswept heath. "So you're Vi's nephew," he said. "I remember you, if you're the same one. Wait a minute and I'll think of your name." (It had been on my card, of course.) "Jimmy? Anyway, I used to bribe you to go to bed so I could sit on the glider with your aunt. Remember that?"

I did not, and am sure that it never happened.

"What can I do for you?"

I told him that I understood he had a copy of *The Lusty Lawyer*, and that I was a collector myself and would like to see it.

"Certainly. Certainly. And here I had been thinking I was the only serious collector in town. Do you advertise in *The*

Antiquarian Bookman, Mr. Weer? I don't think I've noticed your name."

"I'm afraid I don't have the funds to operate on that scale, Mr. Blaine."

"Well, that's a pity. The family fortune is gone, is it? Would you think, Mr. Weer, to see me as you do—this little house, an old man in a bathrobe, one servant—that I am wealthier now than ever?"

"I've always heard that you are an extremely acute businessman."

"Not true, actually. I'm a dilettante—have been a dilettante all my life." He raised his head and looked toward the window, as though he were calling on the sun to witness what he said. I have never been more aware of the skull underlying a man's face than I was of Blaine's then. He had been handsome in a long-jawed way when I was a boy; now that jaw was, very plainly, a bow of bone thrust out from the base of the skull bowl. A movable bow which would not move much longer. "The Depression made us, just as it made about every bank that didn't go under. We didn't go under, though we had to lock the doors twice. We were picking up farms for a song, picking them up left and right. Fertile land. Of course there was no market for it then. The other banks were going crazy trying to sell what they had. Sell at any price. We hung on to ours, told the former owners we felt sorry for them, would let them stay there, keep on working their places; we'd only take half, and we hinted that perhaps eventually they could save enough to buy the places back. Some of them moved out and we gave their land to the others—gave them more land to work, you see. And we took over their marketing. A bank that represents fifty farms can do a lot for the price of produce. Then this juice thing came along, and the demand was for potatoes. This is good potato country, Jimmy. Not as good as Aroostook County, Maine, but still good, and we had no shipping costs—made the men haul them to the plant in their own trucks and wagons. It was less than twenty miles for most of them. When I was courting your aunt, I had the big house—remember that?"

I nodded.

"Vi was the only woman I ever asked to marry me—the only woman I ever wanted to marry. Pretty as a picture, and a shrewd businesswoman, though it was your dad, as I remember, that had most of the money in your family. Roscoe Macafee got the better of her once, though. Do you remember that? Had to do with an ostrich egg from India, an egg all painted with pictures, like an illustrated chapbook Bible. They both wanted it, but he made her give it to him at Christmas. I was there—it was at one of the Christmas parties Judge Bold used to throw before Prohibition. Vi handed over that egg like it was the last hand mirror in the house; I think Roscoe'd thought she'd marry him to get it back, but Vi set her cap for Julius Smart when he went into business here the next spring, and that was the last Roscoe ever saw of her.

"Well, in those days I thought it was incumbent on me to impress people. That's what my father thought, too, I suppose, when he built the place. Then, too, a man that kept a carriage, as I did when I was younger, needed a bigger place—keeping a carriage took more room, and cost more, than owning three automobiles. When the Depression came, suddenly it wasn't wise anymore for a banker to look as though he had money. I sold the place to a real-estate company the bank controlled." He laughed. "Let everybody go except my housekeeper, Mrs. Perkins, and found out I could save a lot of money that way."

With hands like claws, he turned the wheelchair until it faced the window squarely. "Don't ask me what I was saving it for; you wouldn't understand—not if all the Weer money's gone. There's an art about money." He raised a thin arm, and seemed for a moment to be manipulating an invisible marionette. "It is as if I could control the tide by my actions: it ebbs and flows and never stands still. They call it liquid assets, and so it is, but it is the gravitation of men it answers to—men and companies. People—you, I suppose—think I'm selfish, hoarding what I have, and even trying still to swing a deal from time to time. They don't understand that it's the artist in me; I don't want to give a bad performance. Not this late in my life. . . . I'm leaving my money to my books—did I tell you that?"

"No."

"Endow a library, leave it to the university." He coughed, and drew a large soiled handkerchief from the pocket of his robe. "My own books will not circulate. Only they will be displayed, and they may be consulted by scholars. Books are grateful recipients of bequests, Jimmy. I tell you in case you ever find yourself with funds to leave. Have you any children?"

I told him I had never married.

"Nor have I. No son. When I'm gone, this whole town will revert to the Iroquois—did you know that? Determination Blaine bought it, and it was to belong to him, and to his sons, for so long as the moon rose. The fact that the sons were included in the wording shows that it was actually a lease of indefinite length—one that was to remain in effect as long as the line endured. But there are things worse than not having a son, Jimmy. Do you remember the story Julius used to tell? How he broke into the laboratory—"

"It was a bedroom," I said. "A third bedroom on the second floor. The laboratory was in the master bedroom."

"I think I should know better than you. You couldn't have been much more than fourteen or fifteen when Julius used to tell that tale." For a moment a spot of color had come into Blaine's cheeks. I apologized for having interrupted him. "He broke in, he said, and found the deformed body in a tank of alcohol. The druggist's wife, that he had carried out his experiments on—do you remember that? Did you believe it?"

"Yes." I did not mention that for years I have carried a vivid memory (though I never saw it) of the body as it must have looked in its open-topped, methanol-filled zinc coffin, of the soft tissues, and the misshapen head with its blind eyes and open mouth and floating hair.

"I used to wonder if he had strength enough to burst open that door. Julius was active, but he wasn't a big man by any means."

"He bought a crowbar," I said. "After Mr. Tilly died. I remember that quite clearly—his going to the hardware store when he couldn't find a key."

"Anyway, I never believed in the ghost. I think that woman was alive, living by herself in that room until her husband was so frightened of her that he got Julius to stay with him. Probably you've forgotten it, but one time when Julius was coming up the walk he saw the curtain of the front bedroom twitch without seeing any face at the window. Now, that would make you think 'ghost,' wouldn't it?"

"I suppose so."

Blaine laughed. "I've done it myself—before I had to have this chair—when my housekeeper was out and I was expecting someone I didn't want to see. It's too late to prove it now, but you can bet there was a mirror on the wall opposite the window. Sit on the floor under the sill and pull the curtain aside; the person you're looking at can't see you in the mirror because it's too dark in the room. You can bet that's what she did. After her husband died, she did, too—probably took to drinking the alcohol and fell in."

I asked what had happened to Mr. Ricepie.

"Oh, him. Ran away with twenty-five thousand or so. Went to Guatemala, I think we heard. He could have gotten away with a good deal more than that if he had wanted to, but he had worked out some complicated justification for himself. He left it with me, right in my 'in' box under some other papers, but I never read it—just glanced at it and saw what it was and called the police. I suppose they probably still have it somewhere. But you wanted to see *The Lusty Lawyer*, didn't you? I suppose you wonder where I keep my books."

As a matter of fact, I had been wondering, since there were only two books—as nearly as I could see—in the room: a directory under the bedside telephone, and a memorandum book on the rumpled covers of the bed.

"See that door over there? Looks like wood, doesn't it?"

"Yes, but not a great deal like wood."

"Had it put in while I was still president—I'm chairman of the board now. Fireproof vault. See here." Blaine touched a switch below the arm of his chair and rolled forward to open the door for me. The room into which he ushered me was without windows or pictures, and lined with gray steel cabinets. "Fireproof vault, fireproof bookcases," he said. "The bank did all this for me, then wrote it off as a business expense. Had to keep documents in my home, you know—and so I did, so I do. My collection is all here—take a major war to harm anything. Classification by decade of issue, and cross-referenced by author and subject in that card file over there, with notes on price, condition, presumed rarity, provenance, and date of acquisition. What was it you wanted to see?"

"*The Lusty Lawyer.*"

"Nineteenth century. Wait a moment and I'll open the case for you." He had taken a ring of large keys from the pocket of his robe, and used one to unlock a thick-doored cupboard. "Here you are."

I opened the book at random: " 'La,' said Lady Luella. 'Let us not make light of ladies' longings, sirrah.' Llewellyn Lightfoot, the lusty lawyer, knew longings of his own."

"I haven't read it," Blaine said. "And I probably never will. As a collector yourself, Jimmy, you will understand that a book sufficiently valuable to excite my cupidity is too valuable to read."

"That might be just as well." I had closed *The Lusty Lawyer* and was looking at the binding, which appeared (as the bindings of mid-nineteenth-century books are wont to, to modern eyes) somewhat too heavy for the pages it contained.

"Half calf, as you see," Blaine said. "Beveled boards. Not a publisher's binding, naturally. This was issued in parts, as Dickens was, and Thackeray. The reader—if he decided he cared that much for the book when he finished it—took the parts to his own binder and got what his taste approved and his pocket could afford. You can find a thousand different bindings of a really popular book like *The Old Curiosity Shop* or *Nicholas Nickleby*. This is a book the public didn't value, and today the one you hold may be the only complete bound copy in the world."

The pages had loosened on the spine sufficiently that their edges no longer formed a smooth surface at top and bottom. "It's shaken," I said, "and the binding's a bit tattered and stained."

Blaine smiled, two level rows of false teeth, like the plastic edging of a flower bed in a department-store Easter window, springing as it seemed from his old face. "So you're a buyer, Jimmy," he said. "I rather thought so. Five hundred dollars, and I do not haggle over the price of books—buying or selling."

"No," I said. "I was only thinking that it was rather worn for an unpopular book."

"Not reading wear." He rolled forward and took the book from my hand, fanning the pages. "This was stored in an attic, I would say, for fifty years or so. The shaking came from being at the bottom of a heavy stack that was shifted from time to time."

I thought of little Joe in his framed Italian garden and leaned forward, sniffing the binding to see if it smelled of apples, but there were only the odors of dust and mildew.

"As a collector," Blaine was saying, "you should know the difference between abuse and reading wear. There's not one dog-eared page in this, no underlined words, no marginal annotation.

This book has only been read once, if that. Like to see it again? I'm afraid I can't let you borrow it."

"Peace pressed the plantation of perfumed pines as a prince in a parable might pamper a princess; the pines' pliant pinnacles poked the purple empyrean as that princess's pale palms might pat a precious pet. 'Lady Luella,' said Llewellyn Lightfoot—then lapsed into a limpid silence. 'Let's,' Lady Luella softly lisped."

Lois Arbuthnot said, "You saw it, then," when I met her outside the library.

I nodded.

"Have you decided what there is about it that worries your friend?"

"No. It's not pornographic. I suppose it might have been considered a little racy when it was written, but it's only slightly comic today. At base, it's a bad book that deserved to die and did. Listen to me, I'm talking like that myself now. It's infectious."

"Don't despair—dull diction doesn't deserve it. Live and let live. Do you know you're the first person I've met in Cassionsville I've really liked? The first intelligent person."

"Do you mean there are no intelligent people here?"

"No, but the intelligent ones I meet aren't likable—a bunch of bored snobs wishing they were somewhere else without the guts to get there. Some of the unintelligent ones are great—lovable people and great fun. But they're like nice dogs; after a while you get lonesome for the sound of a human voice. You're intelligent, and you're here and not happy; but you don't despise the place and I don't think you really want to go anywhere else."

"I don't," I said. "There's a house in town I'd like to own, but I wouldn't want to move away from Cassionsville."

"You're an engineer, aren't you? I think you said that last night."

"A mechanical engineer. You've heard the joke, I'm sure: 'I

knew we were mechanical engineers, but I didn't think we'd wind up like this.' "

"There's a joke about librarians, too: 'For a librarian she's really stacked.' It's only funny to another librarian."

"The stacks are where you keep the books not on public display—isn't that right?" I stopped for a red light. We were about three blocks from Gold's shop.

"Yes. Why do *you* think your friend is worried about *The Lusty Lawyer?*"

"I think he believes his father overcharged for it. Two hundred dollars is a great deal for a forgotten novel."

"It's a first edition, I suppose."

"And only, probably. It's not autographed, and Blaine himself said there was no annotation. Of course it's perfectly legal for a dealer to sell a book for whatever he can get, but if Mr. Gold made claims with regard to the book that are demonstrably untrue, that would, technically, constitute fraud. And Stewart Blaine is precisely the man to prosecute and send him to prison."

"Did he say why he thought it was so valuable?"

"Not really. He said it was rare, and from what we've found out so far that seems to be the case—it wasn't even listed among Amanda Ros's published works in the biography you have in the library."

"What else did he say?"

"Very little. . . ."

"You're smiling. Now what's *that* about?"

"As I was leaving, he said that it wasn't Mr. Ricepie who took the money and ran to Guatemala. It has nothing to do with the book; it's just that for a few minutes I had enjoyed thinking of Mr. Ricepie drinking planter's punch in a hammock and having a native mistress. But Blaine said later that it was someone I had never heard of named Simpson. I hope he was wrong—I mean right the first time. His memory's failing." There was an open parking spot at the curb three doors down from Gold's, and I eased my car into it, got out and helped Lois out, and put a dime in the meter.

"This is an old section of town, isn't it?"

I nodded and said that the shops had been here when I was a boy. "There's a chance of flooding here, so near the river, so they've always been cheap stores, if you know what I mean. Just a little way up are the better shops—where the department store is, and so on."

While I talked, my mind had been filling with images of my aunt Olivia, who had been killed one and a half blocks from where we stood. She had grown plump within a year of her marriage, eating Milewczyk's cooking instead of her own, buying new clothes each month until she was a comfortable size 14 (or 16—I am guessing), visiting Macafee's and staying, sometimes, for an hour in Mr. Macafee's brown, wooden office, where there was a leather-covered couch and the Chinese egg stood on its squat ebony pedestal in a glass-fronted cabinet on the wall. I have sometimes wondered, as I passed Macafee's (which no longer uses that name), if Mr. Macafee had ever been able to explain to himself why my aunt, who had been impossible of access before her marriage, had become so easy after, and if he connected it, as I did without knowing why, with her increasing corpulence.

In the evenings, when Milewczyk and the maid (neither of whom lived in) had gone home, and Julius was at work in his laboratory in the basement, my aunt soaked in a hot tub, and she often called me into the bathroom to fetch her a new book, or to bring her writing board, pen, and notepaper. The water was opaque with scented oil and foamed with lilac-scented bubble bath, from which her breasts rose and sank with the energy of her conversation. Originally small and pointed, they waxed, in the two years that passed between her marriage and my parents' return, to globes, while her upper arms grew thick as the knees she sometimes thrust above the steaming water.

You must excuse me. I can write nothing more now about the trip Lois and I made to Gold's, or our search for the buried treasure. Everything we do is unimportant, I know; but some things are, if not more important, at least more immediate than others, and so I must tell you (writing alone in this empty room, my pen scratching on the paper like a mouse in a wall) that I am very ill. Sicker, I think, than I have ever been before—sicker, even, than I was this winter, before Eleanor Bold's tree fell.

"What are you writing, Den?"

"Nothing."

"Come on, show Aunt Bella."

"Nothing."

"But such a studious little boy! You must be writing something."

"He can't write yet, Bella—just print his name, and words like 'cat' and 'rat.' But he likes to scribble on paper, and to draw little pictures. He's getting to be quite a reader, though."

"He showed me the book Santa brought him. He can't read that yet, surely?"

"Yes he can—a bit."

"Why that's marvelous. We'll have you read to us in the evenings, Den."

My grandfather said, "Don't tease the child."

"That's something we used to do here when Mother was alive, Den. We'd all sit in the parlor—"

"In the kitchen, mostly."

"You're right—I forgot. In the parlor on Sundays, in the kitchen like this other days, and Mother or Bella or I would read."

"And we're going to do it now," my aunt Bella declared. "I brought a magazine."

Mab said, "Then you're going to have to do it yourself, Mrs. Martin. I'm better at apple pie."

My grandfather snorted, scraping the iron ferrule of his stick across the boards of the kitchen floor. "And you're no great shakes at that, Mab."

My aunt Arabella read: *"Ghost-Chaser Number Three* is the third in our continuing ghost-chaser series. Each of these accounts of real-life adventures with the supernatural is true, though in some cases the names of persons and places have been changed to protect privacy."

My mother said, "Why, Bella, that's not a story, that's an article!"

"No one reads stories anymore, Della; it's not up-to-date."

"Well, we certainly never sat around in a circle and listened while Mother read articles—we'd have felt fools. I'm glad you weren't here at Christmas; you'd have read the hog prices from the livestock exchange."

Mab said, "We had such beautiful snow."

"For each article in this series we have commissioned the services of a reliable and experienced journalist, knowledgeable concerning the occult.

"The Regency, as we will call it, is a new and modern hotel in one of the larger Eastern cities. It towers to a height of fifteen stories above the surrounding buildings, contains three restaurants, a grand ballroom, and many handsome shops. Lighting is, of course, all Edison electric, and there is no room in the entire hotel without plumbing. The lobby has been modeled on the Baths of Caracalla, and contains marble pillars which we believe would leave that emperor green with envy.

"Yet though the Regency is prospering, having attracted the carriage trade from Baltimore to Boston, all is not well there. Though the manager and owners of the hotel are unwilling to own to the fact in public, manifestations adjudged to be supernatural have been observed by a number of distinguished persons—many of whom were ignorant of what others had seen before them. These manifestations have been particularly noticeable on the fourteenth floor—indeed, seven of the ten reported sightings have occurred there, the others having been on the twelfth, sixteenth, and ground floors, respectively."

"A passel of balderdash," my grandfather said. "Old as I am, I never heared of a ghost that wasn't in some house, or else a burying ground."

"Accordingly, your reporter visited the hotel, and, with the concurrence of the management, occupied a room on the fourteenth floor. I found my accommodations as pleasant and commodious a domicile as the hotel's advertising and that sometimes more reliable guide, the word-of-mouth report of the city, had led me to expect. Two windows opened on a capacious airshaft to admit copious sunlight. The furniture and carpet were new, the bed was of the most modern design, and the bath, whose all-enamel tub boasted ball-claw feet and stood upon a floor of sparkling-white hexagonal tiles, was the most modern I have seen. After a light supper in one of the hotel's excellent restaurants, I prepared my room for the vigil I would keep all that night, placing a pair of large candles on the chiffonier, another pair upon the windowsill of the room, and four upon the posts of the bed, where I attached them by their own wax to the elegant knobs that served there as terminals. When all were lit, I made the experiment of turning out the electric lights, and satisfied myself that at eleven o'clock—when, as its custom is (both for the safety of its patrons and to encourage regularity of hours), the hotel should extinguish the electricity—I would not want for light. It yet lacked two hours of that time, and I amused myself with a book (one of cheerful character, the reader may be assured!) until the preliminary blinking of the electric bulbs warned me to make haste to relight my candles. I did so, set my volume aside, and began my watch in earnest.

"All the great hotel was quiet; no sound broke its slumber

save the ticking of the clock. An hour passed, then two. Insensibly I became aware as I sat watching my eight candles of a tumultuous sound—faint at first—which invaded the accustomed quiet. Vainly I tried to convince myself that it was nothing more than the chirping of a cricket in the wall, or the sounds of some sleeper in another room magnified by my imagination. But as the intensity of the disturbance increased, these explanations became increasingly preposterous, and rather than seeking, as I had been, to explain the noise rationally, I lay back upon my bed and surrendered myself to it, letting the fancies it promoted play through my mind without hindrance. Then at last, when (I own) I nearly slept, the thought struck me that the sounds I heard were nothing more than a disturbance on the street outside, and I thought to detect in it the note of a murmurous crowd, and the rumble of a multitude of vehicles on macadam, and the blowing of angry horns. I got up, and wished most devoutly to look down into the street, but alas, my windows, as I have said, opened only upon an inner court of the hotel. In time the noise increased still further, and at last I determined to quit my room, having remembered that the corridors outside had windows opening upon the street at either end to light them. It seemed a bold expedient at the time, and it was with some trepidation that I closed the door of my well-lit chamber behind me and crept down the corridor toward the faint gleam of light I perceived at its termination.

"I reached it at last and, looking down toward the pavement a hundred and fifty feet below, beheld a swimming and irregular glow, as though a thousand carriage lamps were moving to and fro in a mist. Nothing could be seen clearly, and I watched for several minutes before I remembered noticing, at the time the assistant manager (having been warned by the editors of this magazine of the peculiar nature of my mission) had first shown me to the room which would be mine for the night, that these windows were not of clear glass, but of that peculiar construction called 'frosted' or 'pebbled' by which the surface is distorted in such a way that to preserve the privacy of those within; light is admitted but sight excluded.

"For a minute or more I labored to open the window, but it was beyond my strength. In all that time the moving glimmers, which were all I could discern through the irregular surface, continued their dance, and the roaring, babbling sounds I had first heard when I sat in my room increased in volume, punctuated, from moment to moment, by the braying of savage trumps and bombardons, as though the armies of the street were going to war."

"A bombardon is a musical instrument that makes a sound like distant cannon," my mother said to my grandfather, who was looking puzzled. "A deep hooting."

"At last I decided to proceed further down the corridor, hoping to find a window of clear glass. The terror I felt then, as I passed those silent doors though which the clamor of the street still came faintly, I cannot well express to the reader. Most were dark; a few yet showed pencilings of light at their bases, indicating that their inhabitants had brought candles (even as I) or coal-oil lamps to their rooms—scholars toiling in the night, or industrious businessmen perusing even more intently books of another sort. Through one I heard the merriment of an orchestra—or, I should say, a gramophone playing.

"Did none of these men, my fellow guests, hear outside what I heard? Was it audible only to me? Or did each, alone in his room, labor to convince himself that he heard it not, that the roaring and murmuring in his ears resulted from nothing more than overwork and lack of sleep? I was tempted to knock, but I did not.

"At last—for the corridors formed a huge square, and I had made their circuit—I found myself at my own room again, entered and found my candles burning as before. For a long time I sat listening to the noises that had so baffled my puny attempts at investigation; at length they dimmed, and I snuffed out my candles and slept.

"In the morning I questioned my friend the assistant manager, who said that he had heard no disturbance on the street the night before. Inquiring among those members of the staff who had been on duty (for in a great metropolitan hotel someone is always on duty, no matter how late the hour) in the watches of the night, we discovered a page who had stepped outside to smoke at almost the precise hour at which I had left my room. He said that the street had been quiet—a wagon and a motor-truck had passed him, he said, during the five minutes or more he stood there with his pipe, and one or two persons on foot; but that was all.

"I conveyed my thanks to the assistant manager and was about to take my departure when he mentioned, with some embarrassment, that there had been a mysterious occurrence in connection with the fourteenth floor during the preceding night: an unknown person, he said, had called the main desk by telephone, and had complained of unaccountable lights which hovered, so the caller insisted, in the air the room. The room number she gave (for the caller had been a lady) was on the fourteenth floor. I told him that I doubted what he said very much, unless there were—as I had no reason to think—more than one telephone on the floor. For that one telephone was in the hall not more than half a dozen steps from my door, and as I am a light sleeper and was in any event awake most of the night, it seemed highly unlikely that anyone could have rung up central without my being aware of it.

"My friend insisted, however, that the call had come just as he described, and explained that he had sent the page to the room whose number the caller had given, and that the page had reported that he had knocked, but that there had been no answer. He had made a memorandum concerning the event. I examined it and found that the call had been placed at the very time at which I had been struggling with the window, and that the room number given was my own.

"By Arabella Elliot."

"Bella! You wrote that yourself?" my mother exclaimed.

Her sister nodded. "I did indeed."

"And signed your maiden name! Bella, people are going to say you're fast."

"We all do it in journalism," my aunt Bella replied, "and some even sign men's names. There are a good many more of us feminine journalists than you'd think, Della."

Mab Crawford said, "Is it true, Mrs. Martin?"

"Of course it's true. In fact, I didn't tell everything I could have for fear I wouldn't be believed. . . . Look, little Den's going to be a journalist, too, isn't he? He's writing all this down."

And so I am.

I should explain that I have left my office. I opened the door actually hoping (such a thing, as my aunt Bella would say, is the human heart) that I would find Miss Birkhead's desk outside my door, but there was (of course) only the empty corridor. Now I sit in Mab Crawford's kitchen, which was at one time my grandmother Elliot's, but I do not remember her. Sit, still scratching with my little pencil, at her kitchen table. It is as good a place to write as any, though I confess I sometimes wish that I could find the Persian room again, or my own porch room with the fire.

Gold's was an old bookstore, though it had been a bookstore for but a few years. The windows, which were not mullion windows, yet were of smallish flat pieces of glass separated by wooden strips, held new books of which no one but their publishers had ever heard, books about sailing and hunting, and collecting Victorian ladies' accessories. Inside the store, the new books gave way to old; the walls were lined from floor to ceiling with shelving, and it was a very high ceiling, so that the volumes on the uppermost shelves could be reached only by the use of the ladder that had once served the shoe clerks, a ladder that ran on a track.

Between these walls stood bookcases, of soft pine roughly nailed together, eight feet high. These, too, held books, and on the tops of the bookcases, where they were completely inaccessible to any customer, more books still were piled flat: all the outpourings of the English-speaking presses, accumulated and preserved in a pickle of democracy, so that classics stood on the same shelf with books that, though they deserved to be remembered, were not; and these with books justly forgotten; and others that ought never to have seen the light of print. I took one down and showed it to Lois Arbuthnot; it was a memoir by a missionary named Murchison, who had spent a decade in Tartary. "Old and rare books," I said.

"*Ja*," Gold's voice came from behind me. He was not so much looking over my shoulder as under my arm. "That is an old book, and a rare one. I'm sorry, I know you have been here before, but I cannot think of your name."

"Weer."

"Yes, Mr. Weer. Are you interested in that book for the library, Miss Arbuthnot? The Murchisons are a local family."

"I'd have to check first," Lois said, "and see if we don't already have it."

"I doubt that—it's really quite unusual. Privately printed, of course, but not vanity press. Printed by the sect to which Murchison belonged, and sold by them at their meetings to raise funds for their missionary program. A few hundred copies, and that in 1888. Most were probably put beside the Bible, then thrown away by the next generation. This is the only one I've ever seen."

"Then how can you be sure there were only a few hundred copies?"

"Here." He took the book from me and opened it to the last

page. A small block of type in the center read: "Published in an edition of 500 copies by the Letter of Paul Press, Peoria, Illinois, of which this is the ————th copy." In the blank space someone had written in pencil (now so faded as to be scarcely legible), "177."

"I'll have to check," Lois said again. "You're sure the Murchisons are local people?"

"Country people," I said. "I remember them now."

Gold said, "Quite a few have come into town now, Mr. Weer. Country families don't stay in the country these days. Look in the telephone book and you'll find quite a list of them. But this isn't what you came for, I think. I saw you pick it up—quite at random, I would say—from my shelves."

"We're here about Kate Boyne's diary."

"You wish to take it now? Follow me." He led the way to the back of the store, where a small office had been partitioned off; this, too, was piled with books. Gold had a trick of standing with his head and shoulders and little belly thrust forward, as though he were a drill sergeant hazing a recruit. Since he was of small stature, this was not threatening, as it might have been in a larger man, but gave the impression that he was facing a rabble of pygmy trainees invisible to everyone but himself; it was some time before I realized that these were his books.

"Here it is," he said, and picked up a fat little volume bound in a black leather that was now rapidly crumbling away.

I expected Lois to reach for it, but she looked mutely at me, seeming to indicate that since I was paying for it I should examine it first to satisfy myself that my money would not be wasted. "Calf?" I asked Gold.

"Sheep," he said. "That was much cheaper in those days. There was gold stamping on that cover, at one time." He coughed. "'Gold-colored' is what I should have said. Not true gold leaf—a copper compound. Hold it under the light here."

There was a lamp on his desk: a lamp whose center was a magnifying lens framed in a bent fluorescent tube. I put the book under it and traced the words "*The Catholic Girl's 7-Year Day Book.*"

"This was intended as a sort of appointment book," Gold said. "A week per page, and it gave all the information on saints' days, the beginning of Lent, and so on. The girl who had it, Katherine Boyne, had attended school in Boston, and a nun gave it to her as some sort of prize—she tells about it on the first page." Gold had seated himself at his desk as he talked. He rubbed the lenses of his rimless glasses with a handkerchief; his eyes looked dwarfed and weak without their protection, like an elderly mole's.

"Have you read it?"

"The entire book?" Gold shook his head. "I'm afraid I don't have the time to read my books, Mr. . . ."

"Weer."

"Mr. Weer. And this one." (The "one" was almost "vun"; Gold's accent seemed to wax and wane almost with his breathing.) "This one is written very small, and by hand with one of the old crow-quill pens. And peppered over with wrong spellings. But it is so interesting I have almost been tempted. I was saying that it was a seven-year book; the years were 1844 to 1850. But the young lady did not use it as intended—I would guess few of them did. Sometimes she wrote three, four, five pages in one day; sometimes for months she didn't write. As it is, this little book covers twenty years, with the last entry in 1864. You've heard of Liddle Orphan Annie? Not with the *arf, arf.* 'Liddle Orphan Annie's come to our house to stay;/And vash the cups and saucers up, and brush the crumbs away;/And shoo the chickens off the porch, and dust the hearth, and sveep;/And make the fire, and bake the bread, and earn her board and keep. /And all us other children, when the supper things ist done;/Ve set around the kitchen fire, and has the mostest fun/A-listening to the witch tales that Annie tells about;/And the Goblins will get you if you don't watch out!'

"This book, this is Liddle Orphan Annie's diary."

We took it, of course. I spent the afternoon and evening with Lois, then did not hear from her again for almost a week. Then, on Friday evening, at about eight o'clock, she called. I asked how she was feeling, and she said she was exhausted, and sounded like it. I asked if a dinner at Milewczyk's tomorrow night might not cure her exhaustion.

"No, thanks, Den. I've been working double and triple times, and if I can get off tomorrow night, all I want to do is sit at home with my feet up. I called to ask you a question. Are you familiar at all with the country south of the river and west of town?"

"A little," I said.

"Fine. Do you know the old Philips farm? It's about a mile back from the water, on County Road 115, a two-story wooden building. Have you any idea how long it's stood there?"

"About thirty years—perhaps a little more."

I could hear the disappointment in her voice. "You're sure?"

"A man named Professor Peacock used to take my aunt and me out hunting Indian relics; I remember seeing them building the farmhouse there, and searching the fields for arrowheads the first year they were plowed. The land had belonged to one of Ben Porter's cousins, but he just pastured cattle on it."

"Perhaps there had been a house there before, Den. Was there a cellar hole, or an old chimney standing on the property before the house was built?"

"I don't remember any."

"Okay, I guess that's that. Den, about that dinner—I don't want to go out tomorrow, but why don't you come up to my place? About seven?"

I said that that would be fine.

Lois's apartment was the second floor of a private house, reached by an outside stairway. "Small," she said, "but cozy. You don't mind? Just two rooms and a bath, really—the bed folds out of the couch." I said I didn't, and she poured me a drink. "I sent out. Five or six years ago that would have shocked me: having a boyfriend over and sending out for chicken. But I'm too tired to be shocked at anything now. I'll show you what a good cook I am some other time."

"I wouldn't have thought the library here would be so much work."

"It wouldn't be, ordinarily, but I'm on a genealogy kick, as I told you. Remember my telling you about the Philips place? I need a farmhouse, in more or less the same area, that was standing at the time of the Civil War. I'm trying to locate a graveyard."

"Sounds grisly."

"Oh, I'm not going to dig up the graves or anything like that. It's just that you can get very valuable information, sometimes, from old headstones."

"Whose farm was it?"

"That's the trouble—I don't know. All I know is about where it was, and where the cemetery lay from it. A lot of farms had private burying places, you know, in the last century."

The delivery boy came with the food, and we spread a paper tablecloth on Lois's little metal table and laid paper plates and ate. When the meal was over, we sat on the sofa (she with her feet on the coffee table), kissed, and drank Scotch whiskey over ice. She talked about looking for some sign of the old farm-house, and tearing her nylons on the wild blackberries, and after a time took off her blouse and allowed me to help her with the catch at the back of her brassiere, and said that she was going to dance for me; but she was almost too tight to stand by that time, and I talked her out of it without much trouble. She fell asleep a few minutes later. For a woman of thirty-five or so, she had a surprisingly good bust, a trifle small, but still firm and erect. I covered her with a blanket and collected the soiled glasses and greasy paper plates and cartons and carried them into the kitchen. A mattock and a garden spade, shiny-new and unused, stood in the corner behind her refrigerator.

That night I lay in bed unable to sleep. Desire is a strange, wayward thing: when I had been in Lois's apartment, I had felt little for her. Now I was several times on the point of dressing, or of telephoning her. I thought of the two of us tramping through the hills south of the river, remembering my aunt Olivia and the professor. I don't believe my aunt ever yielded to her other lovers before her marriage, but I am certain that on those hiking expeditions she often gave herself to Professor Peacock. He had been young, slender, and handsome; and most important of all he had been of that intellectual and almost pedantic cast of mind for which my aunt had hungered all her life.

But would Lois, under similar circumstances, yield to me? She was an experienced woman, I felt sure; I would not be the first since her divorce. I remembered the warmth the Scotch had kindled in her before it had overpowered her—I would bring a flask, and make certain we had a blanket to spread upon the ground.

She had said the cemetery was near a house standing in Civil War times. A deserted farm, surely—there were many in those hills. The picket fence would be rotted away now, the burying ground overgrown with trees and brush, the tombstones, if they had not used graveboards, fallen forward on their faces.

"See this here? There's a haunt beneath it." Margaret squatting by her stone doorstep, tapping it with one dirty finger.

"There is not."

"Yes, there is so. See this house? This house was haunted by the Bell Witch when we moved in. My pa got the wise woman— she's half Indian and knows all about it—and he prayed and she charmed, and they laid the haunt and set this stone on her. How do you think it feels to be a haunt, with a big rock like that in the middle of your chest? She lays there all the time; we know it's a girl one, because sometimes she used to talk, and threaten what she was going to do—with her arms and legs kicking the ground, only you can't see her. I'm setting on her face this minute, but I'm not afraid. I'm never afraid of her in the daytime except when it thunders."

"That's just your doorstep. Don't you think I know a doorstep?"

"It's from a person's grave. If you turn it over, it says who on the bottom."

Bill Batton has been scratching his head, crossing and uncrossing his legs as he sits on the red leather couch beside the bar in my office. "What was that all about?"

"Mrs. Porter? You heard her—she wants to plant a tree on my grave when I'm gone. That's her hobby: she plants trees of endangered American species on the graves of her friends."

"Yes, but what's it all *about*?"

"Why do I bother with her, you mean? She was a close friend of my aunt's when I was a boy. She was a beautiful woman then, a blonde."

"And you're going to have dinner with the hairy man?"

"Since you're flying back to New York, why not?"

"Den?"

"Yes."

"Did I wake you up?"

"Yes."

"Den, I'm sorry about last night. I'm not usually like that, you know I'm not. I shouldn't have had anything to drink when I was so tired."

"There's nothing to apologize for—except perhaps waking me up."

"Den, I'm going to go out looking again today. I thought you might come with me."

"Not if you're going to dig into the grave."

"What?"

"There's a pick and a shovel behind your refrigerator. I saw them last night when I was cleaning up."

"Den, I was fooling you about the graves. Come over and have breakfast with me and I'll explain."

I showered and shaved and dressed, looking around at my small apartment as I did so. It was cluttered and dirty, but Lois's had been cluttered and dirty, too; it seemed unlikely that there would be much change if we were married—we were too old for children, anyway. Just the two of us in a somewhat larger, cluttered, dirty apartment. I wondered if she would want to quit her job.

"Waffles and sausage, okay? The waffles got a little too brown when I went to make the bed, but at least the sausage is done to a turn. And coffee. Sit down and have some coffee."

I sat, looking at her living room; it was filled with inexpensive, brightly colored furniture.

"I should never have told you that about the cemetery, Den; it isn't true. Can I tell you what I'm really looking for?"

"Something you read about in the book?"

Lois nodded, her brown curls bouncing. "You were bound to guess that, weren't you? When I got so busy after getting it. Den, you remember the day we bought it? You took me out, and when I got back home I wasn't sleepy; I was all excited, and I decided I'd just settle down and read it instead of going to bed. And I did, sitting right here with my feet up, drinking instant coffee. It's not as long as Mr. Gold pretended. Because even though Kate Boyne had a small hand and wrote with a fine-nibbed pen, you can't get as much onto a page in script as you can in type. Most of it was ordinary enough: outings she'd gone on, and who she'd flirted with and her opinions of her employers and their friends—although it was interesting from the standpoint of local history. Then—Den, have you ever heard of William Clarke Quantrill?"

"The guerrilla? Of course."

"He was born near here. You probably knew that, too, although almost everyone thinks of him as a Southerner because he fought for the Confederacy. But he was a Midwesterner, just like Grant and Sherman."

"What about him?"

"He came here with a handful of men in 1863, Den. They were following the old river road that used to wind along the south shore. Kate Boyne says they buried forty thousand dollars in gold here."

"Are you the mistress of this farm?"

"I'm the hired woman. I'm Mrs. Doherty."

"Where's the master?"

"And what is it to you?" She stands her ground, her hands braced on her bony hips, her snapping blue eyes flickering from one to another of the seven rough men on horseback. Her red hair is already shot with gray; her hands are as hard as a ditchdigger's.

The bearded man swings down, pushes past her, pounds the front door with the butt of a Navy Colt.

"There's no one there."

The bearded man lifts the latch and walks in, waving to the others, who tie their horses to the porch rail and follow.

"Do you be gettin' yer filthy boots on me clean carpet!"

They are already through the parlor and into the kitchen, rummaging through her cupboards for food.

"And now," the bearded man says, chewing on a chicken leg, "I think you'd better tell me where the rest are. You wouldn't be the first woman I've shot."

"Mr. Mill and Sean are gone into town; they'll be back soon."

"Ahorse or afoot?"

"They took the wagon."

"Who else lives here?"

"Mrs. Mill's gone back to Boston to see her mother. She took Hannah and Mary with her."

Later that night, when John Mill and Sean were locked in

the shed, and the men had found the whiskey in the harness box in the barn, she heard them talking; and still later, when one of them caught and held her as she came up from the cellar with her jars of pickles and tomatoes, she had taken him to the haymow, and bribed him with such talk as she knew how to make, and kisses and more. She was not that ugly a woman by moonlight.

"So you see it has to be near the river. She mentions it several times."

"It wasn't, Lois. I know where that farm was."

She looked at me, her eyes widening.

"Deer Creek flows into the Kanakessee three miles below town, and Sugar Creek runs into Deer Creek about a mile before it gets there. They called it Sugar Creek because hickories grew there and the Indians taught them to boil down the hickory sap to make sugar. I know you probably think they boiled maple sap instead, but there aren't that many maple trees in this part of the country. Hickory sugar isn't as good as maple, but in the early days that and wild honey were all they had."

"Do you think Quantrill might have turned off the road?"

"In those days he would have had to. Or, rather, that's where the main road would have taken him. It was marshy at the mouth of Deer Creek in the wet season; the road bent south about a half-mile before it got there, forded Sugar Creek, then forded Deer Creek just above it. On the other side it ran back down Deer Creek and forded the Kanakessee at Cassionsville, but if Quantrill only had a few men with him he wouldn't have wanted to come that far."

"That's exactly it! Don't you see, he was trying to get the gold as close as he could to his home."

"There were other towns, farther down the river."

"He must have skirted them—or come straight north from the Confederacy. Den, I want you to help me find it."

About an hour later we loaded Lois's pick and shovel into the trunk of my car, and set out for Sugar Creek.

"Ah Mr. Weer. I had been afraid for a time I would never see you in my little shop again. Have you been away?"

"No. Your son sees me every day."

"But I see little of my son. I work very late here, and Aaron does not like to come. In the old country I would be training him here in the shop to take my place. In this country it is not like that. I am getting to be an old man now, and I would like the old way better, but it iss gone now, drowned in the fire and the blood."

"You are from Germany?"

Mr. Gold nodded. "From Breslau. In 1928 I left."

I reached toward one of the books shelved at eye level, and sensed that the small man was relaxing.

"Something I can help you with, Mr. Weer?"

"I just came to browse, I'm afraid."

"You are always welcome. Perhaps you will bring Miss Arbuthnot next time."

"I'm afraid we won't be seeing her again. She's moved away."

"I'm sorry to hear that. She was a good customer; she bought several of my books for the library. I will have to learn who I should address my lists to now."

"I'm afraid I couldn't help you with that."

"No, naturally not." Gold sidled off down the narrow aisle. When he was out of sight, I walked to the back of the store where his office was. There were several books on his table, and I picked one up. It was Morryster's *Marvells of Science* and, opening it somewhere near the middle, I learned that though it was a mortal sin to do so, the man who wished might, if he knew the procedure, summon devils or angels, "and this not by fayth, for he that doth as he is instructed shall gayn his end, whether he believeth or no." And that angels are not, as commonly pictured, men and women whose shoulder blades sprout wings, but rather winged beings with the faces of children; and that their hands grow from their wings, and in such a way that when their wings are folded their hands are joined in prayer. That Heaven is (by the report of the summoned angels) a land of hills and terraced gardens, with cold, blue freshwater seas; that it is shaped like an angel—or, rather, like many, for (like Hell) it repeats itself over and over again, always different and yet always the same, for each angel Heaven is Perfect, as each is Unique; and that the various angel Heavens touch one another at the feet and wingtips, and so permit the angels to pass from one to another.

And again that Hell is a country of marshes, cindery plains, burned cities, diseased brothels, tangled forests, and bestial dens; and that no two devils are of the same shape and appearance, some having limbs too many, some limbs too few, others with limbs misplaced or with the heads of animals, or having no faces, or faces like those long dead, or the faces of those whom they hate so that when they see themselves reflected they detest the image. But that all of them believe themselves handsome and, at least compared to others, good. And that murderers and their victims, if they were both evil, become at death one devil.

"Mr. Weer. You wished to see me?"

"I was just looking through your books. You have some very interesting ones here."

"These are the rare books. I don't dare put them out front for fear they might be stolen. I sell them by mail mostly, and show them to special customers. You are welcome to look at them."

"You mean you wouldn't sell me one if I were willing to buy it?"

"Many of them are sold already, Mr. Weer. Others are books I have been trying to find for some time for a special customer."

I laid down *Marvells of Science* and picked up another book at random. It was large, rather thin, and was bound in slick, light-colored leather, now discolored by handling. There was no stamping on the cover, and when I opened it I saw that the text, which appeared to be in French, began at once without any title page, or even a flyleaf.

"You are in bad company, Mr. Weer."

"So?"

"That is the Comte d'Erlette's *Cultes des Goules*." Gold spread his hands. "Or maybe I should say that it is the book most often called that, and supposed to be written by the Comte d'Erlette. Really the man was too careful to put down his name, and he didn't give his book a title. That binding is human skin."

"Where did you get it?"

"From a Paris dealer. It was easier to find than I thought it would be—people that have a copy don't often want to keep it long—but it was harder to get it out of France and into the U.S."

"I meant the human skin. Where did you get that?"

"I haven't rebound this book, Mr. Weer. So far as I know, what you see is the original binding, done toward the last of the eighteenth century."

"How much do you want for it?"

"It is already sold, Mr. Weer. To a college library in Massachusetts. The price was eight hundred and fifty dollars."

"You only wanted seventy-five for Kate Boyne's diary, but I suppose this was much harder work."

"I wouldn't argue with you. The Boyne diary I found in a box of books I got from a local man cleaning out his attic. For this I turned the world upside down."

"Mr. Gold, you wrote the Boyne diary."

I had expected him to deny it, but he did not. He had seated himself, as we talked, on the edge of his desk, and he remained there, silent, his small, clever-looking hands folded in his lap. I felt ridiculous, as though I were pretending to be Humphrey Bogart or Charlie Chan. I had never held power over anyone, and now I held it over this preposterous little man—and I didn't want it. "You wrote it," I said again. I said it quite firmly, mostly to convince myself. "I think you found that book—

· 213 ·

empty—in a lot you bought, as you said. You had heard of Kate Boyne, and you looked up records in the courthouse. The date of John Mill's marriage to his second wife would have given you the date Kate came here, and the record of her own marriage would have told you that she was still living at the Mills' farm. Most of your rare books" (I picked up the *Cultes des Goules* and held it in front of his face) "like *The Lusty Lawyer*, I think you make up whole—paper, printing, and binding."

I waited for him to defend himself, but he was quiet. I turned to see if there were customers in the store listening to me, but there were none. "You shouldn't have included Quantrill's buried treasure—"

"Old coins," Mr. Gold said, speaking for the first time since I had begun to accuse him, "are found, sometimes, in the sands of the river."

"That's true. I found one myself, on a picnic, when I was much younger. But at least three steamboats have been lost on the Kanakessee above the town—and the coins aren't all gold —the one I found was a silver dollar—and most of them date from the seventies and eighties."

I waited for him to say something more, but he did not. "You made it too clear," I said, "where the treasure was supposed to be. You said that Kate, standing in the farmyard near the chicken coop, could see the men's lanterns; then you said that when they returned they left muddy footprints on her carpet; and you said that when they had gone the next day, she could see their tracks but couldn't find where they had buried the money. I think that you were just trying to be mysterious, but when Miss Arbuthnot and I went there it was clear that if the thing had really happened there could only have been one explanation: that they buried the gold in the bed of Sugar Creek —and there is only a short section of the creek visible from the farmyard."

Gold said softly, "Colonel Quantrill could have returned and taken it again. Or it might have washed away."

"Quantrill was killed in 1865, but one of the men with him could have come back, that's true; or someone might have stumbled on Kate's book years ago and found it; or, as you say, it might have washed out. But Miss Arbuthnot and I had a disagreement while we were looking for it, and it started me thinking. She had read a part of Kate's book to me to get me to help her, and it said that when Quantrill came, Maud Mill, her daughter Mary, and her stepdaughter Hannah were all away from the farm: Maud had taken them to Boston to see her mother. Mr. Gold, Hannah Mill cooked for us when I was a boy. She would have been in her teens in 1863, and if she'd ever gone as far from Cassionsville as Boston she would have talked about it for the rest of her life. She never mentioned it."

I left him sitting there and went back to my apartment. It was Saturday again; Lois had gone out of my life (I should say that she had left my future—I could never eradicate her from my past, no matter how hard I tried) and there was the rest of the day to get through, and Sunday as well. I wondered what Aaron would say to me on Monday; whether his father would mention what had happened. Sometimes when I felt this way, I called Margaret Lorn; sometimes her husband or one of her children answered; sometimes she. I never spoke, but if she answered she tried, occasionally, to get me to talk, asking what my name was and why I called her, sometimes angry, more often cajoling. I think she actually enjoyed the calls, enjoyed knowing that she had an admirer somewhere. Once I sent her flowers without a card. When we met on the street—which we did less often than might seem possible in a small town—we were polite and formal.

What went wrong? That is the question, and not "To be or not to be," for all of Shakespeare. When I recall my childhood, and forget (as I sometimes do) everything else, it is quite clear what my life was to become. I was intelligent and industrious; Margaret and I loved one another deeply. I would marry her, and enjoy a career that, if not brilliant, would at least be locally distinguished. I would inherit, between the ages of twenty and thirty, my father's estate, an inheritance that would not make me really wealthy, but that, added to what I earned myself, would give Margaret and me a comfortable position in life.

None of this happened, and I found myself instead a poor man at forty, and a very rich one at fifty; and never found Margaret at all. The silver dollar I picked up once when I was on a picnic with her—a dollar from, I believe, 1872, which had the seated figure of Liberty in profile on its obverse—I carried as a pocket piece for years afterward; perhaps it brought me bad luck. Where it is now I have no idea, though I visualize it lying in one of the upper drawers of my old bureau in my grandmother's house, beside my scout knife. I still have not found my way, as yet, back to that comfortable glassed-in porch where the fire was. But I carry my notebook and pen with me, and write, sometimes, in the corridors, and sometimes in strange rooms. One of the rooms I have found is my apartment in the Commons.

My apartment is larger than Lois Arbuthnot's, but not much. I have a living room, a bedroom, and an eat-in kitchenette. (That last phrase is the landlord's, not mine.) My windows— two in the living room, two in the bedroom—overlook what should be Catalpa Street, but which, in winding away from what is now called the old village, has changed its name to Ivy Road. I make my bed neatly when I rise, change the sheets twice a week, and wish my bedroom were large enough to hold an occasional chair, though it is not. My living room (where I am sitting) is ten feet by fifteen. There are two chairs in it, my footstool, a sofa, a coffee table, a radio, and five bookcases. I am thinking about buying a television, and the Commons, I hear, is considering putting up an antenna and running wires through the walls. There is no desk, and so I am sitting in the best chair with my legs propped up on the footstool, writing in my lap.

The buzzer sounds.
"Who's there?"
A murmur.
"Who's there?"
A murmur.
"Lois?"
"I'm *murmur murmur*, Mr. Weer."
I pressed the button to unlock the outside door. My visitor, whoever she was, would be entering the cramped little lobby, trying to decide which of the three stairs she should take. (I have been sitting listening for her step on the thin carpet outside, my book on my lap.) A knock at the door.
"Come in."
She was a girl of sixteen, barelegged, long-haired, wearing a sweater and skirt. Her face was round, pretty, accustomed, I think, to smiles; her hair dark and tawny, between brown and blond. She had a well-developed, somewhat fleshy figure, and today had painted her nails bright red.
"Excuse me for not rising. I have suffered a stroke resulting in partial paralysis of one leg."
Nervously: "That's all *right*."
"Won't you sit down?"
She sat, then stood again at once. The chair wasn't close enough, and yet she was afraid to move it. At last she sat on the edge of my footstool, her knees carefully together, her legs bent back as though to hide her feet.
"I know," she said, "you know what I'm here about. My dad—"
I said, "I'm afraid I didn't catch your name when you rang the buzzer."
"Sherry. My dad . . . He feels *awful,* Mr. Weer. Just *awful.*"
"I felt awful." I remembered standing hip-deep in the hole,

which could actually have been called a ditch or a trench, we had dug in the dry bed of Sugar Creek over the space of two days. My shovel had struck a stone, causing the blade to ring, and in a spot of moonlight I had seen the glint of metal in Lois's hand. I had taken it from her—a little, nickled .25 caliber Colt automatic—when she bent down to see what I had found. She had said she had been afraid I would try to keep everything for myself.

"I guess it's not nice to be fooled."

"I'm told some people like it."

"That's what Dad said. I talked to him about it this afternoon, and he said he's made a lot of people very *happy*, and it hasn't hurt anyone. Five hundred dollars is the most he's ever got, and usually it's a lot less. When you think about the *work* he's done, that isn't so much, is it? I mean he has to write the text. The place in New York that prints them for him would do that, too, if he wanted, but they charge a lot—he says they have to. And it's the same with *binding*. He has to find the old materials and work with them, and a lot of times they're so rotten they'll almost tear when you *touch* them."

"Then why do it?"

"He *won't*. I mean, I promise you, he won't *anymore*. I mean, he *told* me that. He didn't know I was going to tell you—he doesn't know I'm over here. I think he wants to *kill* himself, Mr. Weer, I really do."

I said, "Did he tell Aaron? About my talking to him today?"

"Oh, *no!*" Sherry Gold wiggled as she sat on my footstool; wiggled when she talked and, equally, when I did, as though she were unable to keep still. I noticed that she wore a senior class ring with next year's date; it had been a long time since I had seen a senior ring with next year's date. "They don't get *along*. I mean not at *all*. I mean, I know Ron loves Dad, and Dad loves Ron, but they can't agree about anything, and Dad is so quiet and Ron always *yells*. You know how he is. And then Mom gets mad at Ron for yelling, because she doesn't want the neighbors to hear that we fight, and then Dad fights with her because of the things she calls Ron, and that makes Ron just *furious*, and he goes *stamping* out of the house and sometimes it's a week before he comes back. He has friends who have their own *places*, and I think sometimes he stays with a girl who does. I mean, don't ask does *what*."

"I won't."

Her right hand was moving, though only slightly, toward the waistband of her skirt. The memory of that night with Lois was still so strong that for a moment I actually thought she might be about to draw a weapon.

"You're not going to the *police*?"

To see what she would say, I told her, "I had planned to go to the people who have bought the books; after all, they're the ones who've been defrauded. Mr. Blaine and the library are the only ones I know of now, but I think I can find out who some of the others were."

There was a button, apparently, at the side of her skirt, and she had stepped out of it (still wearing saddle shoes and short socks) almost before I was aware of what she was doing. She had on that cheap rayon underwear sold to girls considered to be socially, though not sexually, immature; and she sat on my lap quite promptly, kicking off the shoes without untying them. "You see," she said, "we can make a *deal*. If you don't tell, I won't." Her young hair was so fragrant that I might have been thrusting my face among the boughs of a blossoming apple tree.

Later she asked if I were surprised that it had not been her first time. I said that I was not.

"I've done it with a boy in school three times. Two boys, really."

I warned her about several things.

"Oh, we're careful. The first time—you know, you're supposed to get drunk or *something*. Or he's supposed to make you—tear your clothes off or *something*. Only it wasn't like that at all.

We had been—you know—in his father's car out on Cave Road, and I just wanted to *so much*, so I said, '*Come on*,' and he took my pants down, and then he—you know—made a mess on himself, and I felt so *sorry* for him, he was so embarrassed. So a couple of hours later, when he was feeling better, and everything, we did."

"You shouldn't talk about it. You'll get a bad reputation."

"Well, I *don't*. Do you mind if I put my panties back on? I want to use the bathroom again and get a glass of water if you don't mind. But you're not going to tell; I mean, an old man like you! If you won't tell about Daddy, you won't tell about me—I mean, why should you? It's the boys you have to worry about because they like to blow off. But they tell so many lies nobody believes them much—you know? But these two have been pretty nice about it, because it's hardly got back to me at all. Wait a minute."

She went into the toilet, and after a pause called, "Can I take a shower?"

"Certainly."

I began to get dressed, and by the time she came out (again in her underpants, but holding a damp-looking towel in front of her chubby breasts) I was finished. She asked, "Are you going out?"

"I think we should see your father."

For a moment she looked frightened. "About me?"

"About the books. If he's as worried as you say, I ought to let him know that I'm not going to tell anyone. We can just say that you came and asked me not to, and I had been thinking about it, and so I promised you I wouldn't."

She nodded, and after a moment began to get dressed. While we were walking around the building to get to the parking lot, she asked, "Do you always keep a gun in your bed?"

For a moment I did not know what to reply.

"I *felt* it. When I was lying with my head on your shoulder.

· 220 ·

I was looking for a good place to put my arm—there's never *any*thing to do with the arm you're lying on when you're like that—so I slipped my hand under your pillow. It was just a little gun, but it *was* a gun. Do you always keep a *gun* in your bed?"

"It was a twenty-five caliber automatic. No, only for the past couple of weeks; I think I'll get rid of it tomorrow."

"What are you going to do with it?"

"Throw it in the river, or the bottom drawer of my bureau."

And that is where my scout knife is, I am sure—in the bottom drawer of the bureau in this room, not eight feet from where I sit. I am not going to look. If it is there, I will be no happier than I am now; but if it is not, I will have to begin the search again. Or perhaps I will look—I am not sure I have the strength of will to walk from this room without it.

"You look so *serious*. What are you thinking about?"

"Nothing."

"Well, I was telling you about me. You know, you said I'd get a bad repu*tation*. Well, I've thought a lot about that—I mean, I really have. Because I'm a nice-looking girl—I mean I'm not the *greatest*, I never thought I was, but I *am* a nice-looking girl—I have this *thing*, comprehend? Down here. I call it the 'magic ring.' And it's going to last from now to about when I'm forty or forty-five. Only if I don't use it I don't get the wishes—you see? Like, I wanted you not to tell about Dad, and you were going to, so I used the magic ring and—"

"Presto chango."

"Yes, presto chango, the world turned upside down, and now you're not. But most people—I mean, most girls—only use it to get a husband so they won't have to work. So they have the *hus*band, and children and so on, and that's it. But I don't *want* those things—I really don't. You cook a roast and baked potatoes, and make a *salad*, and after he eats, you do the dishes and mend socks—*socks*, for God's sake. I mean, who *needs* it?"

I asked her what she was going to do instead.

"Well, *first* I'm going to look around— Hey, where are you going?"

"To your father's shop. Isn't he open this evening?"

"He felt so *bad*—because of you—he closed up. If you want to *talk* to him, you'll have to come to our house. Turn left at the corner and we'll go out Browning.

"Like I was *saying*, I want to look around. I mean—look at my father, for example. He was born way over in Europe, and went to England—"

I said, "I didn't know that."

"He went to England *first*. And he came here and learned a new language, and he's had all sorts of jobs—he was a *furrier* for a while in *New York*, and everything. I mean, he's *seen* things. How do I know what I want to do! I want to travel and find out, and I've got my ticket. You know the immigrant joke? This immigrant writes back to his cousin: 'America! What a country! A person comes here with *noth*ing, no *friends*, can't speak the language, not a *word*, knows *nobody*, the first day eats free in the best restaurant, sleeps in the best, the most luxurious—I tell you, like a *palace*!—hotel, and gets a hatful of money and jewels.' So the cousin doesn't believe all this, and he writes back. 'This happened to you?' and the immigrant writes, 'Not to me, no; but to my *sister*.' You know we're supposed to be Jewish?"

I nodded, although I had never specifically thought of Aaron as Jewish.

"We're washing away—that's the way I think of it. The whole family must be washing away, for God's sake. *Excuse* me a minute, huh?" She reached up and adjusted the rear-view mirror until she could see her face in it. "I didn't bring a purse with me, and all my makeup came off in your shower."

"Did you walk to my place?"

"Rode the bus. I got a token in my bra for the trip back, but you probably didn't see it when I took it off because I did it so it wouldn't fall on the floor. I don't look *Jew*ish, do I? I was looking at myself the other day. What do you think I look like?"

"American."

"Go slow here—it's the middle of the next block, the brick house with the rosebushes. I look *Slav*ic is what I think. So many darn Poles and Russians mixing with us that now we *are* them. We don't go to temple, did you know that? Or keep a kosher house or anything. What we do is, we don't eat *pork*. That's it. My dad has breakfast in a restaurant, the waitress says, 'Sausage?' my dad says, 'No.' That's our *Jew*ishness. The next house, with the light in the front window."

Mrs. Gold (who told me to call her Sally) met us at the door. There was something birdlike about her, and something British as well; I think she knew why I had come, but wished to maintain the fiction that she did not. "My son Aaron works for you, doesn't he?" she said. "He's not in difficulties, I hope?"

I said that Aaron worked with me rather than for me, and that my visit had nothing to do with him—that I had come to see her husband on business.

"Lou's in his study; I'll see if he wants to talk to you." She walked briskly away, holding herself very straight.

Sherry said, "I don't think Ron's come home, or we'd hear him."

"I'm sure Ron can take care of himself."

"Yes, but she *worries*. Listen, I'm going up to bed now; she'll feel better if I'm not around. There's fruit in the bowl, and she'll get you tea as soon as she comes back—she always does." Sherry went upstairs with a swish of skirt and a flash of legs, blowing me a kiss from the top of the banister.

"Very forward for a girl of her age," her mother said, returning.

From somewhere above our heads: "*For*ward, for God's sake."

"Go to bed! Yes, forward for God's sake. Has a ring to it, doesn't it? Like an old battle cry. I don't believe soldiers talk that way anymore, and it might be interesting to find out when they stopped, and why. Do you know what it was that David's soldiers shouted when they charged the Philistines?"

I shook my head.

"Neither do I. But Lou would—that's the kind of thing he knows. He's the most intelligent man I've ever met. I've a degree —I taught in Britain, and I've been substituting here—and he doesn't, but he's far above me; he's the best-educated man I have ever met."

"I'd like to talk to him."

"He said it was all right—that he'd see you. I wanted to tell you something about him first; he's not an ordinary man."

I said I hadn't thought that he was.

"I don't think you're quite an ordinary man, either." She cocked her head to one side to look at me, as though I were a doubtful worm. It was too warm in the house, and the little birdlike woman, and the heat, and perhaps the rubber plant in the corner and the pattern of interlocking green tendrils in the wallpaper, gave me the feeling of being in an elaborate aviary.

"I am a very ordinary man. The most ordinary."

"I don't think so." Suddenly she laughed. "I sound like a gypsy, don't I?"

"A little."

"We could have done that, you know. What the gypsies did. In fact, we could have done it better—we were in Europe earlier, we had the same advantages they did—the more sophisticated culture, the dark looks all the Slavs and Scandinavians and Celts and Teutons found so uncanny. And we had the immeasurable advantage of having provided Europe with its religion without sharing it: Mary, Mary Magdalene, Jesus, Judas, Peter, even Simon Magus—they were all Jews, you know. Think what could have been done with that. The gypsies pretend to foretell the future, but the prophets were all ours—Moses, Joel, Samuel, all of them. . . .

"I'm so sorry. You want to see my husband, don't you?"

I said, "I'm beginning to wonder why you don't want me to go in."

"Just putting off the bad moment, I'm afraid. People don't understand Lou. He's a great man, but he won't be recognized until he's been dead a hundred years."

I wanted to say that I was beginning to think that was true of all of us; that our lives couldn't be viewed with detachment until they were half forgotten, like paintings which can be seen objectively only when the artists are long dead, but I did not.

"You *are* an unusual man, though. I forgot to say that we also have the one really vital element, the sensitivity, the awareness of auras." She paused, watching me, then said, "Lou's study is down the hall, first on your left. It's an extra bedroom, really."

I nodded, and knocked on the door when I reached it. There was no response, so I turned the knob and went in. Mr. Gold, in pajamas and a smoking jacket, was sitting in a leather Morris chair; his feet were on a leather-covered hassock, and he wore old-fashioned red carpet slippers. His gold-rimmed glasses were (as always) neatly in place, and a heavy book lay in his lap. "What kept you?" he said; and then: "I know—Sally. Sit down, Mr. Weer."

I sat in a big, shabby, comfortable chair.

"My daughter came and talked to you, didn't she?"

I nodded.

"Sally told me. Sherry worries about me too much. So does Sally."

I said, "Considering your hobby, I don't blame them."

"You think I might be sent to prison—I really doubt that, Mr. Weer. I've been mulling the matter over since you left my shop this afternoon, and I'm really quite skeptical. In a way it would be interesting, however, if I were tried. I think it would send the prices of my books to much higher levels."

"I suppose it would, but you're not going to be arrested—at least not because of me."

"Sherry dissuaded you, then."

"I like to think I dissuaded myself—at least, mostly. You're doing some real harm, Mr. Gold; you certainly did to Lois and me. But all of us do real harm, and most of us don't have your class."

"I see." He nodded, then lit a cigarette. "There are a great many more of us than you think, Mr. Weer. And we go back a long way. Many of the old books you accept as genuine because you see them everywhere are actually reprintings of the original efforts of people like myself—some of them working many hundreds of years ago."

"Do you know that, or are you making it up?"

"I have good reason to believe it. And books are not our only subject. Everyone knows, I suppose, the story of the Venus of Melos's arms, but—"

"I'm afraid I only know the story of Bonaparte's hand, and I don't tell it very often anymore."

"You must tell it to me sometime. Would you like to? Now?"

"I'd prefer to hear about Venus."

"She wasn't actually Venus, of course, but Aphrodite; and she was discovered, supposedly, in a cave on the Isle of Melos in 1820. The statue is in almost perfect condition except that both arms are missing, and there has been a good deal of foolish conjecture about their position. Since she was a genuine piece of ancient art, you see, it was possible to put her picture in 'family' books, even during the most repressed period of the Victorian era. Thus she became a secret erotic stimulant for a whole generation of little boys—all over the world. Many men retain a lifelong interest in the things that stirred them as children."

"I know."

"In point of fact, the position of the arms—and what happened to them—is well established. It is seldom published, however, because the mystery makes a better story." Gold leaned back in his chair. He had always seemed to me more German than Jew, and never more so than then, as he sucked his teeth and made a little steeple of his fingers—the Prussian scholar at ease, still lecturing in his club.

"At that period, Mr. Weer, the natives of Greece, and of the Greek islands, were rewarded by archaeologists for each example of ancient art they brought in. The archaeologists bought each item individually, I should say. Of course those wily Greeks soon learned that they could increase their profits by knocking their finds to pieces and bargaining for each bit. The same thing was done in this century, by the way, with a Gutenberg Bible, a very poor copy. The owner simply cut the pages out and sold them piecemeal. He realized more than anyone had ever gotten for an intact Gutenberg at that time. You see the principle."

I nodded.

"When the archaeologists were summoned to view the 'newly discovered' statue of Aphrodite, what they found was the famous lady, apparently tumbled from her pedestal, with her arms lying beside her. They struck a bargain for her—a price that was considered quite high at that time. But when they began to haggle for the arms, they found that the Greeks wanted almost as much for each of them as the archaeologists had already paid for Aphrodite herself; they felt, you see, that since the statue would be incomplete and imperfect without them, they should be very valuable."

"I see."

"The archaeologists did not, and they decided to stop spoiling the natives. Then the Greeks threatened to throw Aphrodite's arms into the sea if they weren't given the price they asked for them. The archaeologists, thinking they would not do it, told them to go ahead."

"And did they?"

"Yes, they did. It taught the archaeologists to bargain for lots as lots, and that pretty much ended the custom of breaking up statues. The story is well known; though it isn't widely publicized in the popular press, which finds it more amusing to run pictures of the poor lady scratching herself or making vulgar gestures. What isn't as well known is that she is almost surely a modern forgery."

"Do you know, or are you guessing?"

"I am guessing—but I am guessing, if you like, from a position of insight not many have. Can you imagine—to begin with —a statue falling in such a way that both arms are snapped off cleanly at the shoulder, but with almost no other damage? Can you imagine a statue of that size remaining unknown for almost two thousand years, when it was in a sea cave anyone could have walked into at any time? A sea cave in an inhabited island? Can you imagine anyone moving such a statue into such a cave and leaving it there? Can you imagine a work of art, which is universally admitted to be one of mankind's greatest, existing in the ancient world—on a tiny island—without generating a single written record?"

I shook my head. "I have to admit I can't."

"Yet we are asked, Mr. Weer, to believe all that, and more. No, the great artist—and he was a great artist—who carved the Venus was alive in 1820 when the statue was 'discovered.' It is quite possible that when she was discovered the tools that shaped her stone had not yet been oiled and put away. They should have buried her, and dug her up again, as was done in this country with the Cardiff Giant, but it would seem that in 1820 a sea cave was good enough."

"And her arms?"

"She was holding up an apple, Mr. Weer. The apple of discord, you know, which was awarded her by Paris. Possibly her carver hoped for some confusion with Eve—the newspapers love correcting people, and they would have had a field day explaining the difference between Eve and Aphrodite to readers who had hardly heard of either." He paused. "What was it my wife told you before you came in, Mr. Weer?"

"She said that I was a very unusual man."

"Was that all?"

"I think she wanted to be certain I wouldn't tell the police what you're doing; flattered people are usually magnanimous."

"Sally is a mystic. She likes to think herself psychic, and I believe sometimes she is. She has been making tea in the kitchen, and will come in with it any minute now. Have you heard her?"

I shook my head.

"I have. She had to heat the water, and I heard the teapot sing. A moment ago I heard the rattle of the tray as she got it out of the cabinet where she keeps it. My ears are attuned to this house, Mr. Weer, and I sleep very little. I hear my daughter pacing the floor of her room as she wrestles with questions of boys, and decides for the one-hundredth time that she will finish high school before she leaves home. I listen to them and I write, here late at night.

"Sometimes I sleep here. My head falls forward, and for thirty minutes—or a hundred—I sleep. Often my dreams tell me what to write. Sometimes my wife finds me here in the morning, with my head on my arms."

There was a knock at the door. Mr. Gold said, "Yes," and Mrs. Gold opened it. She had two Russian-style glasses of tea on a tray. "Hot," she said. "Do you know how to drink this?"

I said, "I think so."

"If you want more, just call. There's nice cookies in the kitchen, too, if you'd like some. From Dubarry's."

"I'm afraid I don't care for their baked goods."

"That's too bad. Lou and I think they're the best in town."

Mr. Gold said, "We were talking, Sally. We were speaking with one another."

"Don't worry about me—I can be perfectly happy reading the newspaper or listening to the radio."

"I wasn't worried about you."

Mrs. Gold sniffed, smiled at me, and, waving her tray, shut the door behind her. "A charming woman," I said.

"Twenty-five years ago you should have seen her. I met her in London, did I tell you? The Russian tea—that's London, that's Bloomsbury, not Russia. In Eastern Germany—Poland—

where I was born, Russians are nothing: scum. For Bloomsbury they were very chic. But still, she is a wonderful woman."

"I don't want to take up your evening—" I began.

"I'm keeping you? Excuse it. Like I said, I sleep very little. For me this is six o'clock."

"I just wanted to tell you that I've decided against informing anyone of my experiences with Kate Boyne's journal. Sherry was very concerned about you, and I thought it might be best if I told you in person."

"For that I thank you, Mr. Weer. I"—he tapped his smoking jacket gently—"I am an arrogant man. Proud. I think Gold and his family would have been all right without you. But I'm not such a fool I don't recognize good will when you rub my face with it. I thank you."

"Are you going to keep doing what you do?"

He laughed. "Look at it this way, Mr. Weer. Suppose you were in a court—a court of law; they're very impressive. In England more than here, but that's another story. You get up and put your hand on the book (I've been tempted to make gospels for the other ten apostles, but there's quite a few of them already) and swear you're going to tell the truth, and they ask you, 'Did he tell you he was going to continue?' What are you going to say?"

"I would tell them the truth, I suppose."

"I suppose, too. So I'm telling you now, no more." Gold opened the book on his knees and pretended to read, ignoring me. I asked him what it was he had.

"This book here? The name is Greek. You don't speak Greek; it wouldn't mean a thing to you."

"What is its title in English?"

"Should be, 'The Book That Binds the Dead.' Most people that think they know Greek don't, so they say, 'The Book of the Names of the Dead,' or 'The Book of the Names of Death.' "

"Is it a real book?"

He held it up—a massive thing bound in faded green leather

studded with brass. "What does this look like? A finger bowl?"

"I meant, did you write it?"

"Perhaps." Looking suddenly very tired, Gold put the heavy book on his lap again. "To you I am a fraud, Mr. Weer. An eccentric. To myself I am an artist, shaping the past instead of the future. I write, yes. My hand moves across the paper carrying my pen, and there are words and I try to tell myself they have all come from me. It may be that all mankind, living and dead, has a common unconscious, Mr. Weer. Many great philosophers have thought that. It may also be that more than man takes part in that unconscious. The world shapes itself, I find, very fast, to what I write. Or I write more than I know—perhaps all of us who do what I do. This book on my lap—I just wrote it, but you will find it mentioned in a hundred others. A man over in Rhode Island made up the name and it was taken up —you understand."

I nodded.

"So now it exists. The first book was said to be in Arabic, but there were later translations into Greek (the title, you see, it's really the title of the Greek translation), Latin, and German—all languages I have some knowledge of. The present volume is a collection of rebound pages from several earlier editions; there are some duplications, and some hiatuses, as might be expected."

"Do you have a buyer for it?"

"I might offer it to Columbia; their copy is missing."

"I thought you just wrote it."

"Nevertheless it is catalogued." Mr. Gold removed his glasses and rubbed his eyes. "You remember the remarks with which Dr. Johnson refuted the theory of mechanistic creation? He asked, if that were so, why it had stopped—why we didn't see men spring from the ground, and new races of animals appear. But the truth is that we know little of the process by which entities—all of which, please notice, prove upon examination to be composed of the same electrical particles—come into being. This book I hold in my lap was composed in the seventh century, probably in Damascus, by a native of the ancient city of Sanaa, in what is now Yemen. In 950 it was translated into medieval Greek, and a hundred years later it was burned by Michael, the Patriarch of Constantinople; that should have been the end of it, but two hundred years later a Latin translation of the Greek was placed on the *Index Expurgatorius* by Pope Gregory IX. It was not printed until the Latin version appeared in the Cadiz edition of 1590, and never mentioned in print anywhere until the providential gentleman I spoke of a few moments ago made the entire thing up. Now it has achieved reality, and in another hundred years ten thousand copies may exist."

"You say that the title means 'The Book That Binds the Dead'?"

"Yes. It is a volume of necromancy—among other things."

"Isn't there a danger that someone will really try to do whatever it is the book indicates they should?"

"They may fail, Mr. Weer. Magic is an unreliable thing."

"It seems to me that the danger lies in the harm they may do in failing."

"I would worry about their succeeding, if I were you. It may not be as easy to hold the dead down as we think. But you are becoming restless, I see, oppressed as you are by my spate of foolish talk. Before you go, would you like to hear a passage from the book we have been discussing?"

"I'm afraid I know no language but English, Mr. Gold."

"I will translate for you." Gold pulled his small body erect with what seemed to me to be something of an effort, and opened the book near the center. " 'Then, as the spirit had instructed us, we scattered the ashes to the four winds and what remained in the cup when the scattering was done we ate.' " His voice had gained a depth it did not possess in conversation, with something in the tone that suggested the slow strokes of a hammer striking iron. How much of this was assumed (I knew by now that whatever else he might be, Gold was a consummate actor), I could not tell.

For a long time nothing happened. We stood beside the grave, not looking at one another. A cold wind had sprung up, and the stars were covered, at times, by small clouds like wisps of smoke. Twice I saw late travelers on the road, who, seeing us without robes, took us for *ghuls* and hurried on. I remember my fear that my friend would insist upon leaving, for I would not have stayed alone, and so would have missed—as I believed—all the great secrets, and perhaps left behind me something that would do great harm. At last I heard a whispering, as if many small voices, far away, were singing or humming. I turned my head to find from whence that sound came, and was looking about in that way fruitlessly when I saw that my friend was staring at the ground between us, the top of the grave from which we had (on the instructions of the spirit, of him who leans between the moon and the Dog-Star to speak with men) removed the stones. There the sand was stirred as a woman stirs a pot, around and about, and all the singing I thought to hear in the wind was only the sound of the sand. I reached downward to touch it, but my hand was struck as with a staff, though there was no staff to be seen.

As the stirring continued and the singing grew louder, the sand over the grave rose as dough in a trough, so that it flowed toward our feet. Bubbles appeared even as the bubbles in a pool into which a stone has been cast, and at last an arm of the lich was thrust higher than the sand, and then both arms, and then the terrible head, until at last the man who was dead rose and stood before us, and the grave was quiet again.

The flesh of his head was as the dust, and there remained only his hair, which hung to his shoulders as in life, but had lost its luster and had in it certain of those small animals which the sun engenders in that which no longer has life. His eyes were no more; their sockets seemed dark pits, save that there flickered behind them a point of light that moved from one to the other and often was gone from both, and appeared just such a spark as is seen at night when the wind blows a fire that is almost gone, and perhaps a single spark, burning red, flies hither and thither in the black air. From what the spirit, that mighty one, had whispered to me, I knew this spark for the soul of the dead man, seeking now in all the chambers under the vault of the skull its old resting places.

Then, gathering all my courage, and recollecting what the spirit had divulged to me—that the dead man was not like to harm me save I set my foot upon his grave, or cast aside one of the stones that had sheltered him from the jackals—I spoke to him, saying, "O you who have returned where none return. You waked from the death that men say never dies; speak to us the knowledge of the place from which you have come."

Then he said to us, "O shades of the unborn years, depart from me, and trouble not the day that is mine."

5

THE PRESIDENT

"Your reactions to the cards have been quite interesting, Mr. Weer, but—"

"But rather long-winded."

"Not at all. The greater the response to each card, the more one learns. However, I was about to say that I was going to have to discontinue our little experiment, fascinating as it is. I have to see another patient."

"And what have you concluded?"

"I want to review the notes I've taken before I outline my conclusions to you, Mr. Weer. Could you come back this afternoon? Tell the girl I said you were to have an appointment after my last regular patient." Dr. Van Ness tapped the stack of yellow cards on the surface of his desk, and then, quite deliberately (as it seemed to me), shuffled them. "Was there something else you wanted to ask, Mr. Weer?"

"I was going to ask why Miss Lorn was seeing you."

"I don't believe I have a patient of that name."

"Mrs. Price."

"Is she the Margaret Lorn you told me about? I'm sorry, but I really can't discuss the affairs of my patients. It's nothing serious."

"I see."

"If I were you, Mr. Weer, I'd go home now and get some rest."

A new set of people now occupied the waiting room. One was an employee, and two were wives of employees. I asked the man why he had to see the doctor, and only afterward, while he was telling me, did I realize that he thought I was checking up on him.

At the office Miss Birkhead said there had been no calls. I went inside to my own desk, where I sat with my back to the plant. I had gotten rid of Julius Smart's desk—a heavy, old-fashioned affair with carved legs and front and side panels—when I moved in. The decorator had replaced it with one shaped like saliva on the sidewalk, a blob of walnut. The carpet was orange (I had insisted on that) and a bronze paperweight in the shape of an orange held down the mail. There were pictures from my engineering-department days on the wall—not as many as I would have liked, but all that were available: a candid shot at the drafting board; a somewhat stiffly informal group picture in which another engineer and I stood with Fred Neely, my technician after Ron Gold; a gag picture taken at the company picnic, showing Bert Wise and me fencing with the handles of croquet mallets. There was a built-in bar at one side of the office, and I poured myself a Scotch before sitting down at the desk. I usually drank screwdrivers in public, and the Scotch was a relief.

The first letter was handwritten on ruled notebook paper.

Dear Mr. Weer:

This is to thank you for the nice time you showed me when I was at your place. It surely is a big plant, & I'm glad I got to see it, because I don't get to see that kind of thing much—just from the window of my trailer, you know, when we're going to a new burg, and we pass one of the big industrial plants like yours on the road. And I think—half the people in this country work in a place like that, but I hardly know anything about them. That was what my mother always used to say she didn't want me to do, work in one of those plants, or in a mine. What you said about me being an outsider, and the outsiders being the real insiders because all the inside stuff is swept away in a few years and then everyone is outside it and no one understands it, but they do understand the outsiders who wrote about it or left their impressions, as you said, in some other way, is very true. I have been thinking about it. Dickens was like that, I think. Of course he worked in that blacking place, but if you read *David Copperfield* you see how much of an outsider he was there.

Paperbacked books are very good to me, and to all carnival people generally, because we cannot afford expensive books, and even if we could, we could not keep them with us because we would very soon have a whole trailer full. And we cannot get books from libraries because they do not wish to give us cards (& I do not blame them). Most carnies do not care for magazines except Confession magazines that some of the women like. The rest of us watch the tube a lot and read paperbacks that we can throw away or trade when we're finished. I can't go into town to buy them like most of the others, so I usually have somebody get ten or twenty $s worth and then I read what I want out of that and trade the rest for things I do want. The bad part is that what I want is Dickens and Jane Austen and Proust and Stendhal and the great Russians and that type of thing that you can only get in college towns, but you know what I mostly get. Once I asked Bubba Russo, who is the talker for the Girl Show, to get me what I wanted and he went to one of the college bookstores alright, but he bought nine (9) copies of *Life on the Mississippi*. He thought that was very funny. *Life on the Mississippi* is a good book, sure, but have you ever tried to trade off nine copies on a pony show lot? I still have five of them. (Would you like one?)

The reason I am writing is because of some of the people we talked about that night when you had me to dinner. You will remember, I guess, us talking about Mrs. Mason, the woman that runs the grab-joint with our show, and her daughters. Arline helps her mother with the hamburgers and so on, and Candy used to, but has been with the Girl Show now two years. Candy had pictures of herself taken & she was giving them out to everyone & so she gave one to me and I'm passing it on to you. The other girls in the show all consider this a pretty modest picture because as you have probably already seen, she is wearing a G-string and pasties, which is as far as they are allowed to strip in Sunday School towns where our patch can't fix the cops much. But Candy says she wants to leave something to the imagination, and besides she doesn't want a picture that's going to get her pinched somewhere, by which she doesn't mean what you and I would mean by that, Mr. Weer!

Anyway, if you have any comments on the picture you would like to make, go ahead and make them to me and I will pass them along to Candy; she will be glad to hear from you. She has another picture too, that shows her leaning back on a red velvet table they have, with her keister against the edge of the table and one leg kicked up, if you know what I mean. If you would like to see that I will get one for you.

You remember I told you about this new girl that came to live with Mrs. Mason when we were at Hattiesburg. Her name was Doris, and she was a kid that belonged to Mr. Mason (whoever he was—I myself never laid eyes on him and there was quite a few people around the lot that would have given you nine to five there never was one). She said her father had died, and she was his daughter by wife No. 2, the one he left Mrs. M. for. Her mother was already gone, and her father'd told her she could go live with his first because he had been sending Mrs. M. checks for quite a few years to provide for the other girls, & now she would take care of Doris.

Well, she did, like I told you. I was raised on carney lots myself, and I can testify it's not much of a place for kids; but I've seen quite a few of them and I never saw one having a worse time than Doris. Mrs. M.'s place had always been pretty dirty, even for a grab-joint, before Doris came, but she was not no sooner there than everything had to be spotless all the time and Doris had to do it. I don't get around much, but it got to where everybody was talking about it, even people you wouldn't think would pay any attention to that type of thing, and from where I sit on the bally platform of the ten-in-one I can see the joint (we set up the same way on every lot, as I guess you know) with Mrs. M. and Arline sitting in canvas chairs behind the counter bossing Doris around, and her scrubbing at things when she wasn't frying hamburgers. The worst thing I only found out after I saw you, and that's that Mrs. M. wouldn't let her get enough to eat. She ate in the cookhouse like the rest of us, but Mrs. M. paid, and she wouldn't pay for much, or even let Doris get a hamburger or a doughnut or candy apple at the stand. Bubba Russo told me it got so bad he went over and ordered a burger for himself and stood one for the house, and Mrs. M. looked so mad he thought she was going to knock it out of Doris's hand, and afterwards she raised a big stink with Candy. And Candy went to Regan Reichert (the woman that runs it) crying and said if Bubba didn't stop Mrs. M. was going to quit the show and take all three girls with her. Naturally Regan isn't about to lose Candy, who is the No. 2 stripper—what they call the co-star—and she told Bubba he was going to have to knock it off. After that I heard that Candy was trying to get Doris to turn a few tricks when Mrs. M. wasn't looking, so she could make some getaway money, but I don't know how that worked out.

You remember that when I was at your place we talked about Doris and had fun thinking about what could happen to her that would be good, and decided that one evening some big draw would see her right after they pulled her in to replace Mitzi Schwenk in the ride for life. Doris would have on the fancy helmet and the see-through blouse and the tight leather pants and all of that, and look like a million bucks sitting the big Harley sidesaddle behind Zipper Johnson. Then the big draw (you remember I said it couldn't be me because I already know her too good, so we decided it was going to be Tom Lavine the Canadian Giant) sees her and it's wedding bells, and from there on in all she had to do is clean the trailer and maybe help him pass out his book in the ten-in-one if she feels like it and we got a good crowd. I still think Tom was a good choice for us even if he is as big as a horse and a little weak in the legs, with eyes that aren't so good. He is really a very intelligent sensitive kid (he took a *Life on the Mississippi* off me for cash) that saves his money and won't live long, and those are the main things a smart broad wants in a husband anyway. All right, you're going to say, Tom can't get insurance, but two out of three isn't bad.

So I started working on Tom a little when I got back. I don't think he even knew who Doris was, because he can't see more than two feet in front of his face, but I told him all about her, and then one or two times I took him over to the grab-joint when we were playing the Claibourne County Fair in Homer and the gates hadn't opened yet. I bought him—you know—a hamburger or a taffy apple or something and tried to get Doris to talk. Tom is eighteen and I hear he is slow developing, but it's about time he started getting interested because who the hell could stand having a fairy that was seven foot six around?

So for a while things looked like they were going all right, and I just let them drift along thinking that now Tom had seen how bad Doris had it, and she had seen what a nice guy he was, really, nature would take its course. And everything looked pretty good until we got to Gladewater, which is a little bit of a town in Texas. A lady came looking for Doris there—a woman about fifty, maybe, dressed nice the way country people dress. You know. Well, she had come so early the grab-joint wasn't set up yet, and Mrs. M. had sent Doris off for some hamburg buns, so when this woman asked Jim Fields, a guy that runs one of the front-end flatties, where she was, she was passing right by, and

Jim says, "Over there," and the woman reaches out and nabs her.

We didn't, most of us, know anything about all this until Doris comes back from town, and then she's all dressed nice in new clothes from Sears, some of them with the labels still on. Now you may laugh, Mr. Weer, and I guess some people did, but I was out on the bally platform and saw her, and she looked real sweet. Ethel Fishman, our snake charmer, called her over and talked to her a little, and later Ethel told me this woman was a old girl friend of Mr. M.'s, and when he died— this is what the lady told Doris, but I don't know any reason not to think it's true—he wrote her and said how he was turning his daughter over to Mrs. M., and asked the woman to check up on her if the show ever got close to Kilgore, which was where she lived.

I think that the late Mr. M. must have been quite a ladies' man, don't you?

I don't know exactly what happened after Doris went to work in the grab-joint. Some people say Mrs. M. wanted her to change out of her new clothes and she wouldn't. Others say *she* wanted to change before she got them greasy (which I think is more likely, and I'll bet you do too) and Mrs. M. wouldn't let her. Anyway there wasn't anybody at the joint except one or two marks and Mrs. M. and Arline and Candy, who likes to go walking around the lot in her bathrobe when she's not working. So nobody really knows what happened for sure. But all of a sudden all three of them were tearing the clothes off her, and Mrs. M. was hitting her over the head with the flat side of a frying pan full of hot grease. The way she was swinging it I think she would have killed Doris if she'd been using the edge.

People came running from everyplace, you know how that is, and some climbed down off the bally platform of our ten-in-one, including Tom Lavine. I thought good for you, Tom, but after a minute somebody hit him on the kneecap with something—I suppose Mrs. M. with her frying pan, or he might have been kicked, because Candy was trying to kick all the guys in the balls with her high heels. Candy is a pretty good kicker, but I guess Tom's kneecap would be about as far up as she could reach. Anyway, he fell down and I had to help him up and get him over to the bally again, and he's still wearing a brace on his leg. Poor Doris got knocked down in the mud a couple of times, and all her new clothes tore to shreds. I still felt like things might work out (I'm funny that way, people tell me), because I thought she must have seen Tom running to help her—after all, he stuck way up above the rest—and she'd wonder about how she could be grateful, and one of the other girls around the lot would tell her and there you are. Maybe. Only it didn't work out that way, because last night Doris got into the spark wagon and grabbed the cable connection where we hook into the high tension lines. The woman that I told you about is going to see to her burial here, and the next time we come through I'm going to go by and howl on her grave. (Ha, ha.) (But I really might do it.)

Your friend,
Charles Turner

Two faded sepia photographs tumbled out of the envelope. I glanced at them and pressed the button which should have summoned Miss Birkhead.

No one came, and I rang again. At last an unattractive woman of forty or forty-five came in, and I asked her where Miss Birkhead was.

"She's sick, Mr. Weer. I'm filling in for her."

"Who are you?" She wore a sprig of some fall-flowering plant pinned to her black dress, and had an air of habitual coquetry, as single women in offices often do.

"I'm Amy Hadow, Mr. Weer. I'm Mr. Scudder's secretary. You've seen me there."

I had not, but I said, "That's right, I remember you now."

"What was it you wanted, Mr. Weer?"

"If you had been Miss Birkhead, I would have asked you to look at these pictures." I handed them to her.

Miss Hadow looked. It seemed to me that it was very quiet in the office; I couldn't hear a telephone ringing anywhere.

"Well, the woman is an obvious tramp, though I must say her face reminds me a bit of Carole Lombard's—do you remember her? The tall man—well, what can you say about him? He's terribly tall. I don't think that other man with him is really very tall, but still the other man must be—oh, I don't know. Six foot ten? Perhaps more."

"Are these people alive today?"

"What?"

"I said, are these people alive today? Are those pictures of living people?"

She looked at them again. "I don't think so."

"I don't either, but why not?"

"Well, for one thing, the pictures just look old. I mean, look at the suit the tall man is wearing—that heavy material, and he's even wearing a vest with a watch chain across the front. And he doesn't really look very healthy, with his thin face and thick glasses. The woman has—you know—an old-fashioned kind of hairdo, and she's the kind that gets killed by some man, or gets drunk and wrecks her car. I don't mean to be offensive, Mr. Weer. Is she someone you know?"

"No. I've never met either of these people."

Miss Hadow put the pictures back on my desk. I could see she wanted to question me, but was afraid to. I said, "It had struck me that these were pictures of dead people; I wanted to see if you felt the same way."

"Is that all, Mr. Weer?"

I nodded, and she left the office. I went over to the bar and poured myself a drink.

The second letter in the pile was not mine, but one addressed to Julius Smart, from his friend Professor Peacock. I could not pick it up—it had been nailed to the desk. Outside, through the window, I could see a man with a wrench climbing No. 1 spray tower. Clogged pipes, probably, a fairly common problem.

I drew the curtains, and at once felt sure that the plant outside was an illusion—everything indicated it, even the absence of Miss Birkhead. It was fun to play at president; but every game becomes a bore in the end. I remembered the Persian room and decided to try to find it again, and loll there for a time on cushions smoking hashish and watching my dancing girls. I swirled the Scotch in my glass and tasted it, and it told my throat of savages with spears squatting about a fire of turfs under a mackerel sky.

Outside my door Miss Hadow sat at Miss Birkhead's desk. The familiar corridor, on which lay all the great rooms of my life, was gone, and Dan French was walking up the office hallway beside a stranger. "Mr. Weer," he said, "I'd like you to meet Fred Thurlough. Fred's the journalist I mentioned to you in my note this morning—going to do a story on our plant."

I shook hands with the reporter.

"Fred feels that there will be nationwide interest in what he's going to have to say. After all, American industry isn't doing too well anywhere, and people are concerned. Have you got time to talk to him for a moment before I show him over our setup?"

"I was going to walk around the plant a little myself, Dan. Why don't I come with you?"

"Swell." Dan looked at the reporter. "How about that, Fred? A presidential guided tour. Well, this is the executive suite, as you can see. Carpets only inside the executive offices themselves, you'll notice. We're a little austere here."

I said, "That was the way my predecessor had it, and it's one thing I've never seen any reason to change."

"I'm sure Mr. Weer would be happy to show you his office if you'd like to see it."

The reporter said, "I'd rather look over the manufacturing facilities."

I told him, "I don't blame you. Offices are all pretty much alike."

"You're a one-product plant here, aren't you?"

Dan said, "That's correct. As you know, we make a synthetic orange-type breakfast drink here, which we sell under one of the country's best-known brand names. We are specialists in that product, if you want to put it that way."

I added, "At one time we experimented with a lemon-lime-type product, but public acceptance wasn't good enough to encourage us to keep on with it."

"Our executive offices are at the back of the Administration Building, on the third floor. That's where you are now. This elevator will take us to ground level, where we can walk out into the plant itself."

The reporter said, "Mr. Weer, as you know, the entire valley area is suffering an economic decline. Has this affected your operation as much as it has others in this part of the state?"

"I don't believe it has. We've been affected, of course, but not as much. We make quarterly salary surveys, for example, covering all industries employing more than twenty persons within a fifty-mile radius of our plant. The object is to show that the salaries we are paying our employees are just and equitable. Our most recent survey showed that our people are making 22 percent more than the area average for equivalent jobs. That's very high, you understand."

"Have you cut salaries because of the economic downturn?"

"The union wouldn't permit it. We have signed a contract, which we must honor as long as it remains in force. We'd have a strike on our hands at once if we tried to make a wage cut."

"What about nonunion employees?"

"We've reduced salaries and fringe benefits there somewhat, yes." Dan French opened the elevator doors and you could smell the plant. It is an odor some people find objectionable, acid and piercingly sweet (there are always stories about new hires fainting or throwing up), and I expected some reaction from the reporter, but there was none. "As little as possible, of course," I said. "They know it's for the good of the company—we couldn't survive today without it."

"Your own salary, too?"

"Not yet. The president's salary is set by the board of directors, and I haven't been able to obtain their consent to reducing it. I hope to soon."

"I see."

"Is there any particular part of the plant you'd like to look at first?"

The reporter paused. Dan said, "Sometimes the best way is to work backward. Start with the warehousing and trace the juice upstream through the making operations."

"All right."

"Over here, then."

I said, "Dan isn't just a public-relations man, you know. Before he took over the public-relations function, he used to sell for us, and he worked his way through college by working the second shift here in our plant."

The chill of the coldhouse came through the walls of the offices; the men there wore their coats at their desks, and women wore two sweaters. Some of the cubicles had small electric heaters. "We make two types of product," Dan told the reporter. "Dried and frozen. The dried is sold in bottles, the frozen in fiber-foil cans. Since the cold storage is so much more interesting, I thought we'd show you that. Can storage is—you know—just a bunch of cardboard cartons sitting on the concrete floor in a warehouse. Want me to see if I can find a jacket for you before you go inside?"

The reporter was looking around at the people. He said, "Are you going to wear one?"

"Not me—I used to work in here. How about you, Mr. Weer?"

The Scotch had made me warm; I told him I would be all right.

"Okay, right in here." Dan swung back the big door. "Make it quick—every minute this door's open costs the company ten dollars; that's what they used to tell me."

"What's the temperature in here?"

I said, "Ten degrees above zero."

Dan said, "It has to be cold enough to freeze the juice quickly when the sealed cans are brought in. Otherwise there would be fermentation, and the cans would split. Because it contains sugar, citric acid, and other natural constituents, the juice freezes at twenty-nine degrees, not thirty-two like water. Shall I tell him about the ghost, Mr. Weer?"

I smiled and said, "You'll have to now, Dan."

"Well, back in 1938 there was a kid of eighteen or so working in here—piling boxes and so on, the kind of thing I used to do myself. Of course, we were smaller then, and less automated. Anyway, it was Friday afternoon on a muggy summer day; he was in here alone and the latch froze."

The reporter said, "I thought you could open those things from the inside."

"You can, but you see, the cold worked its way through the mounting screws to the outside of the door; then water condensed on the latch mechanism and froze up."

I said, "We isolate the latch from the cold now, and we have two alarm systems in here in case the door jams, or is blocked in some way."

"Right, but then we didn't. The kid—I forget his name; personnel could tell you—couldn't get out. He was living at a boarding house, and no one reported him missing. Well, you can imagine what happened. They found him Monday morning. He had been trying to break the door off the hinges by piling up the cases to make a kind of tower, then knocking it over so that it would fall against the door. But it was too solid for him."

"Like Injun Joe."

"What?"

"In *Tom Sawyer*," the reporter explained. "Injun Joe is locked in the cave when they put iron doors on it after Tom and Becky

· 247 ·

are rescued. He eats bats while he tries to cut through the oak sill with his knife, but starves to death before he can get out."

"Yes," I said, "like Injun Joe."

"Caves are frightening things." The reporter was walking deeper into the coldhouse as he talked, looking at the frost on the pipes that covered the ceiling. "I did a story on a cave-exploring club not too long ago. Have you ever been in a cave, Mr. Weer?"

"Only a very small one when I was a boy."

"Anyway," Dan said, "the kid's ghost is supposed to haunt this warehouse. Once in a while forklift drivers on the third shift used to say they saw him in the back bays. We started suspending anyone who spread that kind of talk, and that put an end to the ghost."

I said, "If you don't mind, Mr. Thurlough, I'm getting a little chilled; I'm going to step outside. Dan can show you around some more if you like."

The reporter said, "Why don't you both go? I'd like to be in here alone for a few minutes, just to see what it's like."

Dan seemed to hesitate, so I said, "The alarms are right next to the door—just press the red buttons. But you won't have to. The door opens with a push bar; lean your weight against that and it will open every time."

The reporter, who was already twenty or thirty feet away from us, nodded to show that he understood.

Outside I said, "You shouldn't have talked about the ghost, Dan."

"I did that intentionally. Would you like to get some coffee, Mr. Weer? You said you were cold."

I said that I would.

"The break area is just past the foreman's office there. You look kind of bad, and I think some good hot coffee might be the thing for you. About the ghost—if that's all he prints, I'll be happy with it."

"You mean he's that kind of reporter?"

Dan was putting dimes in the coffee machine. "He's doing a story on the decline of industry in the valley, and that type of story isn't going to help the price of the stock."

"I see."

"Here, drink this." Dan sipped his own and made a face. "This powdered stuff's pretty bad, but at least it's hot."

"Were you ever locked in the freezer, Dan?"

"I'm here, aren't I?"

"That latch didn't really freeze, you know. It was a prank. Some of the men who worked with him locked him in. In those days the door had a latch that took the hasp of a padlock, and if it was in place the door couldn't be opened from the inside. One of them stayed behind to let the boy out. He was not much older than the boy they had locked in, and when the one inside started trying to batter down the door, and the hinges and frame bent, he got frightened."

Dan nodded, still sipping his coffee.

"He couldn't imagine, you see, what was happening inside; every five minutes or so terrible blows struck the freezer door, and he didn't know what was going on. The hinges had sprung, and he thought the door itself would give way at any moment. He said he tried to slip the hasp of the lock out of the latch, but it was jammed. He also said he thought the boy they had locked in would kill him when he got out. Have you ever been in here at night—late at night—when the plant is empty?"

"No."

"Believe me, there is no place more frightening than an empty factory at night. I've been in abandoned houses in the woods at midnight—my dad was a great hunter, and he used to insist I go—in just about every place you can think of, and there's nothing else like this plant after dark. It's so big that you can't tell who else is in there with you, or if anyone is, and it's full of catwalks, and metal doors that seem to slam by themselves, and machinery that starts automatically when you're not expecting it. Your footsteps ring on the steel floors, and sometimes you can hear someone else—you don't know who it is—walking a long way off, but you never see him."

"The one that was supposed to let the kid out of the coldroom didn't do it?"

"He became frightened, as I said. He went home. He said later that he was sure the door was going to give way at any moment. But of course it didn't."

"You were here then, weren't you? What did they do to him?"

"Yes, I was a young engineer—two years out of school. They didn't do anything to him; they covered it up. And when the door was repaired, the latch was replaced with one that could always be opened from the inside."

"You want some more coffee?"

I shook my head. "How long is he going to be in there, anyway?"

"I don't know, but he won't freeze in there in ten minutes." Dan wadded up his empty cup and threw it at a trash barrel. "You don't have to stay here, you know, Mr. Weer; I can take care of him if you want to go back to your office."

"I'd just as soon tour the plant with you. I have to see my doctor again this afternoon, and I don't want to get tied up with something I can't leave."

"Again?"

"It's not serious."

"You've been working too hard. Do you know what your secretary told me once? She said she could always tell when you were tired, because you started to drag one leg."

"Believe me, Dan, I've hardly been working at all. I worked a lot harder when I was an engineer. Haven't you ever noticed how many corporate presidents are in their sixties and seventies?"

He nodded.

"Those are men who couldn't possibly continue to work at any job requiring concentration or endurance. I should know—I'm one of them myself."

"You're very democratic, Mr. Weer, do you know that? You're much easier to talk to than Mr. Everitton or the other vice-presidents. Sometimes I have to remind myself that you're their boss."

"Sometimes I have to remind them."

"I'll bet."

"You've been buttering me up, so I'll butter you up—you've got a good smile. You remind me of somebody, but I can't recall who it is."

"The expression is 'a jackass eating bumblebees.' "

"Someone who's dead now. I can't remember. Come on, we're going to get your reporter out before he stiffens up."

Production workers—warehousemen on their break—were beginning to drift into the room. I put my cup in the disposal bin with a hundred other plastic containers of dead coffee and led the way out. Red Harris, the coldhouse manager, came loping up and asked if everything was all right. I said, "Dan and I are showing a reporter around. He's in your freezer."

He looked relieved. "How's it going?"

"Fine."

"There's a bad spot in the floor of Bay Ten. I've had an order in to get it fixed for two weeks."

"I'll see if I can't speed things up for you."

"That's all right. I just wanted you to know that I haven't been neglecting it. The maintenance men don't like to work in there—you know how it is."

"Won't you have to empty the bay and warm it up so the concrete will set?"

"We'll use an epoxy patch. That'll harden if we protect it with a little insulation and give it some localized electric heat."

"I see."

"Anything I can do for you?"

"I don't think so."

"If you need anything, Mr. Weer, just let me know. I'll be in my office."

Dan was swinging back the big freezer door. I said, "I don't think so, but I'll give you a yell if we do." Inside, the freezer felt colder than it had before. Although the interior was well-enough lit for the work done there—mostly stacking pallets of product with fork trucks—the illumination was kept low to reduce the heat generated by the lights. There was an impression of undirected dim radiance, like what we see in dreams when we dream that we are awake by night. Dan called, "Fred! Fred! Hey, buddy!" No one answered. "He's got to be in there somewhere."

"He could have come out while we were drinking coffee. He could be wandering around the plant now."

"He wouldn't do that," Dan said. He had no sooner spoken than the reporter appeared, coming out of a bay and into the main aisle. Dan shouted, "Aren't you freezing?"

The reporter nodded—he was trotting. "This is a big place. I got lost for a while." When he reached us, he stopped, slightly out of breath, rubbing himself with his hands.

Dan asked, "Did you see the ghost?"

"No, but I heard something. When I was way in the back, I could hear a pounding up this way, as though crates of these frozen cans were falling against the door. When I tried to check it out, I got lost."

I said, "Probably some warehousemen unloading the conveyor."

"They weren't there," the reporter said. "They passed me going out—I asked them where they were going, and they said it was their break time."

Outside he wanted to interview someone who worked in the area, and picked a young woman from Red Harris's office. She was of medium height, dark-haired, attractive without being pretty. She was wearing wool slacks, and a cardigan sweater on top of a pullover. Very cleverly, I thought, he arranged that she sit with her back to the room, giving her a psychological impression of isolation, although Dan and I, on the opposite side of the office, could hear everything that was said. He began by asking her name and address, and making certain she did not object to being quoted. "Suppose the bosses hear you," he said. "Are you going to get in trouble?"

The woman glanced over her shoulder at Dan and me. "They can't hear me, can they?"

"Not if you keep your voice down. But if I quote you, I don't want to quote something that will get you fired, even though you could deny it if you wanted to."

"I don't think there's anything I could say that they wouldn't like. Anyway, a person's got a right of free speech, doesn't she?"

"Not really—not if you mean the right to tell the truth, or what you think is the truth, or the right not to speak. Free speech means you can talk about the government as long as you're not against it—don't want to overthrow it. But what I want you to talk about is yourself. How long have you lived in Cassionsville?"

"About fifteen years. We came here from Hylesport when I was twelve."

"When did you come to work here?"

"A year after I got out of high school."

"And you've been here ever since?"

"Yes, I've been here ever since—I mean, I go home at night, and I go on vacation and things. You know what I mean."

"Do you like it here?"

"I guess so. You get used to the people after a while—you know how it is. And everything. You wish something would happen and it doesn't, but you know your way around. It's home, in a way."

"It's dull?"

"Everything's dull after a while."

"Does the cold bother you?"

"Not very much. You get used to it. For us in the office it's not like it is for the men who have to work in it all the time. In the winter we don't dress much different from everybody else;

in the summer I wear light clothes in, then change into these in the ladies' locker room before I come in here. We had a woman here once that wore those gloves without fingers all the time, and that started bothering me after a while—seeing her type. But she left after two years."

"What do you do here?"

"Type and file. Keep the records of the warehouse—you know, how many boxes in and what lot, how many out and what carrier took them."

"How many cartons of juice would you say you've booked in and out since you've been here?"

"I haven't any idea. A jillion, but I really haven't any idea."

"Can't you make a guess?"

"I don't know. I could try to figure it out, but it wouldn't make any sense. Have you seen where they unload them off the conveyor? I go in there sometimes when there's a message for one of the men—his wife's sick or something. Or where they put them on the railroad cars or the trucks. There's a hundred cans to a box, and so many boxes you can't believe it, and it goes on like that all day long. I don't know what they do with it, but people can't be drinking it all—they just couldn't be."

"I've been to other factories," the reporter said. "I know what you mean."

"You think of a woman with a family—she goes to the supermarket, and how many does she buy? One or two cans, maybe five if everybody in the family drinks it for breakfast every day. That's what I think. Then I stand by the conveyor and watch them unload, and I try to think of all the families and there aren't that many people in the world. Just while you stand there—you know, while you say which one's John Boone and somebody says the man in the checkered shirt and you say Mr. Boone and he says just a minute and you say you've got to come to the office, they want you on the phone, it's an emergency—just in that time they load enough for the whole city of Chicago."

"Do you buy the juice yourself?"

"I'm sorry, I didn't hear you?"

"I asked if you bought this kind of juice yourself—for your own family."

"We use the dried."

"Why is that?"

"You're going to laugh at this. . . ."

"Go ahead. Make me laugh."

"It's my hands. We feel—you know—we owe it to the company to use the product, but whenever I reach into the freezer at the store to pick some up, the cold makes my fingers hurt. So I get the dried, the powder."

"Does your family like it?"

"There's just my husband and me."

"Does he like it?"

"He's used to it. You know. I don't think he thinks much about it. Juice, coffee, one egg, and toast. That's his usual breakfast. He reads the paper while he eats, and I don't think he thinks much about it."

"Do you plan to have children?"

"That's funny. I mean, excuse me for laughing, but it is funny. No—not this late. We wanted some at first but I don't think we've talked about it for four or five years."

"Suppose you had a child, a daughter. What would you want for her?"

"I don't know. A real nice childhood."

"After childhood."

"Well, it wouldn't make much difference, would it? What I wanted. I would want her to get married, and she probably would, and then it would be between her and her husband."

"Would you want her to live here?"

"Yes, so I could see her; if she got pregnant or sick or something, I would come over with pies. When I used to think about having children, that was one thing I used to think of—when they were grown I could bring them something when they were sick, and maybe straighten up their houses."

"Do you think this is a good place to bring up children?"

"Well, it's not any worse than anywhere else. I mean, it's not good, no."

"Can you elaborate on that?"

"Well, when I used to think about children I used to remember how nice Hylesport was when I was little but that's terrible now, since the refinery came in. My mother used to tell about growing up on a farm. They didn't have much money, but they weren't *poor*. Do you know what I mean?"

"I'm afraid I don't."

"They didn't have much money, but they didn't need much —you could even pay the doctor in chickens then. They had land and plenty to eat, and they didn't need fancy clothes. For Thanksgiving her father used to kill a deer. That was one of the things my mother always used to tell when she talked about the farm, her father shooting a deer for Thanksgiving. I put little paper turkeys on the table for Joe and I, and I get a turkey out of the freezer."

"I see," the reporter said. I noticed that he had stopped taking notes a long time before.

Dan said, "If you're finished now, Fred, Mr. Weer and I will show you the canning operation, where all those cartons you saw in the freezer come from."

We took him back into the coldhouse instead of going outside and entering Building B in the usual way, walking up the conveyor with him, stepping over the boxes as they came down. He said, "I'm surprised you made this high enough to stand up in. Wouldn't it have been cheaper if you'd just made it as high as the boxes themselves?" I told him men had to be able to get into the conveyor housing to make repairs and clear jams. He said, "I feel like a salmon swimming upstream to spawn and die," and then we were out, and into the noise and bright lights of the packing room.

"Those are the case packers," Dan said. "You might be interested in the way they unfold the boxes, which we receive flat, put the flaps down, and glue them."

"They make the cans line up like little soldiers, don't they?"

"That's right. At the same time they're getting a box ready, they're forming the cans into five layers, with each layer a four-by-five array of juice cans. If we follow the production lines on up, right up here, you can see the seamers. They put the lids on the filled cans, and we use the same type of seamer that they use for beer. Each of these machines will seam thirteen hundred cans a minute without spilling a drop. It's hard to visualize, but if one drop were spilled from each can as it went through the seamer, you'd have enough juice to make a nice little creek running out of the machine."

"I can't hear you."

Dan took him by the arm. "Here, step back from the machine. Is there anything else you'd like to see here particularly?"

"I'd like to interview one of the operators."

I said, "I doubt that you can. Most of these women today are Latin Americans. They don't speak much English." As I spoke, they were watching me with dark Indian eyes, and I wondered if they could understand what I was saying.

"Puerto Ricans?"

"And Mexican-Americans. When I was younger, I used to design the filling machines, and I was in and out of here all the time; the girls were all English-speaking then—girls just out of school and young marrieds, mostly. Now you can't get them to do this kind of work, so we recruit these people and bring them in. Most of them only stay a few months."

"Why can't you hire local people?"

Dan said, "Lazy. Just plain lazy. It's too hard for them, sitting on a stool watching one of these machines."

I said, "This is a pretty ordinary can-filling line, actually. You see the men down there unloading the empty cans and putting them on the conveyor. They go through an inverter and a blowout to make sure they don't contain foreign objects, then under the filling machines where they're squirted full of liquid juice. Over on the dry side, the same juice is run into spray towers. They work just like your lawn sprinkler at home, except that the spray falls a long way through a countercurrent warm-air stream that takes the water out. We store the powder in bins. In the peak season—that's late summer and fall—the making and drying operations run three shifts, the packing rooms two. The rest of the year making and drying run two shifts and packing one."

"Which kind of juice sells best? Dried or frozen?"

"Frozen has always been the leader, ever since it was introduced. Lately dried has been gaining on it, though. We used to be about 75 percent frozen and the rest dried, but now we're 60–40. We're planning now to introduce a new product—liquid juice—to take some of the pressure off the drying towers. It will be packed in plastic fruit, and treated with preservatives and gamma radiation to prevent fermentation. We'll put faces on the fruit, and a child will be able to hold one right over his glass and give it a squeeze to get juice."

"Sounds good."

Dan said, "We have to go over to the next building to show you the making operation, but I'm afraid there's not much there for you to see. Mostly stainless-steel pipe."

When he had seen the reactors and pumps and heat exchangers in the Making Building, we took him to the back of the plant to show him the unloading operation, and the crushers. "Now I've seen the whole thing," he said, watching the gray-brown tubers tumbling down the chute.

Dan told him, "That's right. Most of these are from Maine, now. They plant quick-growing varieties and get their crop in very early—they have to. Here the harvesting season has just begun."

Someone said, "Those are my potatoes," and we all turned to look. He was an elderly man in a sweat-stained hat; he dragged his left leg as he climbed the steel ladder to stand on the platform beside us. "Those are my potatoes," he said again. "Grew 'em not thirty miles from here. My farm."

The reporter said, "You don't work here, then."

"Don't work *here*. I guess you could say I work for them here—work as hard as anybody, and get my pay once a year. Can't telephone and say you're sick either, on a farm. Or retire with a pension. I'm seventy-one years old."

"Have you been a farmer all your life?"

"Yes, sir. Born right there in the room I sleep in now, and helped my dad until he passed on. Raised my family on the farm and live there yet."

"You've seen a lot of changes, then," the reporter said.

"And been against every one of them—is that what you want to hear?"

"No, I was just thinking that this area must have been very different fifty or sixty years ago."

"Some ways, yes. Some ways it's more like it was then than it used to be."

"That's interesting. How is that?"

"Well, there wasn't so many people then—that's one thing. Now the town's a whole lot bigger, but when once you get outside it, there's a lot less. Farms are bigger, and there's a sight of land in soil bank and so on that's not used and no need to live there. Even so, I could show you a many a farm a man was proud to own thirty years past, not in the soil bank, where nobody's living on the place now, and the meadows all growing up in trees. Naturally one reason is the streams don't run like they used to. This place here—and the others like it up and down the whole valley—pump the water up out of the ground; you do that and the streams don't run. Farther back south and east it's mine tailings. Colors the water red and kills everything. My own farm—when I'm gone it's gone. Had three boys and none of them want it."

"Where is your farm?"

"Over towards Milton. When I was a boy, there wasn't anything anybody could have that was better'n a farm, and we felt sorry for anybody didn't have one. If a doctor or a banker could marry a widow that had a good one, they'd stop what they was doing and work it. I tell you I loved my dad, but when he died I had a hard time to cry, just thinking at the funeral that the farm'd be mine now. But the boys—don't none of them want it. You know what did it? Those."

"Potatoes?"

"This here plant opened up and the price went right through the top of the silo, so everybody growed them to sell here. Well, the first thing that did was to turn what had been a interesting business into one that wasn't. And the second thing was that people didn't have gardens anymore, or keep chickens, but just bought what they needed with potato money. Then they started to go down, as any fool could have told they would, but people wasn't used to growing anything else, and wasn't set up for it anymore, and was a little bit afraid they'd forgot how to do it, so they stuck with potatoes. Naturally when everybody grows the same thing, and on all their land, you have a lot of disease —but then that brings the price back up, and so they stick with it. I guess I haven't explained myself, but it's my observation that when a boy grows up watching all that, he don't like what he sees."

When the reporter had gone, I asked Dan to come up to my office for a drink. "Over the rocks," he said, "and no water. It seemed like it went all right didn't it? But you never know until you see the story in print. This is good Scotch."

"I've been thinking," I said, "that I ought to be drinking schnapps, or something of that kind. The Weers were a Dutch family. With your name you should drink brandy, I suppose."

"Or Irish whiskey. I'm Irish on my mother's side."

"I should have guessed it. You're a good talker."

"She was a Doherty, so I'm entitled to carry on about the ould sod."

"Tell me an Irish story."

"You mean a joke—"

"No, a story. The kind one Irishman tells another, or a woman tells her child. Not something someone wrote in New York for television."

"Are you serious?"

"Certainly I'm serious. I have twenty minutes before I have to leave to see my doctor, and for the first time in quite a while I know what I want to do with twenty minutes. I want to hear an Irish tale."

"I only know one. Do you know of the Firbolgs? They were the most ancient people that ever were in Ireland. Before they came, there was no one there but the wolf, the red deer, the birds, and the *sidhe*. You may think you know what the *sidhe* were, but you do not, for there is no word for them in any tongue today."

Miss Hadow came in and asked if I wanted to contribute to the flower fund for Miss Birkhead. I told her not to interrupt me like that in the future.

She said "I'm sorry, Mr. Weer—in Mr. Scudder's office I just come in and go out whenever I please."

"What hospital is she in?"

"She's dead, Mr. Weer. Didn't you see it? It was on the board when you came back: 'Employees will be saddened to learn of the death of Helen Birkhead Tyler, long-time secretary to A. D. Weer. She is survived by her husband, Ben, and two children.' I wrote it myself."

"Order a bouquet in the company's name. Anything up to a hundred dollars. And on the card—I mean the notice on the bulletin board, not the one you send with the flowers—you might add that she was the secretary, at one time, of J. T. Smart, the founder. She was proud of that."

"She was proud of being your secretary, too, Mr. Weer. Anyone would be."

"That's enough of that. Order the bouquet, and shut the door."

"For they were not men and women, as some say, nor gods, nor fairies—there is no other name for what they were. They were not the leprechauns, no more than a man is a plow, for the leprechauns they brought into being to work for them. They were not fairies, no more than a woman is a rag doll; the fairies were the toys of their children, and that is why the few of them that are not broken yet are so sad—the children of the *sidhe* are no more. They could not die save of time: no spear could kill them.

"Now, it so happened that one of the *sidhe*—his name was already forgotten when Ireland was joined to Britain, and Britain to France, but he was very powerful—had children three, two sons, and a daughter, who was the eldest. And he loved them with all his heart, so that it saddened him to think that someday they must die, for he knew that the *sidhe* would pass from Ireland, and from the world, and should his children not pass with them? He thought upon this, and in time the thought came to him that it would be well if those children were to be alive forever, and free and beautiful, as they were then. And so he thought upon it, what thing there was in the world that lived forever, and was beautiful, and free. Now, his house was by Lough Conn—that is a lake that is in Ireland. And at last it came to him that each year the wild geese came to Lough Conn, and to the other lakes that were about; and that though as it might be this goose died, or that, the flock never died, but was beautiful and wild and free, and returned to Lough Conn each year. When he thought that, he knew it was time to act, and he called his children to him and said, 'It is for the love of you that I give you up. Deirdre, when you are all as one, do you watch over your brothers.' Then at once there were no longer any children there, but geese too many to count, and these at once flew away. But every summer they returned to Lough Conn, even after their father died."

"Did they live forever, Dan?"

"No, because when the *sidhe* were gone men shot the geese

with their bows, and so the flock dwindled and dwindled, but was still a flock, and while it lived the children lived. Cuchulainn himself, that great hero, wrung their necks that he might fletch his arrows with their quills, and because they were of that flock the arrows sang as they flew, and wept in the breasts of the slain. St. Columba had a pen that wrote of its own volition, and now you know wherefrom that came.

"In this way, in time, the flock which was the children of the *sidhe* dwindled until at last only a single goose remained. Then this goose thought to itself, How can it be that of all the flock I am the only survivor? For our father's intention it was that we should live forever, beautiful and free; yet when I die the flock will be gone. And thinking these thoughts she flew over Ireland from Inishtrahull to Ballinskelligs Bay, and from Galway Bay to Dun Laoghaire, seeking for one having the second sight who might explain the thing to her, but all such were long since gone from Ireland.

"At the last she came to the cottage of a hermit, and as he was the best she could find, she alighted there and put her question to him.

" 'Little there is that I can do for you,' the hermit said. 'Why did you suppose your father, who could not save himself, could save you? The time of the *sidhe* is long past, and the time of geese is passing. And in time men, too, will pass, as every man who lives long learns in his own body. But Jesus Christ saves all.' So saying, he dipped his hand into a bowl that stood upon the table by him and touched her head with water, making her think, for a moment, of the calm sweetness of Lough Conn, and then of the wild sea. Then he said, 'I thee baptize, in the name of the Father, and the Son, and the Holy Ghost,' and when he had said these words there stood before him Deirdre and her two brothers; but time had had his way with them, and they were bent now and old, and though their cheeks were red as apples, their hair was white as frost, for they had far outlived their time."

I must have fallen asleep—I woke, just now, and Dan had gone. It is time, and past, that I kept my appointment with Dr. Van Ness; but I find the yellow reminder from his office nailed to my desk so that I cannot withdraw it. It is time, I think, that I see the enchanted headrest of the Chinese philosopher looming behind me, and I wait its coming. My aunt's voice on the intercom says, "Den, darling, are you awake in there?"